SUCH

DARK

THINGS

COURTNEY EVAN TATE

SUCH

DARK

THINGS

mira

mira

Recycling programs
for this product may
not exist in your area.

ISBN-13: 978-0-7783-1654-1

Such Dark Things

Copyright © 2018 by Lakehouse Press, Inc.

For questions and comments about the quality of this book, please contact us at
CustomerService@Harlequin.com.

BookClubbish.com

Printed in U.S.A.

To my Michelle.
For keeping me afloat.

To my husband.
For being my Always.

And to my brother-in-law, E.L.
For everything.

SUCH

DARK

THINGS

PROLOGUE

My skin is sticky with blood.

My waistband is wet with it, and I can taste it on my lips. It's splattered on my face, and it tastes like metal that has been rotting in the sun and rain for a hundred years. The night makes me shiver, the cool breeze rustling my hair, and for a split second, I'm back there in that house, standing in that blood. My bare toes feel the warmth of the liquid turn cool as the minutes tick past.

Goose bumps rise on my neck, and a knot that I can't swallow is lodged in my throat. My feet are frozen frozen frozen on the ground, and I can't move.

Their eyes are open and lifeless, although they stare at me. They see me.

Yet they see nothing.

I can't breathe.

My lips are ice, just like theirs.

My heart is pounding and racing and stuttering, and I can't breathe I can't breathe I can't breathe.

"Corinne. You're safe here. *Corinne.*"

And just like that, I'm not there.

I'm *here*.

"There was blood all over me." My words are stilted and fragile, like glass.

I stare at my hand, and even though it's clean now, I see it as it was seventeen years ago, covered in the blood of two souls—souls that were living and that aren't anymore. It's hard to wrap my mind around. First they were breathing, and then they weren't. It happened in a split second. I inhale shakily.

"Think about that moment," the doctor instructs. "Who can you see?"

I think on that. "Melanie is next to me on the floor. Her head is bleeding into a pool. There is so much blood that it looks black." I close my eyes, because it had been the first time I'd seen blood like that, and it terrified me. "Joe is on the bed. His blood is splattered all over the wall. Both of them have their eyes open."

Staring at me.

The emotions welling up in me are like a wave, swelling swelling swelling...until I can't handle it anymore. The horror and the guilt and the pain are just too much.

"I can't do this," I blurt out. "I'm done for the day."

Dr. Phillips looks at me, and he's calm and detached.

"Corinne, why are you here?"

I pause. What a stupid question. "You know why I'm here." I hate it when they treat me with such condescension.

"Humor me," he tells me. "Why are you here?"

I grit my teeth and look away.

He waits.

"You're saying that I tried to hurt myself. But I wouldn't do that."

I look at him now, and he's so fucking emotionless. I look down at my left wrist, at the bandage covering up the stitches.

"I wouldn't," I insist again. "I'm a fucking physician. I

wouldn't have cut my wrist horizontally. If I really wanted to hurt myself, I would've known to cut vertically along the vein."

I finger the gauze. Beneath it, the cut throbs, evidence of something I don't remember doing.

"I'm not crazy," I add. And I don't know if I'm trying to convince Dr. Phillips or myself.

"You're not crazy." He nods. "But you've experienced a mental break. You're here because you need to deal with the causal underlying issue so that it won't happen again. Right?"

He's a fucking asshole.

I stare at the wall. At the whiteness, at the sterility.

"You need some plants in here," I tell him, avoiding the question. "Greenery puts patients at ease. All this blankness... it's maddening."

"I'll keep that in mind," he says wryly. "Corinne..."

I interrupt. *"Dr. Cabot,"* I tell him. "I've earned it."

"Dr. Cabot," he corrects himself. "You're right. You've earned it. You worked a long time to finish medical school and your residency. You're a top ER physician. You have a life envied by everyone around you. You've got to take care of yourself so you can protect this life you've built."

I close my eyes. Behind my eyelids, it's dark and safe. It's black and warm.

"Protect it from what?" I whisper.

"You tell me," he answers. "You've got something inside of you that is triggered now, something that creates panic and a fight-or-flight response. We know what your father did so long ago. What we don't know is *why*...or what damage it has caused in you, damage that seems to be affecting you now."

"I don't know, either," I say helplessly, my eyes opening to the white walls again. "I can't remember. I never could. You know that."

"I know." Dr. Phillips nods again, and he tries to be so fucking comforting. "You have a history of dissociative behavior. You blocked out what your father did so long ago, and it stands to reason that your brain has developed that as a defense mechanism. It's doing it again now. If we don't get to the bottom of why your memories are being triggered now, after all of these years…you'll never have peace. Do we agree on that?"

Reluctantly, I nod.

"So we have to start at the beginning. You have to stay here and focus."

Anger flares in me, red and hot, and I stare him down. He doesn't blink and neither do I.

"Focus?" I ask him, and my words are sharp and I wish they would cut him. "You think it's as simple as sitting down and *focusing*? How dare you sit there and tell me what to do, when you have *no idea* what it's like."

I stand up to leave, but the psychiatrist's next sentence holds me in my place, freezing me.

"Corinne, you promised Jude you'd try."

Jude.

My beautiful, understanding Jude.

I swallow hard. I *did* promise. And I have to follow through, even though the pain it causes me is immeasurable. I owe it to him. I'll do it for *him*. Not for this psychiatrist, but for Jude.

My body folds back into the seat, and I finger the medical bracelet circling my right wrist. Corinne Elizabeth Cabot, Female. It's me, condensed into one stark sentence, yet I'm a stranger to myself right now. That's why I'm here. I don't know myself or my thoughts. My memories are foreign, blocked, nightmarish, out of control.

"Fine." There's nothing else I can say.

Dr. Phillips is quietly triumphant. "Let's begin again. Take a deep breath and close your eyes."

I do, drawing the cool air in a rush over my teeth, expanding my lungs and holding it, before I let it slowly exhale. I do it again, then again.

"Think back to that night, Dr. Cabot. Stand in that room. Tell me where your father is."

I envision it. I see it in my mind like it was yesterday. My father in his bloody steel-toed boots. "He's on the porch, waiting for the police to come."

"He left you alone in the house with two dead bodies?"

"Yes."

"He didn't try to run?"

"No."

"Okay. What did you do then?" the doctor asks me calmly, unfazed by the ugliness of my story.

"I was stunned. I think I was in shock. My hand was bleeding."

Dr. Phillips looks at my hand, because I'm stroking the scar now, an unconscious nervous tic that I often do when I'm anxious. "What happened to your hand?"

"I don't remember."

"Is there a lot that you don't remember from that night?"

"Yes. You know that."

"Yes, I do," he acknowledges. "So you're standing in the middle of a bloody crime scene because your father left you alone. What did you do then, Corinne?"

"I looked out the window," I tell him. "I was frozen. I couldn't move. My feet felt like concrete, and I was afraid if I moved, my heart would explode. So I took deep breaths. I watched the trick-or-treaters walking by. I looked at the blood on my feet. I looked at the jack-o'-lanterns that were lit on porches, and the ghosts hanging in the trees. There was a full moon. There was light on my shoulders."

"Anything else?"

"I stared at the street sign on the corner. All Hallows Lane."

"That's ironic," the doctor points out needlessly.

"Yes."

"How long did you stand there?" His question is quiet.

"Until they came and took me away."

I

Earlier this month
Fourteen days until Halloween
Corinne

There's blood on the wall.

It stands out starkly, a crimson slash of color streaked against white sterility. It's easy to train my eyes on it, easy to focus on that one spot rather than the bloody mess beneath my hands.

People like to think that death is peaceful, that it's calm, that it's beautiful. But from my experience, it's not. It's bloody, it's hectic, it's full of shrieking machines and fluorescent lights and chaos. It's not pretty.

"Dr. Cabot! It's been six minutes."

Lucy looks up at me amid the blood-spattered chaos, elbow-deep in intestines, and with what appears to be brain matter on her brow. Her dark eyes are resigned because she's been a nurse long enough to know what we have to do.

So do I.

It's the story of my life.

I pause and the defibrillating paddles in my hands suddenly

weigh a million pounds apiece. The fluorescent lights are bright and blinding, washing out everything around me but for the blood and the blue curtain circling the gurney. This moment swirls and stands still amid the hospital smells and beeps, and I think of an ancient story from Greek myth.

The Fates—three old women who spin the thread of life, measure the string and then decide when someone will die by cutting it. In this moment, I'm one of them.

My next decision will determine a life.

I'm one of the Fates and I'm measuring the thread and I'm cutting it.

Snip.

I take a breath and stare down at the broken boy in front of me, the one whose life I'm snipping away.

In my head, I know that none of this is my fault. It wasn't my fault that he decided to drag-race down the Dan Ryan and endanger a hundred lives other than his own. It wasn't my fault that he chose to slam five beers in five minutes beforehand. It's not my fault that he's only eighteen and his mother is anxiously waiting on the other side of the double doors, waiting for me to save her son.

It's not my fault that I can't.

He stares at me now, but his blue eyes are vacuous and unseeing. They've been that way for six long minutes. His blond hair is plastered to his face with blood, and it's splattered across his *Live For Today* T-shirt. The back of his skull is smashed in because he wasn't wearing his seat belt, and jagged bone erupts from his hair like bright white arrowheads. Safety glass isn't kind when a human body hurtles through it.

This boy had his whole life in front of him, and because of one stupid decision, it's done. He won't be living for tomorrow... Today was all he had.

He's gone, and it's time for me to wield the scissors.

Snip.

"Time of death, 5:57 p.m.," I say tiredly.

I set the paddles down and take a breath. The boy's bloody hand dangles over the side of the gurney, so I pick it up and place it on his chest. His fingers are naturally curled inward. I straighten them, my gloved fingers lingering on his before I move my hand to close his eyelids.

I feel relief when he isn't staring at me anymore.

"Go to the other one," Lucy tells me. "I'll talk to his mother."

I nod, because that's the right thing to do, because I'm one of only two doctors in the ER right now, and the other boy is waiting for me, and he's not beyond help like this one.

As a physician, I've had to learn how to compartmentalize my emotions, to turn them off at my whim and shift gears, to go from one scenario to the next to the next, all without missing a beat. It's a skill that I learned long ago, beginning in that god-awful house on that bloody night.

I slide the curtain to another room open, and the boy inside is scared, his eyes wide and frightened and alive. He's tall and thin and gangly, although his cheeks still have baby fat, softening the curve of the jaw that will someday be manly.

"Am I going to die?" he asks me, and his voice is so young. He's a little boy in a man's body, and his hands are shaking.

"Not today," I tell him, shining my penlight into his eyes. "What's your name?" He's got blood smeared on his cheek, and I wonder briefly if it is his or his friend's.

"Tyler."

"Well, Tyler, where do you hurt?"

He shows me, both with his words and with unspoken gestures, and I take note. He's beaten up for sure, but not mortally wounded, although we'll definitely check for internal bleeding just to be sure.

"Is Jason okay?" he asks quietly, and his hand taps the side of the gurney nervously, *tap tap tap.*

I hesitate.

Tyler sees the grim answer on my face, and I don't have to say a word.

"Jesus." He gulps for air and I grip his arm.

"You've got a concussion," I tell him. "I'm sending you for a CAT scan. Your collarbone is broken. I can see it poking through your shirt. Based on your level of pelvic pain, I think your hip crest is fractured. We'll get you x-rayed. I don't think you've got internal bleeding, but because of the rate of impact, I'm sending you for a sonogram just to be on the safe side."

He nods and his hand clutches his hip. "It hurts."

"I'm sure it does," I agree. "It will take a while to recover from a fractured hip. You'll have physical therapy, too." I pause. "Apparently, you boys were doing a hundred miles per hour down the Dan Ryan, and not only that, but you were filming yourselves. What were you thinking?"

He closes his eyes and drops back against the bloody sheet. "We weren't."

"You were lucky," I tell him. "You're going to be okay."

"Jason's not," he all but whimpers.

I shake my head and my gut contracts. "No. He's not. I'm very sorry."

I honestly am. I know people make mistakes. I know they have moments when they don't think. I see it every day right here in this room. These walls have seen thousands of people at their lowest moments. Some of them, like Tyler, get lucky. Some of them, like Jason, do not.

"He's been my best friend since kindergarten." Tyler's hands shake as he speaks. "We did Scouts together. We were both going away to Caltech next year. We were going to share a dorm."

Were. Past tense.

Tyler's eyes meet mine, and his are full of shock, of pain, of disbelief.

I don't want to tell him that the real grief is yet to come, when the reality of death sets in, when the absence of his friend is so pronounced that it rips a giant hole in his life. I don't need to tell him. He'll discover it soon enough.

"I'm sorry for your loss," I tell him sincerely, and there's suddenly a lump in my throat because it never gets easier. I've been an ER doc for years now, and death is not something I've ever gotten used to.

It's at this moment that shrill screaming rips apart the ER, a long wail filled with angst and torment. I know who it is without even checking.

It's the poignant grief of a mother, the pain in the scream unmistakable. Jason's mother's sorrow is haunting and raw, and it echoes into my bones, where it vibrates my core.

The sound lodges in my heart, and for a minute, I allow myself to feel it, to know that in a way, I caused that pain. I couldn't save that boy. That mother's life is irrevocably changed. His father's, his family's, his friends'. The wife he might've someday had is gone, the kids, *the life.*

It's not your fault, I tell myself, like I always do.

But that doesn't change the fact that his life dangled in my hands on a string, and I had to cut it.

Snip.

"We'll get you fixed up," I tell this boy, the one who is alive. "Don't drink and drive again."

Tyler shakes his shaggy head. "I won't. Can I see Jason?"

I shake my head. "You don't want to right now. Trust me. Wait until he's been cleaned up."

And the mortician has patched his skull back together.

Tyler nods and closes his eyes, and Jason's mom continues to wail in the background.

I tune it out, because this is my life, and if I don't harden myself to it, I'll go insane. I'll become a whimpering basket case who rocks in a corner because I see this kind of thing every damned day. Chicago is full of accidents and crimes and sickness.

"Do you know where my phone is?" Tyler asks as I'm almost to the door. "It's got the video on it. It's the last time… I mean, it's the last time Jason was alive. Maybe his mom will want to see it."

His mother will want to see the exact moment her son crashed into a stone median at a hundred miles per hour and died? I seriously doubt it.

"I'm not sure where it is, or if it even survived the crash," I tell him. "You'll have to check with the police. They'll be here later to question you, anyway."

He gulps and I take my leave, relieved to escape his pain and fear. Sometimes I can't help but allow those things to leach into me, and the emotions of desperation and grief are exhausting.

Lucy meets me at the nurses' station, and she's cleaned up now and wearing a fresh top. It has pumpkins on it. She thrusts a yogurt and an orange at me.

"You haven't eaten all day."

She's right. I forgot. It happens a lot around here on busy days. When lives hang in the balance, who has time for eating?

"Thanks," I tell her, taking the food gratefully. I hate yogurt, and the orange isn't ripe yet, but it's better than nothing.

"You're going to get too skinny," Lucy tells me, standing in the middle of ringing phones and overflowing stacks of charts. "And your husband probably likes your boobs the way they are. Also, he's on line four. You forgot to call him back earlier."

Damn it.

Jude called around noon. Almost six hours ago.

Son of a bitch.

I grab the phone.

"Babe, I'm sorry," I tell him, without bothering with hello. "It got crazy here today. There was an accident on the Dan Ryan, two kids drag racing… It's been one thing after another…"

"Corinne, it's okay," he interrupts, and his voice is warm and patient. Like always. I feel a pang of guilt, because he really is patient with this stuff, with my schedule.

"I couldn't save one of them," I tell him, and my voice is suddenly small, so very quiet.

"It wasn't your fault," my husband tells me seriously. "You know that."

I imagine Jude's eyes getting warmer with his words, the golden notes flickering amid the depths, almost like the moss in Lake Michigan on a sunny day. His eyes are like honey, various shades of golds and greens, all swirled into one color. That's always been one of my favorite things about him.

"I know." Because I do. I always try my best. I took an oath to heal and protect, and I take that very seriously.

Jude sighs.

"Somehow, I wonder about that. What time are you coming home? Should I wait dinner?"

I eye the orange and the yogurt next to me, and the patient board that is lit up like a Christmas tree.

"No," I answer tiredly. "The board is full, and it's only Brock and me here tonight. I can't get away until later. But I'll be home before bed."

"You need some sleep tonight, Co," Jude points out. "You've been running on fumes this week."

"I know." And God, do I know. I feel a hundred and five

lately, instead of thirty-five. "I'm starting to look like the Crypt Keeper."

Jude laughs, a sincere bark. "You are not. You're beautiful and you know it."

I examine myself in the silver coffeepot next to me. My reflection is distorted with the curve of the carafe, but I get the gist. My blond hair was neat this morning, but now the bun at the nape of my neck is falling apart. There are bags under my eyes, and Lucy is right. I'm going to look haggard soon if I don't watch it.

"You're partial," I point out to my husband.

"Maybe. Just come home sometime today, okay?"

I agree and hang up, and before I can take even one bite of the yogurt, a nurse is calling for me from an exam room.

I yank at my stethoscope so that it doesn't pull my hair as it drapes my neck and walk into exam room five.

"Whatta we got?" I ask the nurses, and I dive into work.

Concussion.

Chest pain.

Neck pain.

Bowel impaction.

At 8:00 p.m., Lucy pokes her head into the room I'm in.

"There was a bus accident," she tells us. "A bus full of kids coming back from a basketball game. No fatalities, but…"

But I'm going to be here awhile.

Abdominal pain.

Kidney stone.

Ankle sprain.

One patient turns into another, from bus accident victims to the geriatric. As always, the clock ticks faster and faster when I'm on the floor, and by the time I take another breath and catch up on charting, it's 11:00 p.m.

Damn it.

I do my charting quickly, scribbling in the pages until my sight blurs.

"You ready, Doc?" Lucy smiles tiredly at me as I grab my purse. She's holding her own. "I'm heading out. We might as well go together, right?"

"Sure."

We're too tired to chat much in the elevator, and I'm so exhausted as I trudge across the parking garage that I feel like my legs won't hold me up. It's dark, and as usual, I keep close watch from my periphery. There is a parking attendant, but he circles the entire garage, and I seldom see the orange lights flashing on top of his car.

"God, I hate this garage," Lucy mutters, her gaze flitting along the secluded shadows.

"Me, too," I agree.

It would take only a second for someone to jump out, for someone to grab me.

"They should film horror movies here," she adds. I chuckle but flinch away from the dark edges of the concrete. I keep moving, one foot in front of the other.

Lucy peers ahead of us. "What the hell?"

There's new graffiti painted on the wall in front of my space. CUNT.

The hateful word drips in neon-blue paint, dried now. In my opinion, that word is the worst thing in the world to call someone. Worse than *bitch*, worse than *whore*. I don't know why. It just is.

I look over my shoulder quickly, scanning the entire dark garage. Shadows move, the wind whistles, but no one is there.

We're alone.

This is just graffiti.

It's not directed at me.

This is Chicago. Vandalism is to be expected.

Calm.

Calm.

Calm.

"That's charming," Lucy says wryly. "I'll call someone tomorrow to have it cleaned, Dr. Cabot."

"Corinne," I correct her. "We're outside of the ER now, Lucy."

She smiles. I wouldn't care if she called me by my first name always, but she's a stickler for the rules.

"Where are you parked?" I ask her. She motions to a few rows away.

"Get in. I'll drop you off."

We get into my car, and we both lock our doors.

Thirty seconds later, she gets out at her car. "See you tomorrow."

"'Night, Lucy. Drive safe."

I'm so tired that I wish I wish I wish in this moment that I lived in a house closer to the hospital, instead of a suburb outside of town. I just want my bed. And my husband. I want to be away from the graffiti and the crime and the noise.

I nose out of the garage, into traffic and toward home.

The lights of the city turn into the tree-lined streets of the suburbs, and somehow I manage to hold my eyes open for the duration of the drive. I punch in our gate code, and the wrought-iron gates swing open, granting me entrance.

Our home is at the back, and it's the only one in the neighborhood that doesn't have jack-o'-lanterns or witches adorning the lawn.

That's okay by me.

I don't do Halloween.

The house standing in front of me reminds me of why I live here, though, and of why I work so hard.

It's for normalcy, for happiness.

For *this*.

Jude and I work hard for this life, for the pleasures and comforts that we have. Our home is proof of that. It's large and renovated and lush. It's four thousand square feet of the American dream, nestled deep in an expansive subdivision away from the bustle and noise of the city. *This* is why I make the drive every day. This home is my quiet sanctuary, my respite from the chaos of my life.

I pull my car into the garage next to Jude's Land Rover and walk quietly into the house. My husband left a light over the sink on for me, but other than that, the house is dark and so silent that the quiet almost seems to buzz.

I creep through the house and almost trip over our dog in the kitchen.

"I'm sorry, girl." I bend and scratch Artie's ears. Her fur has gotten wiry in her old age, white around her muzzle and eyes. She stares at me now, almost in accusation, because I'm coming home so late and disturbing her sleep. "I'm sorry," I tell her again, as though she understands. She lays her head back down and watches me until I disappear into the master suite.

I brush my teeth, but that's all I do. I strip off my germy scrubs, release what's left of my bun and climb into bed naked, like I do every night. Jude stirs, sits halfway up and peers at the clock.

"Well, technically, you *did* make it home today," he says, his voice husky with sleep, and the clock says eleven fifty-eight, so he's right.

"I know. I'm sorry."

"I know."

He's oblivious to my nudity, and I to his, and he lies back down. Before long, he's snoring lightly, and even that doesn't keep me awake. I fall into sleep, and I stay there for hours.

2

Now
Jude

I wake with a start.

My eyes open, and I search the dim room for what woke me.

I skim over the familiar objects in my bedroom. The furniture, the walls, the bold abstract art, before my gaze falls upon my phone.

That was the noise. It vibrated with a text against the wood of my nightstand. I blink the sleep away and reach for it.

I miss you. I hate this place.

My wife.

My head falls back on the pillows, my hand grazing the empty side of the bed. The sheets there are cold. Corinne should be there next to me, her breath even and strong, her hair splayed out on the pillow, her warmth leaching into my body.

But she's not.

I don't know how she got access to her phone.

I miss you, too, babe, I answer. Um. How do you have your phone? Isn't that against the rules?

They aren't supposed to use their cell phones at Reflections, since the devices are considered a distraction from treatment. As a therapist myself, I can't say I disagree with that theory.

I had a bad night, so the day nurse is giving me 5 min to chat with you.

My gut contracts at that, at the notion that she has to get "permission" to talk with me, and once again I wonder if we're doing the right thing. If *I'm* doing the right thing. I pushed hard for her to admit herself so that I wouldn't have to do it against her will.

But the idea of Corinne in a mental hospital kills me.

Are you ok now? I ask.

Her answer is immediate. Not really. I'm ready to come home.

She adds a smiley face, but I know she's not feeling smiley. No one in her situation would.

It'll be ok, I assure her again, as I have four thousand other times this week. I promise.

I'll take your word for it, she replies, and if I concentrate, I can almost see the wry expression on her face as she types. Her blue eyes will be wide, her brow furrowed. I smile. I love you, Ju.

I love you, too.

I gotta go, she tells me. My five minutes are up. See you Saturday?

Yes! I answer. I'll be there.

Who would've ever thought I'd have to schedule a visit to my wife within a two-hour visiting window? Not me. Not her. In fact, not anyone who knows us.

But it's our reality.

I burrow my head under my pillow, as though if I tunnel far enough into my bed, this new reality will escape me. It doesn't, though. The image of finding my wife the way I did, in a pool of blood and insanity, will stay with me for the rest of my life.

I'll never be able to unsee it.

My dog whines two minutes later, saving me from the memory, her bladder having shrunk with her old age.

"Just a minute, girl," I mumble. "Give me a few minutes."

She can't wait, though, and I eventually haul myself out of bed, trudging out into the October cold, opening the back door.

Artie ambles out and relieves herself, taking her time. She sniffs at this and that, and I know she can't see what she's doing. Her eyes are cloudy with cataracts, and she can't hear a thing.

"Come on, girl," I call to her, loudly, shivering. "Get in here. It's cold."

When she's good and ready, she returns to the house, and after I feed her breakfast, I throw some clothes on. I go running every morning. It used to be for fitness reasons only, but now it is also to relieve stress.

Lord knows, these days I've got an excess amount of that.

I run my normal route, through the running trails at the park, through the trees. I can see my breath and my shoes crunch through the dead leaves drifted into piles on the ground. One foot in front of the other, pounding down the path, because this is something I can control. I can run and run and run, until all thoughts evade me, pushed out of my brain by the simple and basal need for oxygen. The need to breathe.

The human body is interesting in that way. It will allow your mind to play its games, right up to the point where the basic need to live overtakes all else. My lungs burn more and more. I ignore it as long as I can.

It's only when they feel about to burst that I finally stop, my hands on my knees as I pull air into my lungs. It takes several long minutes of thinking about nothing but breathing before I come back to the present.

Back to reality.

The Chicago traffic hums in the distance, as people race to work, but I'm removed from it here. This park is secluded and quiet, tranquil and removed. It's a nature reserve, and if you close your eyes, you truly feel like you're alone in the middle of nowhere.

Until a twig behind me snaps.

Startled, I whirl around.

I scan the tree line and the moving limbs, and there's not another human soul here. The wind blows and bites at my face, and there's nothing out there but the sun rising in the distance.

I'm alone, as I always am on this trail at this hour.

No one is here, and Corinne's paranoia has affected me.

I wasn't alone, Jude! she'd told me, babbling until she lost consciousness in the ambulance. *I wasn't alone.*

But everyone knows she was. The alarm hadn't been tripped. No one had broken in. It's understandable why she's paranoid, after living through what she did so long ago, but the fact remains, she *has* grown paranoid.

She *had* been alone that night.

Just as I'm alone now.

Jesus, Jude, I mutter to myself, and I take long steps, jogging toward home, even now fighting the urge to glance over my shoulder. I'm being a dumbass. I take the porch steps two at a time.

My house is a mausoleum without my wife, enormous and quiet, and I hate it. I didn't get married for this.

I'm resentful of my own thoughts as I shower and shave, the fog steaming up the bathroom mirrors. Corinne isn't here to remind me to turn on the exhaust fan, so I don't.

With her gone, I do everything as I always would. Something in my head tells me not to change anything, because to change things while she's gone might set her back.

I don't know if it's true, but I'm not going to chance it.

I let the bathroom steam up.

None of this is Corinne's fault. The very fleeting resentful thought that I had just means I'm a selfish bastard. I'm in a beautiful home in the suburbs, and my wife is in a psych ward. Even worse, I pray every day that she won't remember everything that put her there.

Because I'm a prick.

I feel like even more of a prick when my phone dings a second later and the woman who sent the text is not my wife.

You doing ok? I miss you.

Guilt billows through me like storm clouds, through my gut into my chest. So much of this is *her* fault, this woman who isn't my wife, and while I should stay far far away from her, I can't. For so many complicated reasons, I can't.

I sigh as I head out the door to start my day.

3

My house is silent when I get home from work, and Corinne is nowhere to be found. I check my phone. Nothing. Like always, she has gotten distracted at work and forgotten to text.

The clocks tick, mocking me, as I pace around.

I'm alone. Nothing to do. Nowhere to go.

Fuck.

Seven p.m.

Seven-oh-one.

Seven-oh-two.

Fuck this.

Before the silence kills me, I climb into my car and head out of the neighborhood.

My Land Rover's engine rumbles, and it's one thing I like about this vehicle: it's manly.

Vehicles should reflect your personality. My wife drives a sleek Mercedes sedan. It's refined, like her, efficient and beautiful. It suits her. Mine is aggressive and rugged, two things I think a man should be.

Sure, on the outside, I'm a gentleman. But on the inside, like every other man on earth, I'd like to think that I could hunt an elk and eat it raw if I had to, tearing into its muscle and sinew with my bare teeth. I want to believe that I could protect what is mine, that I could beat my chest and howl at the moon.

Not one of those things are necessary, because I live in suburbia, but I *could* do it. That's what counts.

I head down the highway toward the outskirts of town, toward Immaculate Conception. Its lights are warm and bright, a muted glow from the stained glass windows as I pull into the lot.

It's a large church, as most Catholic churches are, but it somehow manages an air of intimacy, of comfort. When I walk up the steps and into the sanctuary, it greets me like an old friend, and I suck in the familiar smells…of the wood, of the reverence, of the quiet. If silence had a scent, it would be this church.

It smells of wood bathed for a hundred years in sunshine and lemon polish.

At this time of evening, I wasn't sure that anyone would be here, but I hear low voices coming from the confessional, so I sit down to wait my turn. I can't make out the words, only low murmurs.

I cross my legs at the ankles and prepare to wait awhile, but it's only a few minutes before the confessional door opens, and a girl steps out. She's wearing a hoodie, and her eyes strike me.

Big and brown, watery with tears. She barely meets my gaze before she shrugs past and hurries out of the church. Her footsteps fall quickly on the thick carpeting of the aisle, then she's gone.

My turn.

I step inside and take a seat, and through the ornate wooden mesh, I can see the white collar in the dark.

"Bless me, Father, for I have sinned." My voice is loud in the quiet. "It's been forever and a day since my last confession."

I see the priest's white teeth as he smiles.

"Go on, my son."

"Well, how much time do you have?"

He chuckles and waits.

I continue.

"This week, I lied a couple of times. To my wife. I told her I wasn't frustrated when I was. She's at work right now, and so I'm alone. No wife, no sex life." I try to make light of it.

"That's unfortunate." The priest's voice is wry.

"I know you don't know what that feels like, but let me tell you, it sucks."

No answer.

"Also, I was furious at another driver and flipped him off yesterday. He cut me off and didn't even wave an apology."

"Anger is not godly, my son."

"I know," I agree. "That's why I'm confessing it."

"Anything else?"

"So much," I tell him. "But I don't want to bore you. It mostly has to do with looking at scantily clad women and masturbation."

"What have I told you about masturbation?" The priest's voice seems like it is cloaking amusement.

"That the church is against it, but you're not."

"That's right. Are you ready for dinner?"

"You bet your ass I am."

I open the door and step out, and wait for my brother to join me.

Being identical twins, we look exactly alike but for the white collar circling his neck.

Michel smiles at me as he steps out of the confessional.

"How's Corinne?"

I shake my head. "Halloween is coming up. You know how hard this time of year is."

"I know. I've been praying for her."

"Thanks."

Michel pulls his purple stole off and hangs it up. We walk toward the door, and as we step outside, I turn to him.

"Wait. You never absolved my sins."

"Are you truly repentant?" His raised eyebrow betrays his doubt.

I grin. "Not really."

"That's what I thought."

We chuckle and head to the parking lot.

"Do you want to ride with me or drive yourself?"

"I'll drive. I value my life."

"Whatever."

Michel heads to his old death trap of a pickup, and I head to my shiny Land Rover, and we head down the road, as opposite on the outside as we are identical on the inside.

I'm behind him, so when the exhaust from his truck fills mine, I punch a button to filter the air.

At a stoplight, I text him.

Your truck is a piece of shit. Get a new one.

He answers before the light turns green. Mine has character. Yours is soulless.

Tell me that again when your character is broken down and you're walking.

Ridiculous banter with my brother is normal. It keeps me feeling normal…distracted from the current state of my reality. It might sound dumb and detached, but it helps me cope. It's avoidance at its finest.

Within a few minutes of traffic, we pull up to our favorite mom-and-pop café. The glow of the sign beckons me.

Vilma's. The light in the *M* is broken, but you can still read it. Every few seconds it flickers, then dies, flickers, then dies. It's been that way for two years and they never fix it. It would cause a meltdown in someone with OCD.

This place might be small and a bit dingy, but it's also cozy and warm and familiar. I have breakfast here every day after my run and before I go to work. I know everyone here, and they know me, and there is comfort in that.

Vilma herself greets us by name, and I smile at her. She's aging and sometimes crotchety, but she likes me. She cares that I'm here, and that's comforting, too.

She leads us to our normal table, the one in the very back, the one where the wood veneer is peeling and the vinyl chairs are cracked.

We sit down and examine our sticky menus.

"So how was your day?" I ask, studying the list of food that I already know by heart.

"Oh, good. I just got run-of-the-mill confessions today. You know how that goes. Lying. Cheating. Impure thoughts. So on and so forth. How about you?" Michel asks, motioning for the waitress and her coffeepot. I don't understand how he can drink coffee so late in the day and still sleep at night.

"Oh, you know. Same old, same old. Depression, marital strife, OCD."

"Well, here we are," he answers. "The Cabot brothers. Changing lives one soul at a time."

"I'll leave their souls to you," I tell him wryly. "I'll worry about their minds."

Our normal waitress with the faded red hair bustles over with a pot of steaming coffee and fills Michel's cup up to the brim. She knows not to pour me any at this hour.

"You'll have...the corned beef and hash," she guesses for Michel.

He nods. "That sounds good, Meg."

She nods, her pen pausing on her pad as she assesses my mood. "And you'll have...the Texan, medium-well, toasted bun and fried onions."

"That'll do me," I tell her.

She grins because she knows us, then heads to the kitchen to turn our order in. I return my attention to Michel.

"How's Artie doing?"

"She sleeps all day," I tell him.

"Well, she's getting old. A girl's entitled to her beauty rest. Man, she's gotta be... Well, you and Co got her right after you got married. How long ago was that?"

I think about that.

"Hell, I don't even remember. Fourteen or fifteen years."

"That's old for a dog, bro."

I know.

"Her hips are hurting her," Michel tells me, like I don't know that. "She's in pain. That's why she's getting mean."

"I'm not ready to put her down," I answer firmly, because I know where he's going with this. "She's fine for now. She's got a lot of life left. Corinne loves that dog, and so do I."

Michel nods because he recognizes the stubborn streak in me. It matches his own.

"Well, let's meet here for breakfast tomorrow, and you can bring Artie so I can say hi."

"Deal. And I'll buy your dinner tonight as a thank-you for keeping me company."

"And breakfast tomorrow. You're no picnic lately."

"I'm pretty sure priests aren't supposed to be shysters."

Michel laughs. "Hey, you make the big money. I'm just a lowly servant of God."

I roll my eyes, because this particular servant of God plays poker every other week. He *is* a kind and caring soul, but he still pushes the priesthood boundaries.

I'm still chuckling when I notice that he's staring at something over my shoulder. The look of concentration on his face is intriguing, and I turn to see what he's so enthralled with.

Meg is coming back to our table with a girl in tow.

The girl looks to be in her midtwenties. Tight curves in all the right spots, long legs, long caramel hair pulled back in a ponytail, the glow of youth in her cheeks. She's definitely attractive.

"You're not supposed to notice that," I tell him.

He scowls. "I'm a priest, not a eunuch."

I laugh and he punches my shoulder, because we're brothers and that's what brothers do when they notice a hot girl together, even when one is a priest and the other is married.

"Honestly, though, it's not like that," he adds.

I raise an eyebrow because I don't believe him.

"Hey, boys," Meg says, stopping by my elbow and putting our plates down in front of us. "Tonight is my last night here. But this is Zoe, and she'll take good care of you from now on. This is her first night, so be nice to her. Zoe, these are my regulars, Jude and Father Michel."

Zoe smiles and her teeth are white. "I already know Father Michel," she says, patting his shoulder. I feel my eyes widen, and I stare at my brother. He returns my gaze and smiles like a cat who swallowed the canary.

The girl looks at me, and there's something so familiar in her eyes…about her eyes…and… *Is she the girl from the church?* She must've come straight here.

"It's very nice to meet you," she tells me, in a voice that somehow manages to be sultry and youthful at the same time. "I can't wait to start taking care of you."

She laughs because her words sounded suggestive. "I didn't mean that the way it sounded," she adds with a grin, and her lips are impish and full. There's something in her eyes that tells me that she *did*.

She sashays away and her arrogance is a bit annoying.

The girl is full of herself. She's young, though, and attractive, highly sexual. I'm sure she gets lots of male attention, which feeds her ego, and the more she gets, the more she needs. It's a cycle.

"So you got her the job here?" I ask needlessly. Of course he did. There was a Help Wanted sign in the window for two weeks, and it's gone now. I didn't notice when I walked in, but I see it now.

He nods. "Yeah. She's new to my parish, seems like a good kid. She's just down on her luck."

I glance at her trailing behind Meg, her full hips swaying to and fro. "She's too young to be 'down on her luck,'" I observe.

"Eh, you know kids. You used to be one of them, a hundred years ago," Michel jabs. "She's in her ramen-noodle-eating stage—surely you remember how that is. But I can't really say more than that about her. Confidentiality and all."

"Oh, yes. You're nothing if not professional," I answer, gulping at my water.

"You should get Corinne some flowers," Michel suggests, changing the subject. "She needs to know you're thinking about her."

"She's all I think about," I tell him. "You have no idea."

"Does *she* know that?" Michel asks bluntly. "Because you need to tell her. She can't read your mind."

"Sometimes you're a bossy dick," I tell my brother. Michel rolls his eyes.

"Just trying to help. Besides, I'm a priest. I'm supposed to be stern," he tells me firmly. "I've got to lead people to Christ with an iron fist."

"Yeah, because that's what people like," I answer drolly. "An iron fist."

He laughs because he's ridiculous, and his eyes twinkle, and I wonder once again just how in the world he can live his life.

"Are you sure you never hook up with a nun?" I ask dubiously. "I remember your teen years. You blazed a trail through our high school girls a mile wide. You left no stone unturned."

"That's how I got it out of my system." He pats his napkin at his lips, almost primly. "Women hold no power over me now, Jude."

Yet his gaze is over my shoulder, and when I follow it, I find that he's staring at the young waitress bent over a table. I raise an eyebrow.

"Oh, really?"

He laughs. "God didn't make me blind, though. Since I can see, I figure that he wants me to look at *all* of His children. At least the ones who are of legal age...not the actual children. I'm not *that* kind of priest," he adds.

"You're ridiculous," I tell him, lifting my hand to signal for the check.

He is unfazed, like he always is.

Zoe comes to our table with a check in each hand.

"One check or two?" She bumps my shoulder with her hip, and she smiles down at me, waving the checks. Her heat burns into my arm.

"One," Michel says. "My husband is paying."

Zoe's mouth falls open as she stares at Michel's white collar and he laughs, a loud guffaw.

"Kidding. He's my brother. But he's still paying."

Zoe laughs and drops the check in her right hand in front of me.

"At your leisure," she says before she swishes away, her hips swinging wide like a pendulum. Michel watches her go.

"Would you get your eyes back in your head, Father?" I demand. "Jesus."

"Don't use His name in vain," my brother chastises.

"Don't lust after women."

"Fine," Michel counters. "But it's not like I'm going to act on it. She's one of God's children. I truly just want to help her. Her looks are a separate issue."

"Uh-huh." I laugh and toss some bills on the table for Zoe. She's still staring at me, and I try not to notice.

"Have a nice night, boys," she practically purrs, and I swear to God her tits are going to bust out of her top. "I'll be seeing you. Oh, and, Father…thank you again. You're my hero."

Michel grins and I all but drag him out.

"See you here in the morning, you big hero?" I ask as we pause by his truck.

"Yep."

I drive home leisurely, with the windows down and the chilly wind blowing in my face. Soon it will be too cold, so I'm taking advantage of it tonight. I'll never tell Michel, but I do swing by the store and pick up some flowers. They're nothing fancy, just a bouquet wrapped in plastic, but Corinne will like them.

The house is still dark when I get home, and I watch TV until I can't keep my eyes open any longer, waiting for my wife.

Like I have every night for days and days, I fall asleep alone.

4

Now
Corinne
Reflections Mental Facility

I count the ceiling tiles in the night.

The light from the moon illuminates the dark just enough to see them.

From down the hall, I hear screaming, but that's normal here. I'm under no illusions about what this place is.

I hear the nurses' shoes as they scurry toward the noise, and I look again at the ceiling. There are over five hundred tiles. I'm not sure of the exact number, because every time I count, I get distracted.

I'm so lonely, and I know for a fact that I shouldn't be in this room. I'm a physician. I should be medicating whomever is screaming.

But I'm not a doctor in this building. I have no credentials here. I'm a patient, like everyone else. It's a difficult pill to swallow. It's a fact that lodges in my throat and won't go down.

With a sigh, I roll to my side and stare at the wall. It's white and stark, and the sheets beneath me are cold and thin. My bedding at home is luxurious and thick, spun Egyptian cotton, one thousand thread count. It's funny how accustomed I've gotten to nice things over the past few years.

During my childhood and med school, I didn't have anything. Now I pretty much have everything. And in this place, it's a stark reminder of the differences between home and here.

The biggest difference of all is that I'm here, and Jude is not.

It's hard to sleep without my husband. In all the years that we've been married, we've never been apart. We always sleep curled up together, our limbs intertwined. No matter how little we're able to see each other during the day, we always wear each other like a second skin in the night.

I wonder if he's struggling with this as much as I am.

I'll ask him on Saturday.

God, I don't get to see him until Saturday?

What day is it now?

With a start, amid my rambling thoughts, I realize I don't know.

I don't know what fucking day it is.

How long have I been in here?

One day?

Two days?

Three?

Four?

The walls close in on me, getting tighter and tighter, until I squeeze my eyes shut so that I don't have to see them. The only way to survive this is to just plow right through it. I'll do what they want me to do, and I'll breathe, and I'll talk to them, and I'll remember, and I'll get better.

I count, whispering, the monotony lulling me into sleep.

One one thousand.

Two one thousand.

Three one thousand.

The last number I remember is one hundred before I drift into the abyss of sleep.

"Cunt."

The hissing whisper wakes me, and my eyes open wide, and I don't know how long I've been sleeping. Minutes? Hours?

At first, I think I'm dreaming, but then I see the outline of a girl…a woman…in the chair next to my bed.

It's dark, so I can't see her face, but her nail polish glints in the moonlight. It's chipped around the edges. She chews her nails, and she seems so so familiar.

"Who are you?" I ask, a pit forming in the base of my stomach.

"Your worst nightmare."

I sit straight up in bed, trying like hell to adjust my eyes to the dark, and in that one split second, she's gone.

I scramble out of bed, turn on the lights, and the nurses find me moments later crawling on my hands and knees, searching beneath my bed.

"What are you looking for?" they ask curiously as they help me up.

"There was a girl in here…" I tell them, and they look at each other strangely because we're definitely alone now.

"What did she look like?" one asks me as I crawl back into bed.

"I couldn't see her," I have to admit. "It was too dark. And her face…it seemed blurry."

"Maybe you were dreaming," one suggests.

"I wasn't," I insist. "I wasn't alone."

But they don't listen. They turn off my light, and maybe I really am crazy.

I'm on edge for the rest of the night, watching and waiting

for someone to appear, but they never do. My muscles are tight and coiled, ready to lunge out of bed again.

But I don't need to.

She doesn't come back.

I've got to relax. I've got to breathe.

I count my breaths until I finally fall asleep again.

The last breath I remember is number five hundred and four.

At my session in the morning, Dr. Phillips stares at me.

"Who did you think was in your room last night?" he asks me curiously. "Did you think it was the same person who was with you when you attempted suicide?"

He stares at me, waiting, and I recognize the look on his face. I'm sure I've had it on my own with my own patients at times.

He's humoring me.

"There was someone there," I insist. "It was a woman."

"Did she speak to you again? Was she the one who told you to hurt yourself?"

I exhale, then exhale again.

"I'm not schizophrenic," I tell him firmly. "I'm not hearing voices that aren't there. No one told me to hurt myself."

"But you said you don't remember doing it in the first place," he reminds me. "So how can you be sure?"

I'm silent. He knows I'm not sure about anything.

"There was a woman in my room last night," I tell him again, and my words are firm.

He pauses. "Everyone was accounted for at that hour, though," he points out. "There couldn't have been anyone, Corinne."

I stare at the wall again.

"I want to change your medication," he tells me. "Maybe try clozapine."

My head snaps up. "That's an antipsychotic."

Dr. Phillips nods carefully, his expression cloaked. "Yes. It's just a precaution for the time being, Corinne. Your memories are affecting your cognitive function."

"No," I speak out, and then I pause.

Can he possibly be right?

The girl was so real, right next to my bed.

Was she truly not there?

"I…" My voice trails off.

"It's just for a while, Corinne. We'll get a handle on this."

"Am I going to lose my career?" I ask suddenly, because who will want a crazy doctor?

Dr. Phillips smiles. "Our goal is to return you to your regular life unscathed, Dr. Cabot. Let's just focus on the matter at hand, shall we?"

I'm unsettled and disturbed, because I worked so hard for my life, for my career. All of those sleepless nights in med school…they can't have been for nothing. The blood, the sweat, the tears. The student loans, the headaches, the time. All of it.

"Let's return to All Hallows Lane," Dr. Phillips instructs. "Close your eyes. Tell me what you see."

I sigh and stare into space, because I don't want to relive that night. Every time we do, a piece of my soul breaks off and falls into an abyss. I'll never get those pieces back again.

"Your father had been having an affair with Melanie Gibson," the doctor reminds me, as if I'd forgotten. "How long had it been going on?"

"I don't know," I admit. "I'd just found out that day."

"And you didn't tell your mother?"

"No. I didn't know what to say. And I didn't have time, anyway."

He'd killed Melanie and her husband before I could decide what to do.

"Did you like Melanie?"

"Yeah. She was always nice to me."

"What was she doing when you arrived at the house?"

"She was washing dishes. She'd been filling up her candy bucket for trick-or-treaters. Her hands were wet. She was wiping them on a towel when she turned around to greet me."

"She and your dad didn't usually see each other in front of you kids, right?"

"No, never." I shake my head.

"So, what changed that night?"

"I can't remember. I was just there to babysit."

God, it's so frustrating.

My hands clench and unclench, and Dr. Phillips eyes them.

"Calm down, Corinne. It's okay. You're safe here."

"I know that," I snap. "I just... I can't remember."

The memories from that night, the black-edged snippets of time, whirl and twirl around me, and the more they swirl, the more breathless I become. I try to grasp them, to pull them to me, so I can finally look at them, but I can't.

The memories distort, come into focus for just a second, then distort again. Mud. Scuffed leather. Frayed laces.

"I see shoes," I say, breathless, a whisper. "Black shoes."

"Your father's?" Dr. Phillips asks, but I shake my head.

"No. His were brown." A feeling comes over me that I can't describe, terrifying and all-consuming. Something foreboding. I'm covered in sweat and the ceiling is caving in on me and my heart pounds and I suck and suck and suck for air, but it won't come, and I panic panic panic...

When I open my eyes again, the psychiatrist is drawing something into a needle, flicking out the air bubbles and walking toward me.

"No." I shirk away, the needle long and glinting. "I'm fine. I don't need that."

I try to scramble away, but a nurse is suddenly here, and where did she come from?

I struggle, but they hold me down, and there's a sharp prick, then the entire world goes black.

5

"Hey, little sis," I answer my phone midmorning, taking another gulp of coffee out of my favorite mug, the one that says *This might be vodka.*

Jackie takes a breath and then launches into a tirade about her husband, her kids, her maxed-out credit card and her sucky boss.

"Not all of us can be successful like you," she finishes up, as she always does. While I love her, she does try to play the guilt card often. As though it's my fault that I took college seriously and she didn't.

"Jacks, you *are* successful," I tell her, like I do at least twice a month. "You're a CPA. You take care of people's money. If that's not responsible and successful, I don't know what is." Never mind the fact that she finished college only last year, and so she's really just starting her career. Better late than never.

"You know, last year at this time, we were in Cabo together," she points out ruefully. I glance at the wall, at the photo that proves it. Me, Jude, Jackie and Teddy are all standing on the beach, our arms wrapped around each other. The sun was on our shoulders and it had been a good day, one filled with the beach, margaritas, churros and hope.

Teddy and Jude had taken us away from reality to avoid this time of year. God, I wish we could do it again now.

"That was awesome," I tell her honestly. "I haven't had that much fun in forever. And when you lost your passport and gave us all a heart attack, it was so hilarious."

I'm facetious and she chuckles. "That's why having a doctor for a sister is an advantage. You can give everyone CPR."

"Or you could just stop losing your passport," I suggest. Honestly, she's lost her passport on every trip she's ever been on.

"I found it," she defends herself. "In plenty of time to get on the plane."

"You were lucky." I take another sip of coffee and find that it's getting cold. There's nothing worse than that, so I get up to microwave it.

"Do you want to go with me to see Dad this weekend?"

Her question is hesitant, and I don't know why because she knows what I'm going to say. It's the same thing I always say. She should know—she's asked every week for the past seventeen years.

"No."

"Co, please. He wants to see you."

"I don't want to see him," I say as respectfully as I can. "Marion is a three-hour drive from here. I can't spare three hours, and also, I just don't want to. That hasn't changed."

"He's your father," she reminds me. "That hasn't changed, either."

"He's a felon," I answer, and the whole conversation makes me tired. "I don't want to visit him in prison. I don't want to remember what he did. I'm sorry that you choose to, but I choose *not* to."

"Mom would want you to," she points out.

"I know that, but Mom's dead. Therefore, she doesn't get an opinion."

God, dealing with life and death every day makes me cold sometimes. I backtrack.

"I'm sorry, Jacks. I just… I can't. You don't know what it was like. *I* was the one in that house. *I* was the one he left in the house with dead people. I have to cut myself off from that part of my life. I have to so that I can deal with it. If you were smart, you'd do the same."

"He's our dad. I can't."

"As our dad, he *should* want peace for us. Instead, he constantly tries to guilt us into doing more for him, into trying to appeal, into correcting his decisions. We can't do that. He did what he did. We can't change it. He's guilty. He killed people, Jacks."

"I know that." Her answer is steady and solid. "But you know he wasn't in his right mind. That's not who he really is."

I think about my father…the father I knew growing up. *That* father's eyes always twinkled and *that* father had mints in his pocket. Yet that same father is a murderer.

It bends my mind, and I'm silent.

"If you change your mind," Jackie tells me gently, "I'm going on Saturday. I can meet you and we can ride together."

"I'm not going to change my mind," I assure her. "Drive safe."

"I love you, you know," she answers. "Do you love me?"

"Always."

It's what our mother used to always say to us, and Jacqueline and I have kept the tradition alive.

Tradition is soothing and comfortable. We can all use more of that in our lives.

For now, though, I need some air and some exercise. I grab a sweater and Artie, and we go for a walk.

Our neighborhood is quiet, shrouded in trees and forestry, and Artie's nails click on the sidewalk. "We've got to get you a pedicure, girl."

She moves slower than she used to, though, and the clicks slow down by the minute.

I breathe in the fresh fall air, and my boots crunch through the dead leaves. It's ironic that fall is so beautiful. It's beautiful only because everything is dying. I watch the withered leaves tumble from the trees, every breeze carrying yet another one to the ground.

The light is unique this time of year. The sunlight seems as crisp as the air, but yet at the same time, it's muted. It's almost as though it knows its days are numbered before winter. I soak it up while I can, ignoring the niggling thoughts in my brain.

It seems like it did *that day*.

The autumn light.

It's the same.

It's weird how random little things can trigger memories.

My phone buzzes in my pocket, and I almost ignore it, but can't. I have to be responsible.

"Lucy," I greet my friend, after I see her name. "What's up? Do *not* tell me you need me to come in early."

"No." She laughs. "Not this time. I'm coming over to do your nails before work. I saw them yesterday, and they look like something that should be scooping fish out of the lake for food."

"As in bird talons?"

"Now you're getting it."

"Is there any use arguing?" I ask doubtfully, because I already know the answer.

"No."

"Fine. You know the gate code."

"I'll be there in twenty."

It's just long enough for me to finish my walk.

I've also made a pot of hot water for tea and turned the fireplace on by the time the doorbell rings, and Artie is so tired that she doesn't bother getting up.

"Hey, Luce." I open the door. "Come on in."

She's lugging a caddy full of nail paint, and what looks like a tool belt, although it's hard to tell with her baggy sweater. She always dresses like she's wearing flour sacks, and they hang from her body in waves.

"You aren't going to need industrial equipment," I mention. "They aren't that bad."

"Ha. I brought an electric sander just in case."

"Whatever."

After getting tea, we seat ourselves in front of the fire, and Lucy grabs my hand, filing down my nails. I will admit, they're a bit ragged from constant washing, but hardly talons.

"I've got to have some music," Lucy tells me after a few minutes. "I've gotta wake up before my shift. Do you mind?"

"No, go ahead." I wave toward the sound system. "You know how to work it already."

Lucy and I have known each other for a year, but it feels like ten. That's how it is when you work with someone day in and day out. They become like family. She's good to me, oftentimes bringing me coffee at home on her way to the hospital. Her heart is as big as Lake Michigan.

She flips the power switch and fiddles with it as I pick out a nail color. First Bob Marley, then '80s rock. She sifts through the channels. For a minute, the frame is in slow motion. Artie wags her tail once. A bird chirps outside the window. The clouds move. I pick up a bottle. The label says "Do or Die Red."

But then Lucy settles on a station, and the music...when it comes on...freezes my hand, my fingers curled around the curve of the bottle.

Lyrics to the old song "American Pie" fill the air, swirling around me in a flurry of words.

A sudden rush of unexplainable terror wells up in me, illogical and too much to bear. The words, the music, all of it... It pounds in my head, and the memories cave in on me, and I've been here before, yet I haven't.

A sense of familiarity, of déjà vu, of something I can't place, overwhelms me, and a word whispers over and over in my head, husky and urgent and low, and I'm rooted in place.

Cunt.

The word is in my head, as loud as if someone had whispered it. It echoes, and the music and the voice... I know it. But I can't place it.

It's maddening.

A gate opens, and the emotions of that night unleash and surround me, suffocating me. The scenery around me swirls, and I can't breathe. My ribs seem to collapse on themselves, one by one, like taut strings snapping, as the intercostal muscles contract and contract.

I gasp for air, but it won't come. I hear a roaring noise in my ears, and I'm on my knees and all I can see is Artie. She's in my face and she's whining...and I think I might be dying. My heart slams hard harder harder, and my lungs explode.

Then cool hands are on my shoulders, and someone says my name, but the lights are exploding around me, like fireworks.

"Corinne."

I open my eyes and it's Lucy, and she's calm, and she's rubbing my back. Her hands are cool.

"Breathe. Count to ten."

She doesn't ask what the issue is. She's just very no-nonsense. The nurse in her acts swiftly, and my face is buried in her bulky sweater.

I suck in air, letting it out.

I suck it in again, then let it out.

It's minutes before I can breathe, before I can relax.

Minutes more before I can even process what happened.

"I'm sorry," I finally say weakly, and I'm so humiliated.

Lucy stares at me, her pretty face serious.

"Why are you sorry?" she asks. "It's a panic attack. People have them. I'm going to go get you some water."

I nod, and I close my eyes, and I hear Artie growling.

"She won't hurt you," I call out. "She's just old and grumpy."

"Okay!"

Lucy comes back within a minute, putting a cool glass in my hand. "Drink."

I put the liquid to my lips and something something something still doesn't feel right.

"I don't know what came over me," I say. I don't know what else *to* say.

"It happens," Lucy says casually. "Don't feel self-conscious. Lord knows, you're under enough stress at the hospital."

I nod, like that's the reason. No one has to know any different.

"Don't tell anyone, okay?" I say hesitantly. "Please."

Lucy rolls her eyes. "I would never. You know that."

"Thank you. Not even Jude."

She rolls her eyes again. "I still have yet to meet that husband of yours in person. And it's not like I'm going to tattle on you over the phone."

"Okay." I nod, relieved. "Thank you."

"Do you want to ride with me to work?"

She's still concerned, and it's sweet. But I shake my head. "No. By the time I shower and stuff, I'll be fine. But thank you anyway. We'll have to take care of my talons another day."

"You'll do anything to escape pampering yourself." Lucy shakes her head as she puts the bottles away. "I swear. Just don't blame me when the patients start complaining."

I smile. "I would never."

"See that you don't." She tries to be gruff, but she doesn't fool me. She's concerned.

"See you at work, Luce."

She hugs me. "You've got to take better care of yourself. Expect me to start nagging you about it."

"I would expect nothing less."

She leaves, and I'm alone, and I stare out the window, trying to suppress the fear that is bubbling up in me, gurgling to the surface like bubbles in the water.

Am I going crazy like my father?

Is this how it started for him? Irrational panic, and memories that he couldn't explain?

With a gulp, I shove the troubling thoughts away and head for the shower.

At work, I focus on *not* worrying about the panic.

I have to compartmentalize. I have to do that to stay calm. It's never been a problem before, even after the murders so long ago. In fact, that's when I learned the skill. Every day, at school, I weathered the taunts that came from being a killer's kid, and I was brave and defiant. But at night, in the dark, alone, I'd curled up in a ball and succumbed to fear. That was fine for me. As long as no one saw me break down, I could pretend that I was fine.

It's a skill I utilize to this day.

I can do this.

I can be brave, defiant Corinne.

The nurses' station is empty as I grab an orange and peel it, and I sit for a few seconds to rest my feet, checking over my shoulder for Lucy. She's checked on me no less than four times in four hours, making sure I'm fine. It's starting to feel a bit smothering, even though I know she means well.

I take this moment of downtime to check my phone, and a text from my husband makes my heart flutter, and I smile.

I love you today. You're beautiful.

"Hey, what's funny? I want to laugh, too." My colleague collapses into the chair next to mine, exhaling deeply as he drops his head straight back against the headrest. He stares at me from beneath half-closed eyes. "Well?"

I smile. "Nothing's funny. I was just thinking about Jude."

Brock raises an eyebrow. "Good thoughts?"

"Obviously, Einstein. I was smiling."

He lifts a shoulder. "True. Don't judge me. I had three hours of sleep last night. I'm slow on the uptake."

He grabs a coffee cup and gulps it, filling up for seconds.

"Where's Lucy? I might get her to hook me up for a caffeine drip."

I roll my eyes and grab a chart, trying to keep on top of my notes. It's a never-ending task, and the charts end up in a mountain on the nurses' station by the end of the day.

"If she agrees to that, tell me. I'll want one, too." I rub at my neck while I write. "Also, I'll pay you fifty bucks to do my charting."

"Ha. No."

"You don't even want to think about it?" I look imploringly at him.

He shakes his head. "Nope."

"You're not even sorry."

"Nope."

"You're heartless."

"No, I'm not. In fact, here." Brock gets up and stands behind me, gripping my shoulders. He massages, and as he does, the tension leaves my neck in waves and I groan.

"Sweet baby Jesus, that feels good."

"Yeah, I hear that a lot."

He snickers and I ignore it. I don't even care about boyish sexual innuendo. This feels too good. "Don't stop."

"Yeah, I get that a lot, too."

"You're a child."

He agrees. "A child with magic hands."

"Let me guess. You hear that a lot, too?"

"Now you're getting it." He rubs up and down my spine with his fists, and when he's done, I'm almost a pile of goo in the chair.

I close my eyes, and when I open them, I notice two nurses staring at the two of us, whispering.

"Great. Now we're part of their rumor fodder," I say ruefully. "You'd think they'd be too busy for that crap."

They have the grace to look away, but I can feel them whispering long after they walk away. Fantastic.

"Oh, you know how they are," Brock says easily. "They're easily entertained. They were buzzing for days after that chick came in last week with the shower massager stuck inside her. But seriously, they had a point. Who does that?"

I don't know. I don't care. People never cease to amaze me.

"Did you know that Dr. Fields is screwing around with Gabby?"

I stare at him. "Eeew. Gabby is so sweet and Fields is so... eew. And he's on his honeymoon. He just got married. Are you sure?"

I'm indignant on his new wife's behalf, and Brock nods in affirmation.

"Very sure. I got it firsthand from Sara. She was working a double and caught them in the supply closet."

"Gross. What a slime."

"Yep," Brock agrees. "Men are dogs. They can't keep their dicks in their pants."

He says this so cheerfully, even though he himself is in possession of a penis.

"Jude can," I tell him as I return my attention to my chart. "He's got faults, but being unfaithful isn't one of them."

"As gorgeous as he is?" Brock's question seems weird, coming from another man. "You don't ever worry?"

I pause, looking up at him. "Do you have the hots for my husband, Romeo?"

He laughs quickly, turning red. "No. Of course not."

"And no. I don't ever worry." I finish up my chart, proud of myself that it took one minute flat. It's a new record for me. "He never gives me a reason."

Speaking of my husband… I pull my phone out of my purse and start to text him.

Thank you for the flowers. I love you. I hope your day is…

Lucy interrupts me. "You guys, I need you." Her hair is sweaty, stuck to her forehead. "All hands on deck."

She pivots and jogs back toward exam room four, and I slip my phone back into my purse. We rush to help, and for the next twenty minutes, we're consumed with a cardiac infarction, as a forty-year-old man with a high-stress job codes on the table.

I do compressions while Brock grabs the paddles, and the

entire team acts as a unit. We're smooth, we're practiced, we work together with ease.

We get a pulse two minutes later, and the nurses cheer.

Brock bows. "It's all in a day's work, ladies," he says, and they giggle, and I watch him flirt with all of them. He catches me looking and shoots me a sly gaze.

"I have to keep in their good graces," he says sheepishly as we head back out to the desk.

"Must be nice to have a penis," I tell him. "I have to rely on simply being nice."

"Don't be bitter," he tells me. "Just bring them all decent coffee tomorrow. You'll accomplish just as much. My flirting skills suck."

I laugh and he laughs, and once again, I catch the nurses looking at us. It makes me self-conscious. We're not doing anything wrong. It's not like he's flirting with *me*. We're just colleagues. We commiserate together because we understand our jobs in a way no one else can. The phone rings, and he picks it up.

"This is Dr. Lane."

He listens and punches the hold button, returning his attention to his charts.

"It's for you."

I feel a rush of warmth. It's Jude. I've missed him today. The mere thought of this morning makes my stomach flutter, and I pick up the phone.

"Hey, babe."

"Dr. Cabot?"

The voice is not my husband's.

"Yes. Who is this?"

"This is Deb Camden from USP Marion."

My heart starts thumping. It's the prison.

"How can I help you?" Did I just say that out loud, or did I only imagine it?

"Dr. Cabot, this is a courtesy call to inform you that your father won't be available for visiting hours this weekend. He's currently in the clinic, being treated for non-life-threatening wounds he sustained in a fight. After that, he'll be in solitary for a week."

I allow that to sink in.

"Why did you call me, instead of my sister?"

"He changed his emergency contact to you last year."

"He did?"

"Yes, ma'am."

"Why?"

"Now that, I don't know."

"Okay. Thank you for letting me know."

"Oh, and, ma'am?"

I pause, listening. "Yes?"

"Your father is just banged up. He's all right, so there is no reason to worry."

With a start, I realize that I was actually worried. Why? My father killed people, and I haven't seen him in years.

I should feel only disdain for him.

But that's not the case.

I shake it off and hang up.

There's clearly something wrong with me.

6

I watch the new waitress as she waits on someone else's table.

The mom smiles back at her, but the smile is guarded, and I'm sure I know why. She's older than Zoe, tired, and she's let herself go with her baggy Notre Dame sweatshirt and high-waisted mom jeans.

Zoe, on the other hand, is only twentysomething with a tight-ass body. Other women probably don't like her much, especially when she acts the way she is right now. She's shoving her tits against her uniform top so much that the buttons are straining, and she brushes them against the husband's arm as she bends down.

The mom glares, and Zoe ignores her.

"My name is Zoe," she tells him in a low voice. "Whatever you need, just ask."

She makes eye contact with the wife for long enough to see the daggers before she sashays away. I watch the husband's gaze follow her ass, and I can't help but smile a little bit at the drama.

Zoe is smug as she fills ketchup bottles at the side station, very confident in her sexuality. I watch her try not to look at me as she watches the husband. She maintains eye contact with him as she fills ketchup bottles and somehow manages to make it seem suggestive.

She hums as she wipes off the sticky top and hums as she slides her hand along the bottle, holding it tightly in her grasp, sliding it back and forth, back and forth in a very sexual manner.

The middle-aged guy watches her, his mouth open, and the ketchup bottle is clearly a penis, and she's implying the penis could be his, and then it's erupting in a red spurt and she grins triumphantly, licking her lips.

The middle-aged guy looks breathless and weak, and I roll my eyes, raising my hand to signal her.

She sashays over to me, making a huge show of walking in front of her poor other customer. The wife is fit to be tied.

"You know, you might get strangled before you even finish your shift," I tell her, eyeing the guy's murderous wife. Zoe laughs, a sound like tinkling glass.

"That's okay," she tells me, leaning toward my ear. "I like being choked. I like things *very* rough."

Son of a bitch.

For some reason, that's startling, and it actually tightens my groin, not that I'd let her know that.

"Er, charming," I tell her wryly. "My brother, *the priest*, will be joining me. We'll both have coffee to start."

"Sure thing," she says. "Anything you want."

Again with the suggestive tone, and does she ever turn it off?

She pauses and turns back to me. "Oh, and, Mr. Cabot? I

hope I didn't offend you with my talk about rough sex. I just didn't want you to knock it until you've tried it."

She winks and walks away, and my heart is still pounding when Michel arrives a few minutes later.

He's just sitting down when Zoe comes back with her coffeepot and order pad. She makes me feel uncomfortable and invigorated at once. It's an odd combination to feel.

"What can I get for you, sailor?" she asks, and her lip is slightly curled in the way that makes it look like she's pouting. She probably imagines it being sultry, or herself as Greta Garbo.

"I'm not a sailor," I tell her, but I smile. "And my brother is definitely not. But I'll take the smoked salmon and bagel." Michel tells her he wants bacon and eggs, and she lectures him on cholesterol.

"I've got an in with the big guy," Michel tells her, pointing upward. "I'm not worried about little things like heart attacks." Zoe giggles and turns around. As she does, she accidentally steps on Artie's paw, and the big dog growls.

Zoe flinches.

"Don't worry," I tell her. "She's an old softy. She does sense evil, though."

Zoe looks over her shoulder at me. "The old softy is still growling at me, so I doubt it. I'll have to take your word on that. I'll check on you in a while."

Michel and I eat, and Zoe brings our check, and I realize I don't have any money with me. I hand her my credit card.

"Can I see your driver's license, Mr. Cabot?" she asks. "Your card isn't signed on the back."

I'm surprised. "Sure. Thanks for asking."

"We can't be too careful," she says as she takes my outstretched license. "Scammers are everywhere."

She examines it for a minute before handing the license back with a smile. "I'll be right back."

It's not long before she saunters back to the table.

"I have to jot down your phone number, Mr. Cabot. A security measure for the credit card."

I raise an eyebrow. "That's weird. I've never had that happen before."

"Yeah," she assures me. "Amex has been doing that lately. We're supposed to match the number against their number on file to prevent fraud."

"That makes sense. The number on file is my cell phone." I sign the check. "Are we set now?"

"Yep! Have a great day."

Michel and I pause outside the front door, chatting for a minute longer, and Artie looks in the window, growling. I tug on her leash.

"Knock it off, Artie."

Inside, Zoe looks up at me, brushing her long hair out of her face, and smiles.

I ignore the weird sensation building in my chest. I haven't felt it in forever, and I shouldn't be feeling it now.

Attraction.

I climb into my Land Rover and drive away.

7

Ju, Ju, touch me again.

Corinne's voice is sleepy and soft, and I love it when she takes that tone.

I roll over and slide my hand up her thigh, and it's soft and bare and smooth. My fingers search for the moist warmth that I know I'll find, and when I do, my wife arches her back, thrusting into my hand.

I smile into her hair, and she smells like warmth and vanilla and sunlight.

"Come on, babe," I whisper to her. "Cum on my fingers."

I move and she moves with me, and we rock and slide, until she quivers and moans, and her voice is husky as she orgasms against my palm.

I pull away my hand, just long enough to hover above her, and then I thrust into her and...

I wake up with an erection.

I'm startled with the suddenness of reality, then disappointment slams into me as I realize that I'm alone. My wife isn't here. I'm not making love to her. The sheets are cold, the house is quiet.

Damn it.

Damn it.

I stare at the ceiling, calming myself down, slowing my breathing.

I'm alone.

Corinne is across town. In another bed.

I get to my feet with a sigh and let the dog out, and it's as I'm watching her out the window that my phone rings.

"Jude?" It's Dr. Phillips, which startles me. He doesn't usually call this early.

"Is something wrong?"

"Don't worry, it's under control now. Corinne had a bit of an episode last night. She thought someone was in her room. We tried to discuss it at an early session this morning, but she had another episode. We had to sedate her, but she's resting comfortably now."

I'm silent as I process that.

"Jude? Don't worry. It's under control."

"How bad was it?" I ask slowly, imagining the worst.

There's a pause.

"She didn't try to hurt herself again, if that's what you're asking. She had a panic attack and was clawing at her throat. But she was out of it. She wasn't purposely trying to hurt herself."

I suck in a breath.

This can't be my life.

This isn't my wife. It isn't.

"Was it because… I mean, has she remembered?"

"No, she hasn't."

"Thank you," I tell him. "Can I come see her before Saturday?"

Another long pause. "I don't think that would be wise," he finally answers. "In fact, we might want to put a pin in Saturday, too. She really needs to focus on herself right now, Jude. If you're here, she'll be worried about how you are perceiving her, or you could even trigger memories that she simply can't handle right now. Why don't we discuss this as the weekend draws closer?"

I'm numb as I hang up.

Numb as I pour some coffee.

Numb as I pour it down the drain without drinking it.

My coffee sucks ass.

I pick up the phone, and Michel answers on the first ring.

"Can we meet for breakfast early? I don't want to be alone."

My brother's answer is immediate. "I'll meet you in ten minutes."

I make it to the café in nine.

I get my regular table and wait for my brother, and it isn't long before his hand is on my shoulder.

"Been waiting long?" He grins.

I shake my head. "No."

He sits, examining my face. "What's wrong?"

"Besides everything?"

I tell him about Corinne's newest developments as I sip on coffee. My heart feels heavy and hard, and everything seems a little hopeless.

"What if she never gets out?" I ask, and I know I sound crazy. I'm talking about my talented, brilliant wife. That idea is preposterous.

"She'll get out," Michel assures me. "And soon. I promise."

I look away, at the floor, at the wall. My eyes sting, and I don't want Michel to see. I'm not a pussy, for God's sake.

When I look up, Zoe is sauntering toward us. Her eyes are knowing, her hips are swaying. When she stops next to me, her hand is familiar and warm on my back, and she flirts with both my brother and me in her typical fashion.

"What are we having, sailors?"

Michel orders, then Zoe turns to me. Her fingers trail down my back, lingering, and no one can see. I'm the only one who knows.

"I'll have a ham-and-cheese omelet."

"Anything you want, sugar."

She winks and walks away, and Michel watches her go.

"She's taken to this job," he observes, watching her flirt with another patron at another table.

"Yeah, you did her a service getting it for her."

I glance over my shoulder and see her picking up her phone. Her eyes are on mine, and she purposefully walks away toward the bathroom.

Two minutes later, my phone buzzes with a text. I already know it will be from her.

I glance at it, then shift it so no one can see.

It's a picture of her bare tits, her fingers tweaking her own nipple.

Come suck it? she texts next. Please?

I swallow hard and furtively glance at my brother. He's oblivious as he checks his own phone.

No, I answer.

Not right now? she replies. She knows she has me now. She knows my situation is precarious. She knows she can blow it all out of the water.

I put my phone in my pocket without answering. She's the devil in a waitress uniform.

She brings our food twenty minutes later and sits next to us for a minute, and when she throws back her head and laughs, she puts her hand on my knee and leaves it there. There's a weird tension between us, like a live wire flipping around on hot pavement.

Michel notices, and I shrug away from Zoe, her hand falling away.

She looks at me but doesn't say anything.

"Well, I'll leave you boys to eat," she says, standing up and walking away.

Michel stares at me over his coffee cup.

"Anything you'd like to say?" he asks calmly, unruffled.

I shake my head. "I don't know what you mean. You know how she flirts."

"Yeah. I guess." But he's troubled as he eats. I can see it on his face. And he has every reason to be troubled. I am, too. I have no idea how I got into this tangled-up mess.

And it *is* a mess.

The only question is…how am I going to get out of it?

8

I'm walking through the ER, and everything is still.

This can't be right, I think. The ER can't be this quiet.

But it is. It's motionless, silent. I peek into an exam room, and Jackie and Jude are lying on gurneys, their eyes wide-open, their mouths slack.

They're dead and bloody, and I scream. Only, no noise comes out.

Even my screams are silent, and I can't seem to move to help anyone.

I try, because I'm a doctor, and maybe I can bring them back, and I struggle against the air, against unseen hands restraining me.

But I can't. I can't get to them, and they're dead, and I couldn't stop it.

"Corinne!"

A voice, my father's, calls out from across the hall. I'm terrified, and now I can move, but only toward him. Unbidden, one foot steps in front of the other, until I'm standing in front of the curtain. Shaking, I pull it back.

My father sits on the table, his mouth a bloody grotesque mess.

"You haven't fixed it yet," he accuses, and his teeth are missing. "Fix it."

"I can't fix it," I insist. "It's yours to fix."

"No, it's not," he argues, and blood streams down his chin. "It's yours."

I'm confused and I stand still, and the whispers seem to come from everywhere, surrounding me, filling my ears.

Cuntcuntcuntcuntcuntcuntcuntcuntcunt.

They hiss and spin and strike me, and then...

My eyes startle open, and I stare at the ceiling in my bedroom.

I'm soaked in sweat, and my fingers are wrapped in a sheet. I untangle them and allow the circulation to flow back to my hand. Rubbing at it, I stare at my husband. He's sleeping peacefully, burrowed under his pillow, oblivious to my torment.

It's the second nightmare in one night.

It was so real that I thought it *was*.

I sit up in bed and take a drink, then take several deep breaths, willing my racing heart to slow. As I move, Jude hears me and stirs.

"Co?" he asks in confusion. "When did you get home?"

"A few hours ago." I run my fingers through my damp hair, and Jude notices my sweat.

"What's wrong?" I can see his concern, even in the shadows.

"A nightmare."

"Oh, babe." He sighs, reaching to rub my back. "It's okay. I'm here. Nothing bad is going to happen. I won't let anything hurt you."

My husband's fingers feel good on my skin, familiar and soothing, and I'll never want anyone else to touch me but him. I allow myself to relax, to close out the images from my head.

"I'll never forget it," I tell him softly.

He nods. "I know. No one would. But you can move on from it, Co. It doesn't have to hold this power over you."

I squeeze my eyes closed, because my brain knows that. It really does. But my heart… My heart isn't so logical.

"I just wish I could unsee what I saw," I offer limply.

Jude pulls me into his arms, and his warm breath moves my hair.

"You can't," he replies simply. "But we can deal with them, babe. I promise you."

"It's been years," I tell him, and I feel so dejected.

"I know. But the mind works in powerful ways," he tells me. "You know that. Be patient. I really think you should see someone, babe. You need help working through this. You should've gotten help long ago."

"I don't know," I answer doubtfully. "I don't want to see a psychiatrist." I stare at the ceiling and remember my panic attack. "Or maybe I do. I don't know."

I don't say what I'm thinking…that I'm afraid of what I'll find if I poke around my head too much. Something feels like it's there…lurking just behind a wall…waiting for me to find it.

Jude squeezes my hand. "Just hang in there. We'll figure this out. What time do you work today?"

"Second shift."

I know he hates second shift, and so do I. It means I can sleep in, but it also means that I won't see Jude until almost midnight. He sighs, hard, just like I knew he would. When you've been married so long, you can anticipate your spouse's reactions.

"I swear. It won't be for much longer," I tell him, and I mean it. "As soon as they get another doctor in, I'll transition to Family Practice."

"I've heard that before." Jude is wry.

"I know. But I mean it."

He turns to me, his eyes almost green in the early morning light. There's something there in those mossy depths, something I haven't seen in a while.

"Are you sure? Because that would mean that you'd actually have to spend time with me."

His words are pointed, barbed, at the same time as they are insecure.

His implication takes my breath away.

"What are you talking about?" I ask hesitantly, because that's crazy. "You're the most important person in my whole world."

"You have a weird way of showing it sometimes." Jude's eyes are hard, and he's staring at me, and I see the truth in his gaze. He feels neglected.

I taste guilt in my mouth.

"Oh my God," I breathe. "Jude, I'm sorry. I never want you to feel that way. I love you."

Something passes over his face, and he shakes his head, and his attitude is different.

"I know," he tells me, and he sounds so tired. "I'm sorry. I'm just being passive-aggressive because I never see you. This will pass. These hours…everything."

"Do you really believe that?" I ask, and he nods again.

"Yeah. I do."

I grab his hand and squeeze it, his fingers entwining with mine.

"You know, let's make a deal," I suggest. "All honesty, all the time. If something bothers you, just tell me. And I'll do the same. That way, we don't get worked up about things that aren't even true."

He smiles. "I like that. It's a good idea."

"I have them sometimes." I grin back and he chuckles. "In fact, I can go first right now…because I have a concern."

Jude waits, and I continue. "It bothers me that we don't have much of a sex life anymore," I tell him honestly.

He stares at me, and I can practically see him biting back a sharp retort. His tongue must hurt from the effort.

"Okay. Point taken. And it bothers me that you're not home more. It bothers me that we haven't started a family yet, Corinne. We're not spring chickens."

A heavy feeling of dread drops onto my chest like it always does when he talks about having a baby. I swallow hard, then again, then again.

"I promise to come home by dinnertime at least twice a week." I make a spur-of-the-moment resolution, addressing one thing at a time. "Can you promise that we'll have sex once a week? I miss our sex life, Ju. It makes us feel closer, and without it...well..."

Without it, I feel so distant.

He grips my fingers.

"Yes. That's a deal."

We're quiet then, and I almost think I've escaped an uncomfortable subject, but then Jude brings it up.

"What about our family?" he asks after a few minutes.

I swallow again. Hard.

"I...I don't know."

Jude's hazel eyes look more green in the light, as they do whenever he's upset. I try to meet his gaze, to meet the disappointed look there, but it's hard. I look out the window instead.

"You don't know what it's like," I tell him quietly. "Living under the shadow of what my father did. I can hardly stomach the idea of bringing a child into that."

"Into what?" Jude is frustrated now, as he always is when I speak of this. "You didn't commit your father's crime,

Corinne. No one knows us here. Our child would never have to deal with it."

He's right. Of course he's right.

But I'm not telling him the entire truth. I'm not telling him that I'm afraid of genetics. I'm afraid that our child might inherit my father's mental illness... In fact, I'm afraid that I even have or my sister. My father didn't snap until he was an adult.

Jude watches me, watches the wheels turn in my head. "It'll be okay," he tells me, and his voice is understanding. "Our baby would be okay."

I nod. "I know. Maybe soon."

Jude blinks away his disappointment at my non-commitment.

"Want to go get breakfast?" I ask him. "It's almost morning. We can go to your little place—so I can make it up to you for coming home late all week."

He pauses and almost seems reluctant.

"We can," he tells me. "Or we can stay here and spend some quality time together."

He stresses the word *quality*, and I know what that means. I'm so tired, but I don't want to tell him that. I was the one who just asked for a better sex life, for God's sake.

"What do you have in mind?" I flirt, ignoring my exhaustion, and I rub my hand on his leg. Once upon a time, that would've made him instantly hard, but we're not twenty-five anymore, so it doesn't.

"Let me show you." His voice is a growl and he flips me over.

I suck in my breath because this is new—his roughness, his coming at me from the back. His fingers bite into my shoulders, and he pushes me into the bed. His passion is palpable, and it's been so long since I've seen him this way.

Excitement laps into me, and I exhale in a rush.

My fingers curl into the sheets, and I hold on as he slides

his fingers into me, rough rough rougher. One finger, two, then three.

I moan, and he moans into my neck, his chest rubbing my back, his heat leaching into my own. The friction is delicious, and the aggression is pleasingly different.

It's so unlike him, so unlike us, and for a minute, I revel in that. He's taking a renewed interest in our sex life, taking my words to heart.

But then…then…

He grasps my neck from behind. His fingers curl around the sides of my flesh, not truly hard, but hard enough.

I suck in my breath, and for a minute, a strange minute, I feel panicked.

I don't know why. It comes out of nowhere.

I feel subdued, compressed, constrained. It's suddenly terrifying, and I can't breathe.

I can't breathe.

My lungs are hot and I scramble around, pulling away from Jude, turning onto my back and pushing him away. It takes him a minute to realize what's happening. His eyes are glazed over with sex.

"Jude, no." I push at him. "Don't."

He comes to a halt, pausing over me, his forearms shaking with the effort.

His breath comes in pants, then it slows, then he rolls over to the side.

I feel a bit weak, and I'm embarrassed by the panic. What the hell is wrong with me?

"I was just trying something new," Jude says finally, his voice low. "I wasn't really choking you. I would never hurt you, Corinne. Surely you know that."

"I do," I answer quickly. "I don't know what's wrong with me. I guess it was just unexpected. It wasn't like you…and…"

I don't know what else to say. My heart is starting to slow down now, and I feel ridiculously self-conscious. What the hell is wrong with me?

"It's okay," he assures me, but somehow his voice seems empty, or offended. Something seems off. "We won't try rough sex again."

"It's not that," I protest. "Just maybe tell me first next time."

"Okay."

We're silent for a while, and he turns to me slightly, his lips in my hair. It should feel intimate, but instead, it doesn't. It feels like we're a million miles apart. We're doing the right things, but it's lacking substance. We're on autopilot, going through the motions. I wonder if Jude feels the same way, and I wonder why it feels this way.

I feel a moment of panic, because marriage isn't supposed to be like this.

"Jude?"

"Yeah?"

"Do you feel like something is wrong? With us, I mean?"

This rouses him, and I can feel him staring at me, and a weird tension pops up between us. I can practically feel it on my skin, like it's a living thing.

"Maybe."

"What should we do?" My level of panic increases, and my grip on Jude's arm is tight, and the weird tension grows.

"We'll be okay," he rushes to reassure me. "Because we want to be. It's just a slump. Our priorities aren't in order. We just need to get them straight, Co. We'll be okay."

Just as soon as I change my whole life to suit his ideals.

Where did that awful thought come from? I chastise myself. He wants only what every normal person wants—to see their spouse and have children. What is wrong with me? I have no call to resent him.

Minutes pass before Jude gets up.

"I'd better shower for work." He retreats to the bathroom, and the bed is empty without him. He doesn't have time for a run, and I doubt he'll have time for breakfast.

I run my hand over the empty sheets, idly looking at the Jude-sized indentation he left behind. Whatever semblance of intimacy I felt twenty minutes ago is gone now, even though my thighs are still damp from his presence between them.

Something in me wants to go to the bathroom and step in the shower with him, and force a sense of intimacy to return. But something else tells me in a louder voice that I can't force it. It's not there to force. We have to somehow figure out how to rebuild it.

I throw on a robe and trudge to the kitchen to make some coffee, and I pour Jude a go-cup. When he comes out from the bedroom, his hair is still damp, his face freshly shaved, and he has that "clean man" smell. He's long and lean in his black trousers and cream-colored sweater. I kiss his cheek, and his mouth curves against mine.

It's quick, but it's there. A smile.

"It's going to be okay, right?" I hate the uncertainty in my voice. He glances at me quickly, and I remember for the millionth time in my life that my husband is a very sexy man. His hazel eyes glint in the sun warmly, and I search them for truth.

"Of course, Co. It's not even a question."

He's sincere, and he's sure, and I feel a bit better because of that. I watch his black Land Rover disappear from the driveway. Marriages go through peaks and valleys. I knew that when we got married. It just seemed at the time like valleys would never happen.

It'll all be fine. It has to be. We both work too hard at life to not be fine.

I can't shake the uncertainty, though, and so I do the only thing I know to do. I call my sister.

"Hey, you," she answers cheerfully on the first ring.

"Do you and Teddy have issues…in the bedroom?" I ask hesitantly without preamble.

My sister pauses. "Issues as in…"

"As in, you never make time for sex, and when you do, Teddy can't get it up half the time?"

Jackie laughs, a raspy sound. "Of course. That's what happens when you get old, weirdo. The soldier just doesn't salute as easily."

"I'm not old," I tell her. "And neither is Jude."

"Of course not," she agrees. "But in penis years, he's like… fifty-five. So be patient."

"Penises aren't like dogs," I tell her. "They don't have their own time system."

"I disagree. Once a man hits thirty, years double for penises. It's practically a fact."

"Odd that I didn't learn that in medical school." I'm droll and Jackie laughs.

"Do you guys try new things from time to time, to spice things up?" I'm hesitant to ask, but the words come out anyway.

"Hell, yeah. Variety is the spice of life."

Okay. Maybe Jude was right to try something. Maybe I'm a lunatic for freaking out. Something about it, though… Something felt wrong. Really wrong.

We hang up and I take Artie outside.

I stand on the patio and watch her move slowly around the yard. Her muzzle is white now, and her once-strong haunches are thin.

"Artie, come in, girl!" I call, and she rambles leisurely to me. I scratch her ears, and she closes her eyes.

She's been my family for the longest time. Her and Jude

and Jacks. They are all I need in this world. I feed her break-fast before I get ready myself, adding some scrambled eggs to her dog food.

"Don't tell Daddy," I tell her. Eggs give her gas, and she knows it. I think she smiles at me.

I shower and actually have time to get ready for work lei-surely, instead of getting called in early. I blow-dry my hair and put it in a long braid draped over my shoulder, because that makes me feel young and pretty. I still feel the afterglow of sex with my husband, and I want to keep the good vibe going. I apply makeup and lip gloss and the whole nine yards.

When I walk into the ER an hour later, I feel good, I look good, and Lucy stops in her tracks with an armful of catheters for the supply closet.

"You got some," she crows. "I can see it on your face! God, why do I have to be a crazy cat lady? All I get is fur on me all the time, no orgasms."

I laugh without meaning to, and she growls at me. "You don't get to laugh at my pain."

This, of course, only makes me laugh at her again, and she rolls her eyes.

"It's slow today," she tells me. "For once. It's just you and Dr. Lane, and there's a girl in exam room twelve who wants to see a female doctor."

I nod and head in that direction, stopping to pick up the chart from the door. Glancing through it, I get the main facts.

Female, twenty-four years old, presenting with a migraine.

I slip through the curtain and find her sitting on the table, her feet swinging. She's young and cute, and I greet her with a smile.

Because I *did* get some today.

9

"How does that make you feel?"

I ask my patient the age-old question, and he stares at me, dumbfounded.

"It makes me feel pissed. The bitch cheated on me, Doc!"

I don't correct him. I don't remind him that I'm not a doctor, I'm a therapist. And I understand why he's looking at me like I'm on acid. It was a stupid question under the circumstances, but necessary according to protocol.

"I'm sure," I assure him, and he nods because in my own way, I'm validating his feelings. "You have every right to be furious. She violated your trust, and because of that, I'm sure you feel vulnerable."

He nods because of course that's right. I know it's right. I see a hundred patients a year who are in this same exact situation.

"I do," he admits, and he sounds embarrassed. "But I still love her. Isn't that a bitch?"

I have to imagine it is. Sometimes I think the human mind

practically sabotages us into self-destructive behavior. I nod and make notes, and he keeps talking about his feelings.

"It's possible to get over infidelity," I tell him. "If your wife is willing to recommit, and if you are both willing to examine what is wrong in your relationship. Do you think you can both do that?"

He ponders that, and we talk until his hour is up.

"I'll see you next week," I tell him. "Make sure you see Ginny on your way out to confirm your appointment."

"Will do," he agrees, and I'm left in silence but for the trickle of water from the fountain in the corner. Water tumbles over three stacked pots, and it's always on because water is soothing to my patients.

Frankly, listening to it all day makes me have to piss.

I stare at the dark gray walls, at the comforting artwork, at the dark leather furniture. All of it was designed by Corinne, to look dignified and provide a peaceful place for my patients. I have to admit, she's good at designing. When she did it, deep down I felt resentful, like she was trying to control every facet of my life. Even at the time I knew it was stupid. She was just trying to help. Back then I felt like she was too controlling. Now I feel like she's too neglectful. Maybe I'm just a childish bastard who can't be pleased. I have a good life and I know it.

This morning, she wasn't expecting the rough sex. *I* wasn't expecting it. It was something I did on the spur of the moment, and I know why.

The girl at the diner. She had announced so loudly that she loved rough sex. It got my imagination going, and Lord help me, I took that fascination out on my wife.

My intercom buzzes, then Ginny's voice fills my office.

"Jude, you left your cell phone out here. It's been vibrating all hour."

I don't bother to answer; I just get up and head out to my

receptionist's desk. She sits in her pencil skirt, her middle-aged legs still looking decent even though she claims she's allergic to exercise.

"Here you go." She smiles at me, handing me my phone.

"Corinne?" I guess.

Ginny shrugs. "I'm not nosy. I didn't look."

Yeah, right. She's the nosiest person I know, and she probably searched through everything on my phone. But I don't call her on it. Instead, I thank her and head back into my office. Ginny keeps everything organized here and keeps me on track. If it weren't for her, I'd be lost. I'm not going to piss her off.

I scan through my texts.

None from Corinne. I'm oddly disappointed, even though she never texts me during the day. The ER keeps her too busy. But still. I thought she might text after this morning's sex.

One from Michel.

How are you doing?

And several from a number I don't recognize.

Hi there. It's Zoe from Vilma's.

Damn it.

I swallow, and I read her other texts.

You left your credit card at the café this morning.
Do you want to meet me so you can have it back ASAP?

I feel a jolt. First, fuck. I left my card someplace? I can't even remember the last time I did that. How irresponsible.

I practically don't have a credit limit, so a thief could have a field day with it.

Second, how weird that she's texting me. So weird.

I can just pick it up from Vilma in the morning, I answer. Thanks for letting me know.

I see the three bubbles on my text screen signifying that she is answering. So I wait without putting my phone down. The idea of who is on the other end of the phone gives me a jolt, a thrill, even though my initial thoughts about the girl weren't flattering. She might have clear daddy issues, but she has an ass you could bounce a quarter off. It strokes my ego that she's texting me.

I actually have the card with me. I didn't want anything to happen to it. I'm in town running errands. I could meet you for lunch?

Another jolt.

She wants to meet for lunch? Is this for real?

What a kind offer, I answer, and my heart literally pounds. But I would never impose on you like that. If you're working tomorrow, I'll pick it up then.

There are three bubbles. She's typing.

But nothing comes through.

I wait.

The three bubbles are still there, then they disappear.

Still nothing.

I can't help but picture her in her overly tight waitress uniform. The bright blue complemented her skin tone, and her tits were busting out of the top. The skirt was short, and it's quite possible that she made it that way on purpose.

For a minute, being a red-blooded man, I picture that ass bent over a chair, her uniform skirt hitched up to her hips.

Her lacy panties would be shoved to the side…and I think she'd be shaved.

I indulge for just a second, then I push the images out of my head. It's a fantasy. That's all.

I'm normal.

I love my wife.

I miss my wife.

Corinne is my world.

I jam my phone into my pocket as my door opens with *my* next patient.

"Mr. Ford," I greet the elderly man in front of me, the one with OCD who is at this very moment wiping his feet on the carpet as he walks to wipe away all germs from his shoes. He does it a thousand times a day. "I'm so glad to see you. How have you been?"

He takes a seat in the chair across from me, careful to keep his right foot crossed over the left, and for the next hour, I'm immersed in the world of an obsessive man. This week, his new habit is stepping on a particular stair step on his porch precisely four times every time he goes home.

We discuss coping mechanisms, and the chemical reasons that OCD could be at play in his brain, and when we're nearly done, I find him staring at the portrait of Corinne and me sitting on my desk.

"You're a lucky man," he tells me, and his cloudy eyes are pensive. "I lost my Helen a decade ago. I haven't been the same since."

No, he hasn't. His OCD emerged that year, when he was lost in grief.

"I *am* lucky," I agree. "My wife is a brilliant woman."

"She's a looker, too," Mr. Ford observes, and I try to see the picture through the fresh eyes of a stranger.

Corinne's eyes are bright and blue, her hair long and blond.

She's thin, she's trim, she's tall. Her legs are long, her smile bright.

She *is* a looker. Sometimes I forget that.

Probably because I haven't seen her in days and days.

I hide my stress. My patients don't get to hear my very real and very human problems.

We finish our session and Mr. Ford leaves, and I wrap up my notes. When I'm finished, I'm surprised to realize that it's lunchtime.

Ginny pokes her head in. "Hey, boss. I'm going out for lunch. Should I bring you something back?"

I could meet you for lunch?

Unbidden, the texted words flash through my mind, and guiltily, I push them away. Fuck, man. Not cool.

"I'm good," I tell Ginny, and I think my words have a double meaning. I'm good. I don't have straying thoughts about a woman who isn't my wife. Not *real* straying thoughts.

Ginny leaves, and I grab my jacket, and as I do, my phone buzzes, and I think my wife might've texted me back.

I'm startled when I see that I'm wrong.

It's not Corinne.

It's a picture.

Of Zoe.

I was right. She's shaved.

My heart thuds as I stare at the nude picture.

Her tits are big and full, and her thumb is brushing her nipple, her other hand caressing her shaved vagina. Her eyes are big and turned to the camera in a sultry gaze, and she's completely and absolutely naked.

Are you freaking kidding me?

I swallow hard, and it's not like I haven't been hit on before. I have. But this is different. It's so blatant, so outrageous, and frankly, in some hidden and shameful spot, it turns me on.

Fuck, man.

I'm sorry, I'm married, I reply, typing with shocked wooden fingers.

Because I'm good. The stiffness in my crotch doesn't count.

Three bubbles.

That's fine, she answers. Do you want a girlfriend?

Sweet Jesus.

She can't be serious. Is her generation so blatant and direct?

No, I answer. Sorry.

Three bubbles.

Hmm. We'll see.

My heart is beating hard, and it seems to be in my throat and I don't honestly know why. I stare at her words, and every one of them is designed to be flirtatious, to engage me. Somehow, that feels shamefully good.

My wife works so much that we rarely see each other. And here is this girl, this much younger girl…throwing herself at me via message. It's flattering.

It's also pathetic that it somehow makes me feel validated.

God, I'm such a therapist. Can't I turn it off for one fucking moment and simply enjoy that I got hit on by a hot young girl?

Jesus.

I turned her down. I'm good. But that doesn't mean that I can't stare at her nude picture a little while longer. I mean, she sent it to me. She wanted me to look at it. I shouldn't feel like such a perv.

I run to the bathroom and splash cold water on my face, a physical effort to switch gears, to get the forbidden picture out of my mind. Because it *is* forbidden. I'm married, and there comes a point where fantasies aren't good or healthy.

When I come out, Ginny is back.

"Hey, boss," she says cheerfully, a sandwich in front of her. "Your one o'clock is here."

"Send her in," I instruct.

I sit down in my office, stick my phone back in my pocket and get back to business as usual.

My patient comes in, rife with overeating issues, and my afternoon begins.

Once again, Corinne works late and doesn't come home in time for dinner. Michel arrives instead, with his hands full of takeout. We spread out at the kitchen table and eat our weight in Chinese food.

"Don't you think that's enough?" Michel raises an eyebrow at me over the top of my scotch bottle. I scowl at him from across the kitchen table.

"No."

He rolls his eyes. "You know Corinne throws herself into work this time of year, more so than normal. It's her way of dealing with things."

I sigh.

"You don't know what it's like," I insist to him, gulping down the amber liquid. "It sucks. I'm a therapist, and I can't help my own wife. And she won't come home long enough to let me try."

"I know," he says sympathetically. "I know. I'm not judging you. I just think you might want to limit yourself to maybe five drinks. Six is a little over the top."

He's wry, and I gulp down my sixth drink. The room spins a little, and I squeeze my eyes closed.

"Why don't you go to bed, and I'll clean up our dinner dishes on my way out," my brother suggests. I don't argue. I slap his back on my way past, heading down the hall.

"I love you, man," I call over my shoulder.

"I know."

I drop onto my bed, and I hear the back door close ten minutes later and Michel's truck rumbling down the road. I think I'm going to go right to sleep, but I don't.

I stare at the ceiling.

I miss my wife.

I feel empty. Cold. Alone.

I already miss the huge rush that I had this afternoon when Zoe sent me the picture. It was amazing, like the hit of a powerful drug. As a therapist, I know what it was. Dopamine is the hormone associated with pleasure. It's a spark plug in your brain, something that triggers pleasurable feelings and assigns them to objects. It *is* a drug, so to speak, and as humans, we subconsciously do things to access that pleasurable feeling.

Feeling empty, I want to experience that again, to fill the void of my wife's absence. To eradicate the anxious feelings that consume me lately.

So I use my phone to pull up some porn.

It's harmless, faceless. Anonymous.

I go from site to site, one after another.

After a while, I realize something.

All of the girls I'm looking at look the same.

Like Zoe.

Fuck.

I close out of the porn sites because they make me feel like shit, but at the same time, I get a surge of adrenaline. Because Zoe is a real live person out there who wants me. I have proof in my hand.

I pull up her picture and stare at it again.

Between the dopamine and the scotch, I feel drunk on life, and I swear to God the room almost spins with it.

I'm embarrassed to realize as I stare at the picture that I'm not even looking at the girl's eyes. I don't have to. This is porn, in a way, and I don't have to make a personal connection, and I don't have to behave decently. I'm behind closed doors with a picture that a young flirt sent me.

I stare at her tits, and at her hand that is on her own crotch.

The dopamine rises in my blood and I ride that wave, and I'm almost blurry with it when I act on impulse and snap a picture of my erect penis in my hand.

Before I can think twice or clearly, I send her the picture.

Stunned, I watch my phone and see that my text was delivered.

Sweet Jesus.

The room comes into focus and what the fuck did I do?

I've never in my life done something like that. What the hell is wrong with me?

The reality of what I just did…the inappropriateness, the elicit nature of it all… It slams into me and I feel sick. Just in time for three bubbles to appear.

Dick pics don't do it for me. What else ya got?

God.

Holy shit.

Holy.

Shit.

I'm so far beyond pathetic that it's ridiculous. I feel like a complete dumbass. Who in the hell does something like this? I'm utter, utter scum.

I text back and I do the only thing I can do.

I lie.

I'm sorry. That was meant for my wife. Your number was pulled up and I made a mistake. I've had one too many drinks.

I wait.
Nothing.
Still nothing.
So I add, I'm sorry. Please disregard my text.
Finally, after what seems like forever, there are three bubbles.
I wait.
I feel like shit. Like pathetic shit. And finally, words appear.

Too late.

10

"You don't want me to see my husband."

I repeat Dr. Phillips's words, astounded.

He nods. "Just for now. I want you to focus on yourself, rather than on how your actions might affect him."

"How does that make any sense at all?"

Jude is my rock. My world.

Dr. Phillips shakes his head. "It's not that we don't want you to see your husband. It's that we want you to take a few days to not worry about him, but to think of yourself. It's standard procedure, Dr. Cabot."

"Does Jude know? Did he agree to this?"

"He doesn't like it much, either. But he does agree that you should be focusing on getting better at the moment."

I feel deflated, like a balloon that has been stomped on.

"I don't really know how to operate alone," I admit. "It's been Corinne and Jude for so long. Focusing on me, and me alone, seems foreign."

Dr. Phillips nods. "Exactly. Which is why you need some space. Your husband will be waiting for you when you're ready."

I swallow and contemplate that. Why do I feel so anxious about that? Of course he will be. He's my husband. In sickness and in health, for better or worse. We took vows.

"This might cheer you up," the psychiatrist mentions, and I narrow my eyes. "You do get to have a visitor today."

"I can have visitors, just not Jude?"

Dr. Phillips shifts his gaze. "While we feel like Jude might be distracting, I do think it might be beneficial for you to not be alone at this juncture."

I'm still, and when I speak, my words are slow. "Who is it?"

"Your friend Lucy. She's very concerned about you. She calls and checks on you every day. We're truly trying to help you, Dr. Cabot."

He sounds so sincere, yet so clinical.

"Fine," I say simply. "I'm happy for the visitor. But don't forget. I'm here on my own volition. No one in their right mind would hold me here if I change my mind."

"No one plans to," he agrees. "You're here because you know it's best."

"For now," I reply carefully.

Dr. Phillips nods. "For now." He stands up. "Let's go out and meet your friend."

I follow him to the common room, where Lucy is sitting uncomfortably on a sofa, surrounded by patients. She's as out of place as I feel. She looks up and sees me, and I can't help but notice the way she looks at my wrist, eyeing the bandage, probably looking for the crazy.

But she smiles and gets up and hugs me, and she hands me a coffee.

"Your favorite," she assures me. "With an extra shot of espresso."

"Thank you," I tell her genuinely. "This place has shit for coffee."

"Okay, well, on that note, I'll take my leave," Dr. Phillips says. He looks pointedly at Lucy. "Don't forget what we discussed."

She nods but seems a bit uncomfortable. "Okay."

He walks away, and I pull Lucy to a corner to sit in two chairs with me.

"What did you discuss?" I demand as soon as we sit.

She shrugs. "He doesn't want me to focus on Jude, or anything from the outside. I'm just supposed to be a set of ears for you to vent to, if you want."

Her eyes are swimming with sympathy, and I hate it.

"They don't even want me to visit with my sister," I tell her. "I'm surprised they let you in."

"Maybe it's because I'm more impartial," she suggests. "I won't remind you of anything from the past, or stuff like that."

"Maybe."

She sips her coffee, and her feet are fidgety. "Do you want to talk about anything?" she asks softly.

I've been confiding in her for a year, but I don't think I can talk about this. It's just too much. So I shake my head.

"Are you sure?" she asks doubtfully. "It looks like I'm all you've got for now."

I think about that, and it's honestly tempting. I've never wanted to talk about any of it, but I was out in the world and surrounded by the hustle and bustle of life, and it was so easy to distract myself. In here, there's nothing to steal my attention. Nothing I can do to keep my mind busy. And I decide that's the method to their madness here.

They literally force you to think of nothing else but your issues.

"My panic attacks weren't caused by the hospital," I begin. "I let you think they were, but they weren't."

Lucy nods. "Okay."

"They're from other issues. Old issues. Issues from a long time ago," I continue, my words slow. "My dad was cheating on my mother, but I didn't know it. By the time I found out, it was too late."

She waits, her legs crossed and her fingers wrapped around her coffee cup. "Too late?"

I nod. "Yeah. My father killed his mistress and her husband. I was there babysitting. I was eighteen."

"Oh my God. Corinne." She's stunned, as anyone would be. "I didn't know. I would never have guessed. Oh my God."

I look at the floor. "Yeah. So apparently, they say I've suppressed issues and memories, which I know I have, but they've caused me to sort of implode now. As you know."

Lucy fidgets uncomfortably.

"But I swear to you. I'd never try to kill myself. Never. I don't know what happened."

Lucy's eyes are drawn to my bandage again, and self-consciously, I hide it under my other arm.

"You must've just been…" Her voice trails off. "I don't know. Overcome?"

"With what?" I ask desperately. "With crazy?"

She shakes her head. "Of course not. Don't say that."

I'm silent. I take a drink. I look at the floor again.

"You really don't remember anything at all from that day?" she asks, and her eyes…they're both dubious and fascinated.

I shake my head. "No."

She stares off into the distance, her slender fingers drumming her knee.

"Why haven't you told me about this stuff before?" she asks gently. "We're friends, Corinne. I like to imagine that we're good friends. You could've trusted me with this. Trying to deal with this alone…that's a heavy burden to bear."

My eyes well up. She has no idea.

"That's what Jude says. Sorry. I know I'm not supposed to focus on him."

She fiddles with her cup awkwardly.

"Well, thank you for listening today," I tell her, and honestly, it did almost feel good. "You won't mention this to anyone, will you?"

She shakes her head vehemently. "Of course I won't. Ever."

"Does anyone know where I am?"

She shakes her head again. "Not that I know of."

"They don't know why I've been gone?"

She looks away. "I'm not sure."

"Lucy."

She looks at me reluctantly. "They know about the… incident. You were brought into our ER, Corinne. You know how gossipy some of the nurses are."

"Great."

She's silent. She can't fix this.

"I think our time is almost up," she says now. "Can I come visit you again?"

"Of course you can." I hug her. "And bring some more coffee."

She laughs and stands up, and her pants almost fall off. I roll my eyes.

"You seriously need some new clothes, Luce. You're so beautiful. You should act like it, not dress like you're eighty-five."

She grins. "I'm doing mankind a favor. If I unleash this—"

and she gestures at her body "—they would all be devastated by my natural beauty."

We're both laughing when Dr. Phillips walks over.

"Can I escort you out?" he asks her. She nods, and I do sense reluctance there, but she's in a loony bin. Of course she's reluctant.

"I'll see you soon," she tells me. And then she pauses. She turns around, and her mouth is next to my ear.

"You don't have to worry about Jude," she tells me. "You know. What your father did. I know your husband would never do that. He loves you. So while you're in here, don't worry about him at all."

I have to chuckle at that.

There are many things in life that I worry about, but Jude being unfaithful isn't one of them.

II

Last night, I texted the waitress a picture of my dick like a fucking slimeball.

That's the plain truth of it.

Now I'm standing at the door of Vilma's, watching that very girl wait on tables, and trying to decide how to handle this situation.

I'm not going to shirk away from it. God, no. I come here every day, and this is my place. She's new, and it was simply an error in judgment. I'd had too much scotch, and fuck it. I'm not going to make excuses. I'm married. I love my wife. I made a dumb mistake, and that's that.

I stride inside.

Vilma is hunched over the hostess desk, her gnarled fingers adding up tickets. I smile at her when she looks up.

"Can I have the window table?"

"Of course." She nods. "Follow me."

Zoe is in the kitchen, and so I'm relaxed as I decide upon

coffee and toast, and when I look up, she's bustling back through the kitchen doors.

Fucking-A.

I'd forgotten how blatantly sexy she is. She's like a bright neon sign, blinking on and off that she's got young, firm tits and that my dick should stand up and take notice. Her uniform is tight, her legs are long. She's curvy, and I can tell that in ten years, she'll be plump. But right now, her curves are like a ripe peach, just perfect for biting into.

I swallow hard as she bends over at a table and her ass strains against her short skirt. I can see the outline of her butt cheeks, and she's not wearing panties. She's a bit on the trashy side, but in a young and immature way, like she's wild and unrestrained. When I think of it that way, it doesn't repel me like it did the other day. In fact, it gives me a strange rush.

I gulp hard, right as she glances up and meets my gaze.

She stops in her tracks, her temples damp from rushing around, and for a minute, it's just her and me in the middle of the busy café, frozen as we stare at each other.

An invisible tether connects the two of us, her eyes to mine, and she seems real now, instead of the vague abstract that she was last night on my phone screen. Her face is flushed in an attractive way, the glow of youth radiating from her. Her lips are full, her eyes are bright. There is something there, an unreadable something, but she masks it and smiles. The world unfreezes, the sounds and smells coming back to life around me.

I smile politely back, and she walks straight to my table, holding my credit card in her hands. She offers it to me.

"I'm sure you're wanting this. If you see strange shoe purchases, don't blame me." She giggles and I roll my eyes.

"Thank you for holding it for me."

"Not a problem. This isn't my section," she tells me. "But I'm gonna take care of you anyway."

She grins again and her tone is a bit suggestive, and I'm wondering if that was on purpose. *She's gonna take care of me.*

"About last night…" I don't know what to say.

She grins again, waving her hand. "Forget about it," she tells me lightly. "*I* already have. You clearly were texting your wife while drunk and accidentally sent it to me. It happens."

Except that's *not* what happened, and I think she knows that.

But I play along because she's giving me a generous out, and neither of us mentions that she sent me a picture, too. I'm the married one here. It's *my* job to be good.

"Exactly," I tell her. "I'm sorry. I hope I didn't make you feel uncomfortable."

She dips her head until her lips practically brush my cheek. "On the contrary," she whispers, and her breath smells like spearmint. "Your wife is one lucky woman."

I feel a pang in my gut and I flush, and when she straightens, Michel is standing behind her with a glib look on his face.

"Hey, bro," I greet him, pretending that my dick isn't stiff with Zoe's implications. "Have a seat."

"I'll go get your coffee," Zoe tells us before she sways away, and Michel looks at me knowingly as he sits.

"Someone looks nice this morning." He watches her go, and he laughs and I laugh, because that's what brothers do, even when one is a priest. "I think maybe Jezebel had a hand in designing that one."

I watch Zoe pour coffee into mugs, and she leans over so that I can see her tits better, and I decide Michel is right. Zoe is a modern-day Jezebel. She's showing me her goods on purpose and trying to make it seem innocent, and this all has the very real possibility of crossing a line.

That makes me uncomfortable. Having a fantasy was fine, but reality… Well, reality isn't.

I try to ignore her eyes when she comes back and sets our

cups down in front of us. I bury my face in my mug and don't look up.

I catch her watching me a few times, but I don't stare at her. In fact, I make sure I don't look at her.

I'm good.

I'm good.

There's a strange feeling in the air, a very tangible knowledge that if I wanted to, I could cross a line with this woman. It's in the way she stares at me pointedly, in the way she moves around me.

It makes me feel awkward at the same time as it's a bit exhilarating and flattering. It's a strange feeling, half unpleasant and half amazing. I could have those curves in the palm of my hand, and I... God. I push the thoughts away.

I'm good.

"How's Co?" Michel asks, drumming his long fingers on the table. His fingers are identical to mine, and I find myself spacing off as I watch them. "Jude?"

I look at his face. "Yeah. She's okay."

"Sister Esther was in Mercy ER the other day. She fell and broke her arm after hours. Corinne set it. Esther said the place was a madhouse, but that Co was very kind."

"She *is* kind," I agree. "And the place *is* a madhouse. I swear it's sucking her lifeblood out."

"Maybe it *is* her lifeblood," Michel suggests. "Maybe you should remind her that there's more to life than work. Take her on a trip or something."

I think about that for a split second, but then Zoe comes back, and she stands very close to me. Her eyes meet mine, and she smiles.

"What can I get you to eat?"

We give her our orders, toast for me, an omelet for Michel, and then she's gone.

"I remember when we were that age," Michel muses as she walks away. "We were just snot-nosed kids. We didn't know a thing."

"Nope."

"You still don't," he adds with a grin.

"Bite me."

"I'm a priest. I would never," he announces.

I roll my eyes.

"I'm starting to wonder, you freak."

He laughs.

The food comes, and he eats his eggs, and I bite my toast.

"How about this... I'll come over for dinner this weekend," Michel suggests. "We'll cook out and drink some brews. Just you, me and Corinne. It'll give her a reason to be a hostess. You've got to do some normal stuff, man."

I nod. "Okay. She'll love that. Consider yourself invited."

"Good. I'll bring the wine."

I shake my head. "Uh-uh. I don't want shitty communion wine. You can bring dessert."

Michel rolls his eyes. "Whatever." But he's busted. I can see it on his face. That was totally his plan. I chuckle and pick up the check. I make sure not to leave my card this time, and I feel Zoe staring at me when we walk out. Her gaze impales a spot between my shoulder blades, burning a hole, daring me to turn around.

I don't.

For some reason, it makes me feel like a saint.

When I get in my car, I text Corinne, just to pound home the thought that I'm good. I'm fucking good. It doesn't matter if Corinne can't see the text right now. She'll see it after her shift.

Hey, babe. I hope you're having a good day! I love you.

She doesn't answer, and I drive to work.

I'm just a normal man, doing normal things. It doesn't matter that the waitress hit on me and I've fantasized about her a couple of times.

I'm normal.

It's all okay.

My day is long. Boring.

My drive home is uneventful, and the house is dark, as I expected.

Artie meets me at the door. She practically head butts me, so I know she desperately has to go out. I open the patio door, and she bounds to the backyard, faster than I've seen her move in a long time.

"Girl, we've got to get you moving. If you don't use your muscles, you're just going to get stiffer. I think I'll try taking you jogging with me again. Would you like that?"

She stares at me from the shadows, moving slowly as she squats.

I'm not sure she can actually jog, but we can try.

"Tomorrow," I tell her. She's unfazed as she slowly walks back inside. I dump some dog food into her bowl. She doesn't lunge at it like she used to. In fact, she sniffs it and lies down next to it. It's almost like she's saying, "I don't want it, but God help anyone who tries to take it. I'll just sleep right here and guard it."

I smile and scratch her ears, then check the clock.

Six o'clock.

I wonder what Corinne is doing. Is she coming home soon?

I call to find out. A nurse answers.

"Hello, this is Jude Cabot. Is Dr. Cabot available?"

The nurse is kind and pleasant, and her voice is very familiar. I think her name is Lucy. "I'm sorry, Mr. Cabot. She's out on the floor. Can I have her call you back?"

"Nah," I answer. "Just tell her I called."

"Will do, Mr. Cabot."

"Thank you," I say.

She hangs up, and I hang up, and I'm alone again, staring at the wall.

12

Jude and I haven't sat down for a meal together in weeks.

I make sure I do my charting early, chipping away at my mountain of binders by four o'clock. It gives me plenty of time, and the influx of patients has been slow for once. Chicago seems to agree that I need a night off.

I text him by six thirty. Hey, I think I can come home soon. Let's meet at your little café for dinner.

He answers immediately. Absolutely!

Great, I tell him. I'll text you when I leave.

I'm smiling, and Lucy grins at me.

"Got a big night planned?"

I smile back. "Just dinner with the hubs."

"Your hubs is hot, though, judging from the pictures," she points out. "I certainly wouldn't kick him out of bed."

I laugh because, to be honest, when you've been married so long, it's easy to forget how lucky you are. Jude *is* hot. I've just grown accustomed to it. He's been in my bed a long time.

"I don't," I tell her. "I don't kick him out of bed."

"Good girl, Doc."

She eats a bite of yogurt, and the clock ticks, and I only hang around to wait until another doctor arrives to relieve me. I'm the only one here, since it's slow.

"Who's coming in tonight?" I glance up at Lucy when I see her getting ready to leave.

She checks. "Looks like Fields."

"Oh, good. That should make Gabby happy."

Lucy's gaze is sharp. "You heard about that, huh?"

I nod. "Everyone has. He's on his honeymoon, and Gabby is his side thing here."

"I'm going to talk to her," Lucy assures me. "She knows that dating a member of the staff is against the rules."

"Someone should talk to *him*," I mutter. "Fucking around on your new wife is against the rules, too."

"He's a slime," Lucy agrees. "But you can't fix that. Once a cheater, always a cheater. God help his wife."

I shake my head, and I've got only four charts to go. I finish them up in ten minutes.

Fields still hasn't arrived.

"He's five minutes late," I tell Lucy. "Can you call him?"

She nods and picks up the phone.

I check on the patient in exam room one. An infant with suspected rotavirus. We're waiting on the labs to confirm it, and in the meantime, she's got an IV drip with fluids. She presented with dehydration and a fever.

"She's doing better," I assure the young mom. The mother looks up at me with red-rimmed eyes. She clearly hasn't been sleeping, but what young mother does?

"Do you promise?" Worry is evident in her voice, and I pat her back.

"Absolutely. Fluids work wonders. If the results come back

as I suspect, rotavirus positive, we'll admit her overnight to observe and get her hydrated. At this age, dehydration can rapidly accelerate. We've got to be careful. But rest assured, we're on top of it."

She nods and exhales, and I slip back out, sliding my stethoscope off, preparing to leave.

Lucy stares at me, though, her face grim.

"What?" I'm afraid to ask. Around here, it could very well mean that someone has died.

"He lost his passport. He's stuck in Barbados."

I stare at her mutely. "Fields?"

Lucy nods.

"He's not coming in?" I ask dumbly.

"No. He's waiting on the embassy to issue him a new passport so he can reenter the country."

"God, what an idiot. That's literally something my dingbat sister would do."

Lucy agrees. "I tried to call Schmidt and Lane, but can't get ahold of them. I'll keep trying. Until then…"

"Until then I'm the only one here."

"Yep." Lucy is apologetic, but it's not her fault.

"Fuck."

"Should I call Jude for you before I go?"

"No. I'll talk to him. Just have whoever is coming in for you find a replacement for me."

She nods and heads for the nurses' station, and I head for the doctors' lounge. I drop into a seat and text my husband.

Slight delay. I'm still trying to get out of here.

I mutter a prayer that God will still get me out on time. I mean, it's six thirty-five. I could still make it.

K. I can't wait to see you.

Jude answers immediately. I smile at his words and close my eyes just for a second. It feels like I haven't slept in a thousand years.

13

You still alive?

I text Corinne at eight. I've been waiting at a table for an hour, sipping on water, reading the news.

Vilma stops by my elbow. "I'm so sorry, Mr. Cabot. I know you've had to wait. Both of my evening-shift girls called in sick, so we've been trying to cover. My morning girl just arrived, and so things will pick up soon."

Fuck. Her morning girl.

But I smile at her. "It's fine, Vilma. No worries." She pats my arm and takes her leave, and I text Corinne again.

Do you have an ETA? Should I order for you?

I put my phone on the table, and as I do, Zoe sees me from across the room. Her eyes light up, and she literally stops what she's doing. She makes a beeline straight for me, and it's like

I'm the only one on the planet who is important. A thrill shoots up around my heart, causing it to pound.

"Hey, sailor," she murmurs when she reaches my elbow. She smells like drugstore perfume, but it works for her, a tangy loud scent of flowers and fruit. She's got on too much, but that's her personality. She's blatant, she's obvious.

"I thought we established that I'm not a sailor." I arch my eyebrow, and I can't help but smile. She's flirting with me. Who wouldn't enjoy that?

My self-rationalization knows no bounds.

She shrugs. "I like sailors, though."

She pauses, her pen above her pad. She takes the tip of it in her mouth and nibbles on it, then her pink tongue darts out to swirl around it, round and round.

"What would you like?" she almost whispers, and her breathy tone reminds me of Marilyn Monroe. *Happy biiirrrthday, Mr. President*... I bet JFK didn't give one fuck about fantasizing.

I clear my throat. "I'm waiting on my wife. But I'll have a salad to start, I think."

She smirks a bit. "Why have salad when you can have steak?"

I feel my heart pounding against my ribs, threatening to break them.

"Are you the steak?" I ask bluntly, and the blood rushes through my temples in a roar. There's no sense in pussyfooting around this.

Her lips part. "Maybe. Although I do know a guy with a great sausage."

I startle at her bluntness because she's referring to my dick pic, and I thought we were done with that. She throws her head back and laughs, sliding her hand down my arm as she slips into the seat next to me.

Her fingers are warm, and the heat bleeds through my shirt

into my skin, making an imprint. I feel it throb, a foreign object in a place it shouldn't be. I'm like a deer in the headlights, and I'm frozen.

"I'm sorry." She giggles. "But the look on your face is priceless. I didn't mean to have fun at your expense. I won't mention it again. Probably."

She giggles again, and I can't help but chuckle, too.

"I deserved that," I admit. "I really did. I'll be more careful who I send pictures to from now on."

"Not *too* careful, I hope," she answers, and her carefully sculpted eyebrows are raised, her eyes staring boldly into mine without flinching.

Now I'm really stunned, and I can't help but engage. I can't help it. Her bluntness draws me in. It's refreshing and we're just talking.

"I thought dick pics don't do it for you."

She smiles, a grin that stretches from one side of her mouth to the other.

"Maybe I liked yours," she tells me. "It's everything I like… long, strong and hard."

Jesus.

She doesn't miss a beat, as though she doesn't know my heart is pounding a million miles per hour.

"I'll go get your order in."

When she stands up, she slides her full tits along my shoulder, and there's suddenly a lump in my throat as I watch her walk away, her young ass perfectly formed, like an upside-down heart.

This is wrong. I'm a dumbass. I should run.

But wait, the devil on my shoulder whispers. *You're not doing anything but talking. What's the harm? Your wife will be here any minute. You're good. You're just here to eat with your wife.*

I shove my misgivings away, and I lock them closed with a key, mentally handing it to my internal devil.

Fuck it.

As Zoe takes care of her other patrons across the room, I feel her watching me. It's like a heated cord, running between the two of us, tying us together. I watch her smile at a middle-aged man, and as she flirts with him in front of his wife, she watches me from her periphery. I wonder if she's trying to make me jealous, or if she's vying for a bigger tip. Either way, she's pissing off the wife.

Zoe sways when she returns to me with a glass of water. As she sets it down, I look at her. "You know, you don't have to flirt for tips. Good service works just as well."

She's surprised by that but masks it quickly. "Oh, I perform *very* good service."

Jesus, she never turns it off.

"But thanks for looking out for me. I'll be right back with your food," she purrs. "It just came up."

A minute later, she's setting a juicy steak down in front of me.

"Life is too short for salads." She smirks, and I know she's not talking about my meal. "I mean, if you really wanted the salad you ordered, I'll go get you one. But I think you really want the steak."

She's the steak. She knows it, and I know it.

"This is fine," I manage to say, and she laughs, trailing her hand across my back as she leaves to attend other patrons. I watch her sway and laugh and flirt, and I try not to, but my gaze keeps getting drawn back to her, over and over and over.

Her hips sway as she works the room, her skirt tight as she bends over. I picture what I would do with that ass, and… fuck.

My phone rings and I pick it up.

"Babe, I'm so sorry." It's Corinne. "Fields is stuck in Barbados, and he didn't let us know until tonight. Lucy is trying to get someone here to take over for me, and I fell asleep in my chair. I'm so sorry. I'll just have to see you at home."

"That sucks," I tell her honestly. "I wish I had known. I would've just stayed home."

"I'm so sorry, Jude," she says, and she sounds so sincere. "I'll make it up to you."

"Okay. Just try to get home early, okay? Maybe we can still salvage the evening."

"Deal." She hangs up, and I look up to find Zoe watching me, a strange look in her eyes.

I've got to get out of here.

I wolf down my food, and just when I look up to wave her over for my check, she's in front of me with a drink in each hand.

"I don't know what you like to drink," she admits, setting one down in front of me. "But the rum and cokes aren't bad. I'm off work now, so I need a drink, and you look like you do, too. Vilma's drinks aren't fantastic, but at least she has them. Most of these hole-in-the-wall places don't."

Son of a bitch. I didn't get out of here fast enough, and here she is at my table, tucking her legs up under her. With her short skirt, I can actually see her crotch if I try. I pointedly look away.

"That's one of the reasons I started coming here," I tell her, watching the condensation drip down my glass. "Vilma's has a liquor license. My wife used to like to come here on Sunday mornings for Bloody Marys with breakfast."

"Oh?" Zoe's eyebrow is raised again, and her lips are plump as she runs her tongue along the rim of her glass. I follow that pinkness with my eyes, imagining the wetness of it. "Why doesn't she come anymore?"

"She comes sometimes."

She giggles. "I'd think so, with a sausage like that in her bed."

Damn it, I can feel my cheeks flush. I haven't spoken with anyone like this but Corinne in fifteen years. It's a rush that I can't ignore as the blood pumps hard through my groin.

"I've had no complaints." I sound smugger than I am as I gulp at my drink. Half of it slides down my throat in one big swallow.

"I bet."

She smiles again and takes another sip, and this is okay. I'm talking about my wife, for God's sake.

Zoe examines me over the rim of her glass, and she twirls her hair in her fingers.

"Tell me about you, Jude Cabot. You seem fascinating."

"I'm not," I assure her, but she's already shaking her head.

"That's a lie," she protests. "You're sexy as sin, you're married, yet here alone talking to me. You're confident, you're strong. You're in the prime of your life. That all sounds very interesting to me. Tell me your story. How long have you been married?"

She sips at her drink again, and this is all very conversational. She's just a girl and I'm just a guy and we're just having a chat. That's all. I'm not wrong. This isn't wrong. It can't be wrong because we're literally talking about my marriage.

I smile back.

"Fifteen years. Since college."

"So..." Zoe counts on her fingers. "That should make you...what...thirty-five? Thirty-six?"

"Yep. Thirty-six." I eye her clear skin, and the face that is unmarred by a single line or blemish. "You're...twenty-five?"

"Bite your tongue, heathen!" She laughs. "I'm twenty-four."

"That's a fun age," I tell her. "I was still eating ramen at that age, I think, while my wife was in med school, but it was good."

"Your wife's a doctor?"

I nod. "Yeah. In the emergency room."

"She sounds very important."

Somehow, Zoe's words are complimentary, but her tone is unimpressed, almost droll.

"She is," I tell her. Because Corinne *is* important. And smart and beautiful. But Corinne isn't here right now, and this isn't about her.

"What do *you* do?" Zoe asks now, and she's so interested as she waits for my every word. God, it's flattering.

"I'm a therapist. Marriage and family, obsessive disorders, depression, etcetera, etcetera."

"*Etcetera.*" Zoe laughs. "How modest."

"I'm a very modest guy," I tell her. "Just ask me."

She laughs again, and she's so enthralled with what I'm saying that she literally is sitting with her face in her hands, waiting for me to speak. I'm trained in body language, and she's turned toward me openly, tossing her hair every once in a while, her eyes smiling along with her mouth. She's in this moment, and she's enjoying it.

I'm her sole focus.

I can't lie. It feels fucking good.

"Being a therapist must be so gratifying." She sips at her drink. "You get to help so many people through their issues."

"Well, I'm not a doctor like Corinne, but I make do." Now I'm the droll one.

Zoe rolls her eyes. "You're more important in your own way, I think," she tells me. "You heal people's *minds*."

"Well, it's all I ever wanted to do." And that's the truth. "My parents wanted me to be a psychiatrist, but I never wanted that.

They end up being pill pushers. I wanted to learn to actually help my patients, not just overmedicate them."

"That's commendable." Zoe nods. "You hear about so many people who are just fed antidepressants and that's the end of it."

My phone vibrates, and a message pops up. Zoe and I both glance at it.

I'm definitely not gonna make it. I'll be home later.

Fuck.

Zoe takes a drink and stares at me over her glass. "Are you happy, Jude Cabot?"

It should be a simple question. It really should be. But here I am, talking to this girl while my wife is at work, and suddenly, I don't know.

"Yes," I tell her finally. "Of course I am."

But am I? The question actually makes me uncomfortable, and I want to change the subject.

"Enough about me. What about you?" I ask. "What's *your* story?"

I'm surprised to realize that I'm actually interested in hearing it. For the first time in fifteen years, I'm enjoying a conversation with a woman other than my wife over dinner.

Corinne was supposed to be here and she's not.

I'm not doing anything wrong.

I'm not.

14

I twist and turn, but I can't get away from the blood. It's everywhere.

It's spattered on the walls, on the floor, even on the ceiling. Worst of all, it's on their faces.

My horror is immense, so much so that I feel deadly calm. My heart is a cold pool and my feet are blocks of ice as I move through the bloody rooms.

Why would my father do this?

But my stomach knows.

My heart knows.

"Miss...you can't be here," a policeman calls out, his face white and a drop of orange vomit on his mouth. He already threw up from the horror here. Why haven't I?

I let him take my shoulders and lead me out, and that's when I see my father. He's sitting in a cop car, in the back, and he's got blood everywhere. It's smeared on his face, on his hands, on his shirt.

He looks at me, and his blue eyes are so cold and empty that I have to close my own. I can't look at him.

"Fix this," he whispers, and somehow, I hear him through the glass and across the yard. "Fix this. Corinne? Corinne!"

Then I realize that it's not my father's voice, it's Jude's.

I wake with a start, and I'm unable to shake the uncertain feeling all day.

"Why would Jude tell you to 'fix this'?" Dr. Phillips asks me in session later in the afternoon. I fiddle with the arm of the chair.

"I don't know. Maybe because I let our marriage go lately... this year. I was so focused on working, on trying to build our life, that I forgot we already have one."

I feel helpless and restless, and Dr. Phillips shoots me a sympathetic look. He rarely shows warmth, so it surprises me.

"You do know that a marriage is comprised of two people, right?" he asks me simply. "You weren't...aren't...the only one in it, Corinne."

"I know." I rush to defend my husband. "Jude was always wanting me to come home early for dinner, though, and it seemed like I always had to work second shift. I never wanted to tell the hospital no. But I ended up telling my husband no all the time. My priorities had gotten skewed."

"Did Jude talk to you about this?"

"Frequently," I answer. "Maybe not 'talked,' but definitely mentioned. It upset him, and I guess I never really understood how much. I feel awful, because I remember my father..."

I trail off and I'm lost in memories, and Dr. Phillips waits patiently. Finally, he prompts me.

"Your father?"

I look at him. "My father used to mention to my mother that she spent so much time on our stuff—me and Jackie—that he felt like he didn't have a wife anymore. And then..."

I can't finish the sentence.

"And then he was unfaithful and became a murderer?" Dr. Phillips lifts an eyebrow. "Are you under the assumption that those were causal factors? Are you saying you're worried that would happen to Jude?"

He's in disbelief, and I guess it does sound dumb out loud. I smile a little.

"I guess not. I just… I neglected him. A lot. More than I realized. I was always so busy at the hospital that I sometimes forgot to answer his texts and whatnot."

"Do you feel that your marriage with Jude was beginning to mirror your mother and father's marriage?"

I shrug. "I don't know. All I know is that I took Jude for granted for so long. I'd give everything I have to be able to call him right now."

My kingdom for a simple phone call.

15

My phone rings and I glance at it.

It's Corinne. A surge of resentment wells up in me. She already told me she couldn't meet me. There's no reason to rub it in or apologize further. Actions speak louder than words.

I let it go to voice mail and return my attention to the girl in front of me.

She's fluttering her fingers as she speaks, playing with a strand of hair and sipping at her drink.

"You want to hear about me?" She smiles. "I'm boring. Same ol' thing you always hear, I'm sure. Trying to make ends meet so I can get a degree and make something of myself. Yada yada yada."

"That's commendable," I tell her as a waitress comes to clear my dinner plate and check on our drinks. The waitress smirks down at Zoe, and Zoe rolls her eyes.

"That's all, Beth," she says, and I get a glimpse of her snotty side. As Beth walks away, Zoe leans toward me.

"The other girls hate me here. I don't usually play well with women."

"I can see how that would be," I agree. "They must feel competitive with you."

She shrugs again, unconcerned. "Maybe. But there's no competition, really. Once I decide on something, that's how it will go."

"My, what modesty." I grin. She giggles and leans over as if to wipe my mouth. It happens before I can even pull away. And then, instead of wiping her fingers off on her napkin when she's finished, she slides them into her mouth, sucking them clean.

I'm mesmerized even though I try not to be.

"I do have one girlfriend," she tells me, changing the subject. The air practically snaps with electricity, and I try to ignore it. "We've been friends forever. I admire her, honestly. She's so pretty and stubborn, strong-willed. But she's gone down sort of a wrong path. She's a stripper now. I'm really a sexually open person, but God, I'd never be a stripper. You can't choose what kind of men you have to deal with, y'know?"

I process the information about her friend.

"She's gorgeous, though. This one time…" Zoe drifts away into her thoughts, staring into the distance. "We were talking all night and drinking…and I told her how beautiful I thought she was, and one thing led to another and we kissed."

My groin immediately tightens because I'm a fucking man.

She shakes her head, like she's shaking the memories away. "It's the only time I've made out with a chick, but I have to say, I liked it. I'm not gay, though."

She stares at me thoughtfully, then laughs nervously, her fingers fluttering to her hair.

"Oh my God. I can't believe I just told you that! I've never told anyone before. It must be because you're a therapist. You're so easy to talk to."

"Am I?" I'm wry now because I'm hard, so I adjust in my seat so my dick isn't constrained by the seam of my pants.

"Yeah." She plays with the straw in her glass. "I worry about Chelsie, though. Like I said, she makes bad choices, and right now, she's staying with an abusive boyfriend. I keep trying to talk to her about it, but she gets mad at me. Any professional advice?"

I can't turn the therapist in me off. "Well, if she's a stripper and attracted to abusive men, I'd say that she has issues from her childhood. Maybe abandonment issues, maybe her father was abusive. It's hard to say. All you can do is be loving and kind to her, and maybe encourage her to talk to a professional."

God, I sound old.

But Zoe doesn't seem to notice. She chews on her lip. "She doesn't have any insurance. I think most doctors want insurance. Do you see patients without it?"

I nod. "Sure. I offer a discount to cash-paying patients."

Again, I feel ancient. But she smiles beatifically. "Awesome. I'll tell her to look you up." She props her face back on her hands and turns toward me. "But back to us."

"Us?"

"Yeah, us." She smiles, and she grips my knee under the table. Her fingers are warm and firm, and she lets them linger on my leg. I glance around, and no one else notices, and I don't know anyone in the café. Thank God.

"There's an us?" I play dumb, because once again, this feels wrong.

But I'm not doing anything. It's not like I'm going to fuck this girl. Right?

She nods. "Yes. I told you. Once I set my sights on something, it's mine."

"But I'm married," I remind her.

She grins. "I know."

She's unconcerned. I pay the bill for both of us, and Zoe watches me with satisfaction.

"See? We just had our first date."

I shake my head and roll my eyes, and Zoe wipes her mouth with her napkin.

"I wonder, though…" she muses. "If you can handle me."

I snort and roll my eyes. "Whatever, little girl. I've got more years of experience than you've been *alive*. Not that this is going anywhere, because it's not."

She chuckles like the joke's on me.

"I like it rough," she announces, and she doesn't even lower her voice. The old lady at the next table clears her voice, and I'm fascinated once again by Zoe's directness. "I like choking and bondage and I like being spanked, because I'm a bad girl, Jude. A very bad girl."

She looks so innocent as she says it, and she grabs my knee again, her fingertips biting into my leg, driving home her point. *I like it rough.*

God, that's hot. I've never been turned on by *rough* before, but new is always exciting. However, we're in a diner, in a place I regularly frequent, and I'm a married man.

Gently, I grasp her hand with my own and remove it from my leg. Pointedly, I set her hand on top of the table. Letting her touch me is wrong. Fantasy is fine, reality is not.

"Sorry," she tells me, although she doesn't sound sorry at all.

"It's okay. Many get carried away by my wit and charm." I joke it off. She laughs, and we get up and walk toward the door.

"Did I scare you away?" she asks as we step onto the sidewalk. "By telling you what I like, I mean."

"Your sexual interests aren't my business," I tell her, but she smirks.

"They *will* be," she answers. "Can you walk me to my car? It's dark out here."

"Of course," I answer, because it *is* dark, and it wouldn't be right to let a girl walk to her car alone. I'm a gentleman.

She leads me to a black car, and I frown at the parking spot. "Don't park all the way in the back when it's dark out," I tell her. "Park under a light."

She smiles now. "Is that concern I hear?"

"It's just common sense."

She opens her door, leaning on it. "I had fun tonight," she tells me, her eyes glued to mine. "You're very interesting."

She wants to linger, I can tell. But I can't. Because there's electricity in the air, and if we linger... I don't know what will happen, but it won't be right.

I'm good.

I'm good.

"Drive safe," I tell her gruffly.

She stares up at me, and the light glistens on her lips. She licks them.

"Aren't you going to kiss me?" she asks softly, and I physically rear back.

"Of course not!" I'm startled and she laughs.

"That's okay. You will someday."

"I won't," I tell her firmly, and she grins like she knows better.

"Good night, Jude Cabot," she tells me softly. "You can go home to your wife now."

I do go home, but my house is empty.

My wife doesn't come home until well after I've fallen asleep.

16

"How did you get in?" I ask Michel curiously. On my lap, I finger the books he brought me, the crosswords and the magazines. His eyes crinkle at the corners, and he glances over his shoulder.

"I insisted that you needed spiritual guidance. But Jude also listed me as an emergency contact, so they kind of had to."

"Is Jude okay?" I ask him quickly, because Jude is my first thought, always. "I hate all of this, Michel. When I think about the effect it's having on Jude…it kills me."

Michel flinches. "You know Jude," he says offhandedly. "He hides his feelings and goes through the motions. He'll be okay."

There's something in his voice. It stands out to me, and I examine him, his eyes. Something is there, hidden in the hazel depths.

"You're hiding something," I observe. "Tell me."

Michel shakes his head, and he's so very like his brother. "I'm not hiding anything," he assures me. "Jude misses you. That's all."

I'm not sure whether to believe him, but it's clear he's not going to elaborate. He's always protected his brother. He isn't going to stop now.

"Are you making sure he eats?" I ask hopefully.

Michel laughs.

"Since when does my brother not eat?" He raises an eyebrow, and he has a point. I laugh. "We've been eating at the café a lot, and I think he's been ordering pizza, too. He's not starving, Co. Don't worry about him. Let's just focus on you."

This makes me stare at my hands. Focusing on me is nerveracking.

"How are *you* doing?" Michel asks, and he reaches out to grasp my hand. His is strong and warm, very like Jude's, and if I close my eyes, it's almost like Jude is talking to me.

"I'm okay," I lie. "I'm fine. I'm just trying to figure things out so that I can get home."

"What can I do to help, Corinne? I'll do anything, you know."

His voice is warm and genuine, and I hug him. "I know. There's nothing, though. If there were, I'd tell you."

"Do you want to talk?"

"No." My answer is immediate.

"Okay." He relents easily. "Don't get upset. It's okay."

He placates me automatically, his tone soothing. I have to laugh.

"Are you worried that I'm going to lose it while you're sitting here?"

His expression is so startled and open that I laugh again.

"You are!"

He chuckles now, too. "I don't know what to think," he

admits. "I'll just be honest. You're the strongest person I've ever met, and it confuses me now, because you're here. I don't know what to do."

I shrug. "There's nothing for you *to* do. Don't worry about me, Michel."

"Ha. Too late."

"I'll figure out the holes in my brain," I tell him firmly. "You just worry about Jude for me."

"I've always worried about Jude," he admits to me. "That's not going to change now."

We chat a bit more, and when he stands up to go, he looks at me strangely.

"Corinne, I know they want you to focus on remembering the past. But I don't know that I'm on board with that. Maybe you should just focus on the future. The past is behind us, anyway."

I pause. "I know. But they think that I have to process the past in order to move on to the future."

Michel shakes his head a little. "I'm not a therapist. But I don't agree. I think sometimes the past can just be hurtful. I don't want you hurt, Corinne."

"Thanks, big bro," I murmur, and I don't know what to think. Does he know something I don't?

"Wait," I call out to him. He pauses, then turns.

"Are you afraid of something, Michel?"

He flinches, almost, and his mouth is grim. "Yes," he answers simply. "But it's going to be okay, Corinne. I have faith in that."

I just watch him walk away, once again reminded of how very much he is like my husband.

17

Now
Jude

My brother texts me.

Just saw Corinne. She looks good. Pale, but good.

Relief floods me.

I don't have to listen to the doctor tell me not to see my wife, but if they think it will help, I'll do what they recommend. It comforts me to have Michel there holding her hand, letting her lean on him. He's almost an extension of me sometimes, and if I can't be there, at least he can.

Thanks, I answer.

She's worried there are things we aren't telling her, he adds. I don't like lying.

My gut constricts. I don't like it, either, and it seems like that's all I've been doing for weeks.

We're protecting her, I answer. She'll remember in her own time, IF she remembers at all. It's the way the doctors want it.

It's the way YOU want it, my brother answers. I flinch because I can't deny that it does help me, too.

"Jude?"

The sun is shining on Zoe's hair as she looks at me, and it's clear from her voice that it's not the first time she's said my name.

"I didn't hear you," I say, sliding my phone into my pocket. "Yes?"

She rustles around in a bag on the picnic table. The breeze flutters the edges of the bag, and she holds it down. "I was just asking if you want a mayonnaise packet for your sandwich."

"Oh. No, thank you."

She smiles and hands me the sandwich, and the park is completely still. For noon on a weekday, that's a little unusual. It's usually busy during the day.

"You're distracted," she tells me as she scoots next to me, the warmth from her hip bleeding into my own. I try to hide my distaste. I don't want to be here. I don't want to be here with *her*.

"I'm sorry," I say automatically. "Issues with my wife."

The dismay on Zoe's face is immediate, but she tries to hide it. I don't know why she bothers. I know her feelings about my wife.

"Tell me about her," she says, taking a bite. "It'll make you feel better."

Talking about my wife to Zoe doesn't feel right, and I tell her that. She rolls her eyes.

"We're both adults, Jude. It'll help you to get it out. Trust me. You should know that. You're the therapist."

"Haven't you ever heard the old saying…painters have the peeling houses, gardeners have weeds in their yards, etcetera, etcetera?" I ask.

She rolls her eyes again. "So you're telling me you aren't

emotionally healthy?" She chews for a minute. "Well, you *are* having a lunch date with a woman who isn't your wife. So maybe I'll give you that."

"Thanks," I say wryly.

She puts her hand on my leg, her fingers squeezing my thigh. She moves them upward ever so slightly, and even though I know I shouldn't, my body reacts. I try not to show it, but my groin contracts, hardens.

She leans upward, her mouth grazing my jaw.

"Tell me about it," she tells me, and her voice is soft. "I won't judge."

"I don't feel like I can ever talk about it," I tell her. "I don't like to discuss it with Michel, because he knows her and loves her. I don't want him to look at her differently. You know?"

Zoe stares at me, waiting.

"My wife is an amazing person." I make the statement simply. "And I love her."

Zoe is silent for a second. "Then why are you here with me?"

That, of course, is an excellent question. There are a couple of reasons. The most important is that Zoe would ruin everyone's lives if I wasn't. She has very subtly made comments that she wouldn't hesitate. So I have to bide my time until I figure things out, until I figure a way out.

"I'm not sure," I tell her honestly. "I guess I'm just a scumbag."

She shakes her head. "No. You're not. But let's not focus on that. Tell me more about your wife."

I don't know why she wants to know, and for a minute, I don't care. Although I don't even like this girl, it does feel good to talk to someone who doesn't know Corinne, who can't judge her, who can't examine her under a microscope.

"She was raised in a tiny town a couple of hours from here,"

I tell her. "And when she was in high school, her dad killed two people. A woman he'd been having an affair with and her husband. Corinne was there. She was babysitting, and apparently, she saw everything. The trouble is, she doesn't remember it. She disassociated with it almost immediately. It sometimes happens to people with PTSD when they've been through a significant trauma."

"That's terrible," Zoe says quietly, and her fingers reach for mine. I let her hold my hand, and I stare into the distance.

"Corinne was taunted terribly while she was still in Stratton Bay. Teased mercilessly by the kids at school, because her dad was in prison for murder, and because she couldn't remember what happened. They called her crazy just like her father."

I pause and take a breath. Zoe chews on her lip.

"And is she?"

Her question is hesitant.

I shake my head. "No. She has some lingering issues, of course. Anyone would. But crazy? No."

"But didn't she... I'm sorry, I don't mean to pry, but I heard at the café that she attempted suicide."

Zoe squeezes my hand, and ice shoots through my heart, because the mere words startle me every time. Corinne did attempt suicide. My beautiful, confident wife. It's something I still can't comprehend.

"I can't explain that," I tell her. "Neither can Corinne. She doesn't remember. Her brain is protecting her again, disassociating from everything that might cause her pain."

Zoe is sympathetic, her gaze soft, and her grip tight. "God, Jude, I'm sorry. You're going through so much, because even though she can't remember, *you can*. I'm glad you're talking to me. I'll do anything I can to lighten your load."

She's quiet for a few minutes. Pensive.

"Has she talked to you about what happened with her father?"

I nod. "A little. She knows he was having an affair. And she remembers showing up at his mistress's house to babysit. But that's pretty much it. She remembers the blood, she remembers waiting for the police. But other than that, she says it's like her brain has holes."

"God, how miserable for her," Zoe murmurs. "I can't imagine."

"Yeah. Me, either. I tried to convince her to get therapy for years, but she never wanted to. It was like she was too afraid of what she might discover. But here lately, she kept getting triggered and started having panic attacks. She thought she was going crazy, and then…well, the suicide attempt."

"Jesus."

"Yeah. It's hard. I'm not going to lie."

"So that must be why you're here," she suggests. "With me. You're searching for comfort. Or a distraction."

"Let's not overanalyze it," I tell her. Because thinking about it makes me sick. The idea of being here makes me sick. I should leave. Right now.

Yet I can't. Because I don't know what Zoe would do, and Corinne isn't in a strong enough place to bear it. I just have to wait this out.

When I look at Zoe again, her eyes are soft, and she's staring at me, and she reaches for me, pulling me into a tight hug. Her hands rub at my back.

"I'm here for you," she tells me. "For as long as you want me to be."

I close my eyes and ignore my guilt, my pain, my reality.

I feel her lips on my cheek, then they meet mine, and I keep my eyes closed. That makes it better, more palatable. I feel less of a prick if I don't actually look at her.

Her arms tighten around my neck, and the kiss deepens, and my traitorous body reacts.

Against my will, my dick hardens. I don't even like this girl as a person. I know that. I'm getting ready to push her away when...she starts shrieking.

Jumping up, she waves her arms around like a madwoman.

"Get it, get it!" she yells.

I'm confused for a minute until I see the bee buzzing around her head.

"Stop flailing," I tell her calmly. "Be still."

She stops moving and follows the bee with her eyes.

"I'm deathly allergic," she tells me. "Can you kill it? Please?"

I watch the insect, following it. "Do you have an EpiPen with you, by chance?"

She shakes her head. "No. I'm allergic to epinephrine."

"Well, that's an unfortunate pairing of allergies," I tell her, and I have to admit, I'm doubtful. Part of me thinks she's being dramatic to get attention. The bee lands on a nearby plant, and I squash it under my foot. It curls onto the ground, lifeless.

"There. It's taken care of. You can relax."

She goes limp and exhales shakily. If she's acting, she's good at it.

"Thank you. I was stung when I was a kid, then they gave me epinephrine, and I almost died. If they hadn't figured out I was allergic, I would've."

"Well, it's gone now. Don't worry." I eye her, and she seems sincere.

She grabs my hand and we walk back to my car.

"Thank you," she tells me, kissing my cheek as I drop her off. "You're my hero. Can I see you tonight? I could come over. We could watch a movie or something. I was supposed to go to a movie with Chelsie—you remember her, right? But she canceled."

"Yeah, I remember her." *Of course I do.* "I'm not sure what my plans are tonight. I'll text you later."

She nods, then she's gone, and I drive home, hating myself the whole way.

I hate myself. I really do. I don't know how I've let this, whatever this is, continue. I don't know...but I do.

It was one moment that pushed me over the edge.

One moment that led me down this lustful path. One moment that changed my mind about this girl and led me to risk everything just for the sexual thrill.

One. Fucking. Moment.

I'm pathetic.

18

I love mornings.

Of course, I don't decide that when I'm groaning as my alarm goes off, or as I'm getting dressed in the dark with bleary eyes, or when I'm sucking down quick gulps of coffee to wake up.

No, I decide that as I'm jogging down my front steps with my dog by my side, as the cold breeze hits my face and I enjoy the silence. It feels like I'm the only man in the world as I stride down the sidewalk out of the subdivision and through the park to the running trails.

The silence is golden.

It feels so good every morning to not have to listen to talking. I love my job, I do. But there are days when the endless talking grates on me, getting to me in a way that makes me feel like going postal.

But every morning, I balance myself again with this.

A silent jog through silent woods with my trustworthy sidekick.

I slow my stride down so that my aging sidekick can keep up. We'll take a truncated jog today so that she doesn't overdo it.

Like every other day at this time, the world isn't awake yet, the horizon is still dark. Orange fingers stretch from the dark ground up to where the sun will soon be. The only noise is the sound of my feet and Artie's paws hitting the pavement, pounding and clicking, step after step after step.

I suck in the brisk air and release it in a fog around me, in and out, as I jog my way down the trail. The remaining leaves on the trees rustle drily, and somehow, I find myself aligning the sound with my breathing. In and out, in and out. With each breath, I fall more and more into balance. I feel each muscle in my legs constrict and contract, pushing and pulling, propelling me through the park.

Then, in the silence, there's something.

A foreign noise. Something unusual, out of place.

I hear them before I see them, and it takes me a minute to recognize the sounds for what they are.

Sex.

Artie perks her ears and so do I.

A low voice murmurs, "Yes. More."

A woman.

Then another woman. "Show me."

What the fuck?

Two women?

I pick up my pace, and as I crest a small hill, I see them.

It's like the Heavens parted and God Himself is smiling down on this park, because two completely nude women are having sex on a picnic table in the broad sight of anyone who might pass. They're slender and long, with bare limbs and tender flesh, writing and moaning in front of me. Their nipples are taut and erect in the cold morning air.

I'm instantly hard, and I pull to an abrupt stop, holding Artie close to my side. She starts to whimper, but I shush her so the girls won't know we're here.

I step back into the trees so they don't see me and stop what they're doing. I see them, though.

Holy shit.

A brunette kneels over a blonde, her face buried in the other girl's crotch, her tongue darting out to lick with long strokes, her fingers kneading at the other girl's thighs.

"Like that?" she asks, her voice low.

"Just like that," the other one answers. Her fingers are entwined in brown hair, pushing her face, pulling it back, then pushing again. "Jesus, Zo. You always know what I like."

Zo?

Startled, I'm frozen, my eyes glued to the scene in front of me. It's like slow motion, yet fast-forward at the same time. Fingers slide, moans and groans, whimpers, tongues. Pale skin, plump tight flesh, tits and ass.

God.

I can hardly swallow my own spit as I watch the girls in front of me, and it can't be. *It can't be Zoe.*

Yet the brunette lifts her head from between the blonde's legs and looks over her shoulder with wide eyes, and those eyes hunt for mine. It's like she knew I was here, and knew I was watching, and *it's definitely Zoe.*

The second our eyes meet, hers narrow in satisfaction, and she smiles.

Her hair is a long curtain, and she flips it back so that I can see better, and she does it on purpose. She wants me to see her tongue flicking down, she wants me to see her lick, lick, licking. She wants me to see it all.

I know it.

I can feel it.

With another soft smile, she flips around and straddles the other girl's face.

"Lick *me* now, Chelsie," she says, and her friend obliges, quickly and easily. With slender hands, she cups Zoe's ass as she buries her tongue inside Zoe.

Zoe is facing me now, and her eyes are flooded in pleasure, and they don't waver from mine. She holds the stare and holds it and holds it.

She squirms and rocks against the other girl's tongue, whimpering and moaning as the girl reaches up and cups Zoe's tits. The blonde alternates between pinching and pulling Zoe's nipples and kneading at the tender flesh until...until... Zoe arches upward, slamming her pussy into the girl's face, crying out as she orgasms against the blonde's mouth.

The sun rises around her, and it's like a scene from a movie as the light frames her.

Zoe couldn't have planned a more erotic scene.

She quivers in the light of dawn and then collapses onto the girl, her eyes still glued to mine as their arms and legs entwine, and they clutch each other, their tiny breaths forming ethereal clouds around them.

"Chelsie, you're amazing."

Chelsie. It's the girl she'd been telling me about.

"I know." Chelsie giggles, reaching over to trail her fingers over the curve of Zoe's generous ass. "You love me."

"I do." Zoe admits this, and with each word, her eyes search mine. Hunting for what? Surprise? Repugnance? Rejection?

She'll find none of that.

I keep my expression completely empty, but I don't flinch. I bend down and stroke Artie's head.

"It's okay, girl," I tell the whimpering dog. "It's just two girls."

Just two girls having sex in a park.

Chelsie startles at my voice and sits up, her eyes darting around the trees to find me, but Zoe, of course, is unsurprised. She knows full well that I'm here, and maybe that was the point.

"Zoe, someone's here," a voice calls out, and a guy steps from the sidelines. He looks to be homeless, dirty and tattered.

"I know, Gil," she answers him. "Thanks for standing watch."

This is weird. Too weird.

I begin jogging again, even though it's difficult with a rigid dick, and I hope to hell that they don't see it. Only a freak would stand there and watch that scene, yet I did. And only freaks would lie in the middle of a public park and have sex in front of a homeless guy, yet they did.

Maybe we're all freaks.

I feel them watching me as I leave, and I hear whispers, but I can't tell what they're saying. It doesn't really matter, though. What matters is that I had a real live porn scene unfold in front of me, and the excitement of it was fucking overwhelming. I jog straight for my house, leaving the dog in the kitchen.

Corinne is still fast asleep in the bedroom, and I pass through to the bathroom. In my hurry to disrobe, my fingers fumble the string to my shorts, and I forcibly shove them down over my rock-hard penis. The need for release is almost pathetic. I feel it, the pressure, building in my balls, and as soon as the water is hot, I jump in the shower.

As I masturbate, I replay the whole scene in my head.

"God, Zo," the girl had moaned, her fingers reach, reach, reaching. Her fingertips had circled Zoe, and she was tight and small and perfect, and... Jesus.

I stroke myself, my eyes so tightly closed that I don't notice my wife watching me.

She clears her throat, and the sound breaks through my concentration and I drop my dick.

"Errrr, I didn't mean to interrupt." Corinne has the luxury of being glib, because she's caught me quite literally with my pants down and my dick in my hand. "I heard the shower and thought I would join you, but I see you're busy."

She's annoyed, but I defuse the situation as best I can.

"You can join me," I suggest, and God I hope she does. I need release right now. Standing here talking when I need to cum is killing me. "I didn't want to wake you because you worked so late, but I'd always rather have you than this." I hold up my right hand and she smiles now.

"Really?" She's surprised.

"Of course. Get your pretty ass in here."

She drops her robe and joins me, and I hate to admit that I have sex with my wife against the stone shower wall all while thinking about Chelsie and Zoe.

I can't help it. I'm normal, right? Any man would've been turned on by what I just saw. Any red-blooded man.

It's evolution. Or genetics. Or whatever the fuck it is that causes men to be men.

I'm thinking about them as I cum into my wife, but of course Corinne doesn't know that. She thinks this is all about her, and I should feel guilty, but I'm overcome with my climax instead. She smiles when I'm finished, her wet fingers clutching my shoulders.

"Well," she murmurs, "this was a nice way to start the day."

"It was, wasn't it?"

But a part of me isn't talking about sex with my wife.

It's talking about watching a lesbian sex scene in the park, because that's really how I started my day.

I can't look Corinne in the eye as I get ready for work, although I kiss her goodbye when I leave. It's chaste, but it's still on her mouth.

"I'll call you tonight," she promises. But she won't. I know that. For the first time in a long time, I'm okay with that. I'm not annoyed, because I've got something else to focus on. Maybe this weird flirtation thing with Zoe is actually *good* for my marriage.

Ha. That's rationale at its finest.

I drive down the road, and I get the first text when I'm sitting at a stoplight.

Did you like that?

It's Zoe.

I stare at the words, knowing that the girl who just licked another girl is typing them. She's focused on me now, and she's wild and unrestrained. It's the most exciting thing that's ever happened to me.

The light turns green, and I don't text her back, because I might be perverted, but I don't text and drive. It's another five minutes before I hit another red light and I can answer.

Of course. Wasn't that the point?

Because I truly think it was. Something tells me she did it on purpose. She somehow figured out where I would be—did I mention to her that I jog in the morning?—and made sure that I'd see. It should make me uneasy, but instead, it turns me on. She went to all of that trouble just for me? The blood pulses through me, and I feel alive for the first time in months.

There are three bubbles now. She's replying. But the light turns green, and even though I hear the ding of a new text,

I fight the temptation to look until I pull into my parking spot at the office. I'm barely parked before I yank the phone up to read it.

It was—it was all for you. Smart boy.

I was right. She meant for me to see them. The exuberant feeling carries me through the morning, fueling me through my appointments. The memories of what they did together keep me hard on and off, and I have to fight to keep my focus on my patients.

At lunchtime, I'm like a little boy at Christmas when I pull my desk drawer open to check my phone.

There are two texts from Zoe, and none from my wife.

God, it turned me on to have you watch us.
I'm going to show you how much.

As I hold the phone, three bubbles pop up, and I'm practically shaking in anticipation when a third text comes through. A video.

Zoe is in her waitress uniform, standing in a public restroom. She's fingering herself, and the camera zooms in to her fingers. She's so wet that I can hear it as her fingers move.

God, I want you, Jude, she murmurs in the background.

I swallow hard, because all of a sudden, this is real.

I'm really in my office watching a girl masturbate while she whispers my name.

I'm married.

I'm married.

Yet Corinne hasn't called or texted all day. If I'm out of her sight, I'm out of her mind, and that's so fucking frustrating.

This girl, though… This girl is making it difficult.

I watch the video again, then again.

God, I want you, Jude.

The whisper imprints in my head, and I hear it again and again through the rest of the day. The feeling it invokes is like a drug, and I can't help but want more of it. It lights a fire in me that I haven't felt in such a long time, and it's no excuse, but I want to feel more of it.

That's why, after work, when I get another text from Zoe and it says, I want to see you tonight, I answer her.

What time?

I lay my phone down before I can change my mind, before I can ponder what an asshole I am.

And then my phone rings. I startle, thinking Zoe is calling. But it's not her. It's my wife.

A pang of guilt shudders through me, and I let the call go to voice mail. I can't talk to her right now. Not right after I set a date with another woman.

She'd hear it in my voice. She'd know.

And that would kill me.

19

Jude doesn't answer his phone.

I don't know why. But something feels odd, something nameless is heavy in the pit of my belly. I can't place it, I can't name it. It feels like something is wrong. Only, I have no basis for that feeling whatsoever.

I guess it's because he's never not answered his phone before.

I leave him a voice mail, then look around the ER.

It's quiet for once, almost still. Brock comes out of exam room one, and he pauses to look at me.

"You look like shit, Cabot."

"Thanks."

"Well, you do." He sits next to me, opening a chart. "You should go lie down. I've got this."

I don't argue, because while I might look like shit, I guarantee that I feel five times worse. I head for the doctors' lounge, to the soothing darkness, and collapse onto a cot. My stomach is rolling, uneasy and nauseous. Saliva pools in my mouth, and I fight the urge to vomit.

Surely it's not just because my husband isn't answering his phone.

That's dumb.

"Jude is fine," I whisper to myself. Nothing is happening to Jude. He's safe. He's just busy. There's no reason to worry.

I close my eyes and try to ignore the feeling of foreboding in my gut. After a while, I open them again to distract myself, to watch the crack of light under the door, to watch the shadows pass by with the nurses as they walk, allowing it to lull me into sleep.

Before long, I'm dreaming. Only, my dreams are memories.

"Your father was supposed to be home for dinner," my mother tells me, pacing by the phone. "I don't know where he is."

Jackie and I look at each other, nervous and edgy. I think I know where he is, and I can tell Jackie does, too.

My mom stops at the sink, her worn dress hanging from her thin frame. She's been smoking too much lately. She's losing weight.

"Mom," Jackie starts out, and she's hesitant. "I saw him earlier. He was in the park with Melanie Gibson."

I kick her under the table. We did see him, when we were walking home from school, and he was too close to Melanie, way too close, but we shouldn't tell my mom. I don't know what's going on, but it can't be good. Not with the way Melanie was looking at him with stars in her eyes.

My mother's head snaps up, and she stares at Jackie intently.

"What do you mean, Jacquelyn?"

Her words are abrupt, pointed. I kick Jackie again and she winces.

"Nothing, Mama," she says now. "I thought I saw him, but I don't know."

"You were mistaken," my mom says. "He was at work earlier. He couldn't have been in the park, you silly girl."

She paces again, though, and she lights one cigarette after another, smoking them in a chain.

She dishes macaroni out onto two plates and hands them to us. "Jackie, are you trick-or-treating tonight?" she asks, trying to sound normal.

Jackie nods. "Yes, Mama. I'm going with Trish." Her best friend.

My mother nods. "Good. And you, Corinne? Are you still baby-sitting for Melanie?"

She tries her best to sound casual, but her words are loaded. She knows that I am, and she knows that something is going on with my father and Melanie. I can see it in her eyes, and I can hear it in her voice. I know I should tell her what we saw, but I can't. Because she'll hate us for it.

"Yes, Mama," I answer instead.

"Well, see that you're not late," she tells me. "Hurry up and eat your dinner."

The dream morphs and changes and I awaken with a start, and as I try to calm down, I force the images from that night out of my head.

I had eaten my macaroni, and I had not been late.

I didn't say a word to my mother about what I knew...or what I *feared* I knew.

And I'll always wonder how things might've been different if I had.

A bit of vomit rises in my throat, and I swallow it down, the bile bitter and gross. I gulp some water and curl up on the cot, my skin clammy. I wish I were home with Jude, curled up in our soft bed instead, where he could hold me and tell me that everything is going to be okay.

Because for whatever reason, I feel like it's not.

As crazy as it might sound, I feel like something terrible is about to happen.

20

What am I doing?

I stare into my rearview mirror, and my eyes are hooded and closed.

What am I doing? I'm meeting a woman who isn't my wife for dinner.

The muted lights from Olive Garden shine onto the hood of my car, and I wait for her to arrive. Every time headlights swing into the parking lot, I think it's her.

Every minute, I try to talk myself into leaving.

I almost do, in fact. I'm just starting up the Land Rover when she pulls in next to me, as stealthy as a shadow.

I don't know if I'm pleased or disappointed.

"I don't know what I'm doing here," I admit as we meet on the sidewalk.

She smiles confidently. "You're here to see me."

She's dressed in a tight skirt and tight top, the top two

buttons undone. I can see the swell of her breasts and the top of a lacy red bra.

"I shouldn't be," I say simply. "It's wrong."

"Don't think about it," she advises, and she pulls me through the doors. "I'm hungry, you're hungry, and we're across town from anyone who might know us. Everything is all right, Jude. We're just having dinner."

"We're just *eating*," I tell her pointedly, and she rolls her eyes.

"A booth for two," I tell the maître d'.

He glances up. "And are we celebrating anything in particular?" He looks from Zoe to me.

Zoe nods. "Yes. It's our anniversary."

I want to elbow her, but don't.

"Oh, happy anniversary, my dear," our waiter tells us as he guides us into the restaurant. "What number is this?"

"It's our second date of many to come," she says as she sits down, and my stare pierces her. "I'm celebrating them all."

The waiter smiles like it's the most romantic thing he's ever heard, but all I want to do is bolt from this place. This was a mistake. A big one.

"Two long islands, please," I tell the waiter. "And make them strong."

My thumb taps the tabletop. I'm nervous, and I hate that. I'm letting a twentysomething kid intimidate me?

But it's not that.

It's the knowledge that I'm risking my marriage to be here, and how fucking dumb is that? Zoe looks at me.

"What's your middle name, Jude Cabot?"

"That's an odd question."

She shrugs. "I just want to know about you. Is that wrong, too?"

I shake my head. "No. I suppose not. It's Ashton."

"My, isn't that fancy!" She laughs and our drinks arrive.

She holds up her glass. "To Jude Ashton Cabot. Maybe I'll call you Ash."

I clink my full glass to hers and take several long drinks.

"They used to call me that, actually," I tell her, and I stare across the room. In my head, I see my old football field, and I hear the chanting crowd. "In high school. Ash, I mean. It was on the back of my football jersey."

"You were the quarterback, I presume? King of the field?"

"Of course," I snort. "If I do something, I do it right."

"Oh, I'm sure." She's glib now. "Did you play in college, too?"

"Only for a while. I got injured sophomore year and Corinne didn't want me to play anymore. It worried her too much."

"You quit playing football for your wife?" Zoe is incredulous.

"Well, she wasn't my wife at the time," I amend. "But yeah. It worried her too much."

"Do you always stop doing things she worries about?" Zoe arches her eyebrows, and her question seems sarcastic, and I know she's talking about being here with her right now. I look away and she laughs.

My belly churns with a dark sort of excitement, and I hate it and love it at the same time. My desires are so dark and seedy now. It's new, it's novel.

"Look," Zoe says, as if she knows exactly what I'm thinking about. "The best thing about this dinner is that reality is out there." She motions toward the window with a fluttery hand, and her bracelets jingle. "We're in here, and we don't have to acknowledge it or think about real life. Isn't that awesome?"

I'm still silent, undecided.

"We can be what we want in here," she adds softly. "I won't judge you, and you won't judge me, and we'll just *be*. No expectations, no rules. You're not a therapist and I'm not a waitress, and we're just Jude and Zoe. Does that sound good?"

I hate to admit that it does. I don't have a wife who has issues and is never home. I'm just Jude. I can separate the aspects of my life. My dinner with Zoe doesn't affect my marriage with Corinne. I'm just passing time. I'm not *really* going to do anything.

She raises an eyebrow. "Does it?"

"Yeah, actually."

She smiles.

"Good. Let's get another drink."

I order two, one for each of us, and she studies me.

"You know, you look exactly like your brother. What's it like being a twin?"

"Come now. Surely you're more original than that. Everyone asks that question."

"Okay. What's it like to have a priest as a brother?" she amends. "Does he judge everything you do?"

"Nah. Michel doesn't judge. He doesn't even seem like a priest, to be honest."

"Does he take your confession?"

I snort into my glass, and the ice cubes tumble against each other. "Uh, no. Not for real. Every once in a while, I'll do it for a joke. But my real confession might scare him."

It's her turn to snort. "Whatever. I can see in your eyes... you're not scare-worthy."

I can't help but laugh at that. This girl doesn't know me at all.

"Whatever makes you think that?"

"I'm a good judge of people," she says.

I laugh at that. "You're too young to have acquired that particular trait," I tell her. "You're still wet behind the ears."

She rolls her eyes. "Seriously. I've learned from the school of hard knocks. I know people, trust me." She pauses and looks at me. "For instance, you. You're unhappy in your marriage right now, and you don't know how to fix it, but you still love your wife. On the other hand, you're still here with me because you're curious. Yet you're torn about it because the guilt is eating you up." She pauses again. "Am I close?"

I look away. "Maybe."

She snorts. "Okay, Mr. Therapist. If you're so experienced, read me."

I gulp at my drink until it's half gone, and I signal for another from the waiter.

"You're a girl who requires a lot of male attention, probably the result of daddy issues from your youth. You like to appear confident, but on the inside, you're insecure. You put a lot of stock in your looks and your ability to get male attention. Without that, you'd be bereft."

She raises an eyebrow. "Maybe. Maybe not. I do have issues. You'd have a field day with me, I'm afraid."

I laugh, and it's a jaded sound. "Nothing surprises me anymore."

"Can I try?"

"Sure. Go for it."

"You're not going to judge me, right?"

"I would never," I assure her. "There's no judgment here, remember?"

My wedding ring gleams in the soft light, and I wonder if the waiter noticed it? Zoe isn't wearing one.

"I lost my virginity to my foster father when I was fourteen." She states it casually, like she's talking about the weather. "My foster mom worked second shift, and I always went to bed early because I had to get up early for school. Every night, he would stand in the doorway and watch me sleep. I would wake up sometimes and see him, but I always pretended that I was sleeping because I didn't know what else to do."

She pauses and waits for my reaction.

"Did you tell your mom?"

I shake my head. "No. Because I liked it."

That does shock me, although I make a point not to show it. Instead, I ask a simple question, something that I would ask in my office if I were talking to a patient.

"What did you like about it?"

"I don't know. It gave me sort of a sense of power, I guess. He was a grown man, and apparently my mom wasn't enough for him, because he was coming to me for his kicks."

"Didn't that make you feel trivial?" I ask her curiously.

"No." Her answer is simple and immediate. "I felt powerful."

"How long had you lived with them?"

"Since I was nine. They were like my parents. If they had the money, they would've adopted me. As it was, they wanted to keep the government payments they got from taking care of me."

That part doesn't surprise me. "Go on."

"One night, I woke up to find my dad there, watching me like usual. Only this time, I was prepared. I had gone to bed naked. I pretended like I was flinging my sheets off in my sleep, but I was wide-awake. I arched my back and showed him my boobs, and moaned like I was having some sort of erotic dream."

She looks at me, waiting for permission to continue, and I nod, curtly, once.

"My eyes were closed, but I could smell him. His penis. It was right in front of me. He'd apparently pulled it out and was holding it in my face. I started sucking it with my eyes closed, because somehow, I knew that's what he wanted. It was instinctual. I'll never forget the taste of it. Like salt and…him. I never opened my eyes, even when he came all over me."

"And the whole time, you pretended to be asleep?"

She nods. "Yeah. That went on for a while. Night after night, I'd give him blow jobs 'in my sleep.'"

"But it escalated."

"Yeah. One night, instead of standing next to my bed, he climbed in with me," she says softly. "I pretended like I was sleeping, like always, but I wasn't. He slid his hands everywhere, along my breasts, along my thighs. He kissed my nipples, and I didn't know what to think. I'd never done that before, and it turned me on. He pressed his hard dick into my side, and I wiggled against it, and then he had sex with me. I never opened my eyes."

My fingers are steepled on the table in front of me as I process this. "What happened the next day?"

"We both pretended like it didn't happen," she answers. "I pretended like I didn't know—because remember, he thought I was sleeping. We acted like normal. He teased me about this and that, and gave me shit about not doing my homework, but that night, he came back."

"Did you tell him no?" My question is solemn and quiet. "He was an adult and you weren't. Regardless if you liked it, it was wrong, and illegal." I shake my head.

"No, I didn't. Because I liked it. I liked the feeling of power, I liked having him inside of me, and I liked knowing that he wanted me and not his wife. He came back again and again, and for a long time, I pretended that I was sleeping. Every night, he pretended he didn't know I was awake. It was our own wicked little game."

She pauses for effect and reaches for her drink, but it's empty. She orders another, and then we order our meals. I order lasagna and she orders soup and salad.

"Was that meant to shock me?" I ask finally. "Because it doesn't."

"I was just sharing. I've never told anyone that before."

"Because you feel ashamed?"

"No. I'm not ashamed. I just don't feel like it's anyone's business."

"Did your mother ever find out?"

"No. I'm very good at keeping secrets."

I eat my bread stick and analyze her.

"Did you ever stop pretending that you were sleeping?"

She nods. "Yeah. After a couple of months. I opened my eyes up wide when he was fucking me and stared right into his. He didn't know what to think, but I just pulled him close and told him to fuck me harder."

Lord, this girl. She's trouble. I know it right now, yet I can't seem to stand up and walk away.

"I started getting what I wanted around the house, though," she admits. "If he told me to do something and I didn't want to, I would just raise my eyebrow and look into his eyes, and he knew. He knew that I could blow his life out of the water if I wanted to."

I raise an eyebrow. "Did you ever?"

"No. I liked fucking him too much. And my life got really easy after that. He intervened whenever my mom gave me a hard time, and he always took my side. It was awesome."

"When was the last time you had sex with him?"

"A couple of years ago. I went home for Thanksgiving and fucked him in the laundry room while my mom cooked in the kitchen. That was hot. But he's getting too old now. He doesn't turn me on anymore."

It's rare that I see a woman who seems so detached by the sexual act. Generally speaking, they tend to assign much more emotion to it than men do. But not this girl. It's fascinating.

"I'm not bad," she insists. "I just know what I like. And it was nice to have an older man teach me the right way to do things. I still like older men. They're established and confident, and they're over all the bullshit that younger guys are into."

I can't help but ask. "Such as?"

"Such as...playing video games or having penis envy. Older

guys know what they want and how to get it. You do, don't you?"

Our food is delivered, and I don't answer. We're quiet for a time while we eat.

I finish mine before she does, and the whole time, I analyze her. She doesn't have attachments, she doesn't form emotional bonds. That means she wouldn't have any qualms about breaking up my marriage for her whim.

I push away from the table.

"This was a mistake," I tell her, motioning for the waiter. I hand him my card. "I'm sorry, but I can't do this."

"Jude, stop being a child. We're just having dinner. You're helping me with my issues. Isn't that what friends do?"

"You're not my friend." I sign my name to the bill and stand up.

She stands up, too, leaning up to whisper in my ear. "But I really want to be. I don't have that many. Please."

She sounds sad, and I have no idea if it's an act or not. If it is, it's a damn good one. But this girl's issues have issues. It's time to go. I turn around and walk to the door without waiting to see if she's following.

I look when I reach the door, and she is, so I hold the door for her.

She walks through.

"I really hope I didn't offend you," she says meekly. "I wasn't trying to."

"Of course you didn't." I'm curt now. What was I thinking coming here? I'm a dumbass. "Have a good night."

I turn to walk to my truck, but she grabs my arm and moisture is pooling in her eyes.

"Please, wait."

I pause without looking at her again.

"Can we just talk for a few minutes…about anything else? I

feel really shook up. I haven't thought about that stuff in years. I'm rattled." Her hand is shaking on my arm. I can't help but notice, and something tugs at my gut. My conscience, I guess. The therapist in me can't leave her like this.

"I guess that wouldn't hurt. Just for a minute. Until you gather yourself."

Without another word, she opens the passenger door to my Land Rover and gets in. I hand her a tissue, and she dabs at her eyes.

"I thought you liked it."

I stare at her and I feel like I'm dissecting a puzzle, and she shrugs.

"Maybe that's just what I tell myself so that I don't feel so disgusting. Or maybe I did like it, but I don't like the way it makes me feel now. I just don't know anymore."

She thrusts herself into the crook of my arm, burying her face in my sweater, and her shoulders shake as she cries. I finally cave in and wrap an arm around her, giving her as much comfort as I can.

After several minutes, she sniffs again.

"Can you make me laugh? I don't want to think about ugly stuff."

I think for a minute.

"What do you get when you cross a snowman with a vampire?"

"I don't know."

"Frostbite."

She rolls her eyes. "Seriously?"

I shrug. "I'm bad at jokes."

"But you smell good."

She looks up at me, and I look down at her, and I see so much in her eyes, things that shouldn't apply to me, things I shouldn't even be here for. Lust. Want. Need.

"Jude…" she whispers, and her hand flutters to my chest.

"Zoe, I can't do this. It's wrong. I've made a lot of mistakes in my life, but fucking you isn't going to be one of them."

I'm so blunt that it's almost painful.

"It's not that you aren't beautiful," I rush to say. "Because you are. But it's just wrong."

"You don't have to fuck me," she says slowly. "I just want to feel close to you. Please. If we don't have sex, then we aren't doing anything wrong, right?"

Where is she going with this?

"I just want to spend some time with a decent human being," she adds. "My life sucks. It would be nice to have a bright spot in it."

She puts her hand on my knee. I purposely pick it up and lift it off.

"Okay," she says quickly. "I won't touch you. And you don't have to touch me. Is it okay if we touch ourselves, though?"

That was unexpected, and the rush of adrenaline that courses through my veins is shameful. The very thought of masturbating in this truck while someone watches and masturbates at the same time is a turn-on like I've never felt before. And I wouldn't be touching her. So that means I'm not cheating on Corinne.

She digs through her purse and pulls out a condom. "Put this on."

"Um," I start to say, but she holds up her hand.

"Trust me, we're not having sex, and I'm not going to touch you."

Curiosity is getting the best of me, and I seriously consider it.

"Just do it, Jude. I promise. I'm not going to touch you. But if you touch yourself while I watch, that's not wrong, is it?"

I'm quiet as I turn the condom over and over in my hand.

"Right?" she pushes.

I'm silent.

"Look," she says, and her voice is very small, very quiet. "I want you, Jude. I do. But I respect your marriage vows, so I don't want to do anything you're not comfortable with. But I'm here. Your wife isn't. Please. Let's just… It's not wrong."

She isn't wrong. She's here and Corinne isn't, nor does Corinne seem to want to be.

"I'm here, Jude," she murmurs. "I'm here because I want to be here with you. Touching yourself isn't wrong. I want to watch you. I want to pretend that your hands are on me. Can we please do that? Please?"

"Uh. Maybe." I'm wavering. The moonlight glints on the red lace of her bra, and the swell of her breasts is creamy soft. I want to touch it, but I don't. *No touching.*

"Please?" She reaches over and lifts my hand, placing it on my dick. "Touch yourself for me. If you won't let me touch you, at least let me pretend."

I can't help it. My testosterone kicks in, and I'm doing this.

"Now what?" I ask when I'm big and stiff. She smiles.

"Put the condom on."

I do.

"Keep playing with yourself, and watch me while I watch you. It's basically porn, Jude. There's nothing wrong with that."

She strips off her shirt and pants and slides her hand through the side of her underwear. I play with myself and she watches, her eyes hungry. I stroke myself and she watches, her tongue sliding along her lips. I get harder and harder, and she breathes heavier and heavier. Her eyes are heavy-lidded as we fog up the windows.

"Jude, I want to watch you cum," she whispers, and her voice is husky with want. She arches her back and closes her eyes. "Jesus, that's good." She moans as she orgasms, and she says my name as she cums, and it's my undoing.

I spurt into the condom. I'm silent, and I'm still.

What the fuck did I just do?

After a minute, I slide the condom off.

"Don't tie it," Zoe says quickly, taking it from my hand.

"What?" I'm confused.

She holds the full condom, eyeing it.

"It's still warm," she observes.

And then she drinks it.

She fucking drinks my cum.

She licks her lips when it's gone and then throws the empty condom out the window.

"See? I told you we didn't have to touch each other. So we haven't done anything wrong."

She smiles victoriously. "I'll see you soon." Without another word, she gets out and closes the door behind her.

At a stoplight on my way home, I check my texts. There are a couple from Corinne, wondering where I am, and two missed phone calls. I feel instantly guilty. I'm very seldom out of reach when it comes to Corinne.

And then a text from Zoe comes in.

You are delicious.
Call me in the morning?

I don't know what to say. All I can think of is Zoe playing with herself in my truck and then drinking my cum. I hate myself for it.

I don't answer for another two stoplights.

But on the third, even though I hate myself for it, I do.

Ok.

21

My house is dark when I get home, and Jude's car isn't in the garage.

What the hell? He's never out this late.

The first thing I think of, the first thing I always think of, is the worst. What if he's lying in a ditch somewhere? What if there was an accident? That's the product of being an ER doctor. I see terrible things all the time. But those things are rare. Those are the exceptions.

The likelihood of something being wrong…it's slim. I mentally calm myself. Surely nothing is wrong with Jude. He's fine.

I text him, and there's still no answer.

I let Artie out, then pet her when she comes back in.

"Where's Daddy, girl?"

She stares at me blankly, her white muzzle nudging me. I pet her again.

"I'm going to lie down while I wait. I have the plague."

She stares at me before she lies down by the back door, and I collapse into my bed. Every cell in my body feels sick and the room spins. My forehead is so sweaty, my hands are so clammy. I'm in bed for only a few minutes before I have to lunge to the bathroom and retch my guts up.

"Fuck." I wipe my mouth and lie on the cool tiles, my cheek pressed to the stone.

The walls spin, and it feels like the worst hangover in the world, and I fall asleep on the bathroom floor. I only know that because the next thing I know, Jude is waking me up.

I know it's the middle of the night because the bathroom door is open and there's no light coming in from the bedroom windows.

"Corinne?" Jude is alarmed, and I don't blame him. It's not every day you find your wife sprawled on the bathroom floor like a dead person.

"Ju!" I breathe, and I can feel the sick on my breath. "You're okay."

"Of course I'm okay," he confirms. "I'm just running late."

"I have the flu," I tell him weakly as I sit up. The room spins. "You should probably sleep in the guest room tonight. I don't want you to get it."

"Let's get you to bed," he suggests, and he helps me up. His hands are cool against my skin, and I lean into him.

He flinches.

I pause, staring at him.

"What's wrong?"

"Nothing," he insists. "Why?"

He seems detached. But I'm probably crazy. He just doesn't want to catch the flu. I'm at the edge of death, after all.

He guides me to the edge of the bed.

"Sit," he instructs. He grabs my nightgown from my dresser and strips off my scrubs. I lift my arms and stand, then obligingly slide my nightgown over my head. As I do, I catch a whiff of something…different. Almost feminine.

I stick my nose back in Jude's shirt. I smell it again. It's faint, but it's there.

"What?" He looks at me, curious.

"You smell like perfume."

Is it my imagination that he looks terrified?

But then he's shaking his head, and he's normal, and he's calm. "I hugged a client earlier, Co. And also, I'm using a different deodorant."

Oh. Relief passes through me in a wave. Of course. What the hell is wrong with me? He helps me into bed, and nothing is wrong.

"Thank you," I murmur as my head hits the cool pillow. Jude pulls the covers up to my chin.

"Do you need anything?"

I shake my head. "No."

He presses his mouth to my forehead, and his lips are cool. "You don't have a fever. You've probably just worn yourself out finally. I'll get some ice water and put it on the nightstand. If you need anything else, just shout."

I nod and close my eyes. But then open them.

"Wait!"

Jude pauses at the door. "Yeah?"

"Why were you running late? I never get home before you."

He hesitates, and there's something on his face again, something that niggles at me, and then it's gone, the same look he had before.

"I had dinner with a colleague. I told you about it last week."

I don't remember that at all.

"You did?" I ask groggily.

He nods. "Yeah. You don't pay attention to me much anymore, Co."

He's wounded, and I'm sorry.

I tell him that.

"Just get some sleep." He turns the light off on his way out, and sleep takes me quickly.

When I wake, the clock says it's 6:00 a.m.

I sit up, taking note of how I feel.

The room isn't spinning anymore, which is a good thing.

My stomach, however, is a different story.

I run for the toilet and dry heave.

"Fuck." God. I lean on the sink for a minute, examining myself in the mirror. I'm paler than normal, and dark circles rim my eyes. Perfect.

I brush my teeth and make my way to the kitchen, expecting to find it empty, but it's not. Jude is at the table with a cup of coffee and the morning paper.

"Hey," I greet him, confused. "Why aren't you jogging?"

Now *he* looks confused. "Because you're sick. You never get sick. I was worried, so I'm staying home."

"Seriously?"

I'm astounded and it must show. He rolls his eyes.

"Corinne, we're married. I'll take care of you. In sickness and in health and all that. Sit down."

He pours me a cup of chamomile tea and makes a piece of dry toast.

"No butter for you," he tells me as he sets it down in front of me. "It'll just make your stomach angrier."

"Not possible," I groan. Jude rubs at my back, then holds his hand against my cheek.

"Still no fever," he says. I could've told him that, but he's trying to be nice, so I don't mention it.

"I think I might be dying," I say instead. "I hope you have my life insurance paid up."

He chuckles. "Drama queen."

"I feel bad that you're here babysitting me," I tell him hesitantly. "Although it's nice to spend time with you."

"It is nice, isn't it?" he says easily. He doesn't point out that we could've been doing this all along if I'd just chosen to come home at decent hours.

He's being so sweet and understanding that it makes my heart twinge a little. This is my Jude. *This* is the Jude I fell in love with and married.

"Thank you," I say limply. "I don't know why you're being so nice, but who am I to question it?"

He rolls his eyes. "Let's get you on the couch and we'll start a movie."

"I'm not going to argue with that," I tell him.

I get settled on the couch, wrapped in a blanket, and Jude sits by my feet. His hand rests lightly on my calf, and he looks at me.

"Can I ask you a question?"

"Of course."

"Do you even still like me?"

Shock slams into me, and I stare at him wordlessly.

After a minute, I gather myself.

"Do you really feel like I don't? Have we really been reduced to that?"

Jude looks away. "I don't know. You just never want to come home to me, Co. What else am I supposed to think?"

His hazel eyes are clear and bright, and my heart breaks a little at the thought that I've made him feel this way.

"You are my entire life." I reach over and take his hand. "*This* is."

Something crosses his face, something I don't quite recognize, but it's there for only a minute. It's probably shock. He nods.

And I have to vomit again.

"God," I groan as I jump up and run for the powder room. I kneel, and as I vomit, I feel Jude's hands holding my hair out of the way. I motion for him to leave, but he doesn't. When I'm finished, I sit back and lean against his chest.

"This is how you know it's love," I tell him wryly.

He grins. "I'm not gonna lie, though. I'm gonna wash my hands now."

I giggle in spite of myself, and he helps me back to the couch. "God, the room won't stop spinning."

"You're probably dehydrated, Dr. Cabot." He looks at me. "Take a drink of Gatorade."

"I hate Gatorade."

"Yeah, but you hate being dehydrated even more. That's probably why you're dizzy. Come on, take a drink for me."

I scowl, but he's right, so I take a sip from the straw. "Thank you for taking care of me."

He smiles. "It's in my job description."

That might be true, but he has never done this before. I have to say, I like it.

"Do I get soup for dinner?" I ask as I snuggle into the cushions. Jude looks at a loss but quickly nods.

"Of course. I'll just…Google how to make it."

I giggle again and close my eyes. "It's not hard. You'll have to use a can opener, though."

"I'll manage." He's droll and I laugh, and somehow, even though I feel like death warmed over, I like this. We feel like a unit again, for the first time in a long time.

"This is nice," I tell him. He agrees, and I'm comfortable next to my husband. I fit exactly right in the crook of his shoulder, and his hand rubs light circles on my back. It lulls me into sleep.

I sleep on and off all day. I wake up when I hear his phone

ringing against the coffee table. The vibration is loud, and Jude is nowhere to be seen.

I sit up and rub at my temple, and his phone buzzes again. It's a number I don't recognize.

"Hello?" I hold it to my ear. Silence. "Hello?"

The call ends, and Jude walks through the door, staring at me questioningly.

"Wrong number, I guess." I hand him his phone, and he hands me a bowl of soup in exchange.

"This looks edible," I tell him.

He's smug. "It happens to be delicious," he answers, sliding his phone into his pocket. "I tried it."

"You're husband of the year."

"I am, aren't I?" he agrees. He's so cute it's ridiculous.

I reach over and grab his hand, pulling it to my chest. "Snuggle with me."

"You should eat," he says, but he obliges and wraps his arms around me. "Fine. Let's rest for a bit. Rest is important for you, too."

"You just want to nap," I mumble, but I don't care because he's warm and we're comfortable. We must sleep undisturbed for a few hours, because when I wake, it's evening.

Something woke me, but I don't know what.

Then it happens again.

Jude's phone buzzes with a text, then buzzes again and again against my hip. He's snoring in my ear, but whoever it is seems insistent, so it must be important.

"Jude." I nudge him sleepily. "Your phone is blowing up. It's probably your office."

He snores again.

"Jude."

His phone buzzes again, and he startles awake.

"It might be an emergency," I tell him again. "You should get it."

He nods blearily and gets to his feet, while I close my eyes again. God, it feels good to not be the one handling a crisis for once.

He slips out to handle his emergency, and I slip back to sleep.

22

With my wife curled up in our home, I stalk down the driveway, pacing by the mailbox.

What do you need? I text Zoe, without even reading her texts.

Three bubbles appear, then disappear. Then a frowny face.

I was thinking about drinking your cum, and it was sooooo good.

I pause, phone in hand, as I stare at the dying landscape around me. Dead leaves blow across the yard, and I can't think of what to do.

Last night was a mistake, I text. I'm sorry.

My phone rings immediately.

"Hello," I answer gruffly.

"You can't mean that," Zoe says, and she's urgent. "It wasn't a mistake. You didn't do anything wrong. I didn't touch you, Jude. You touched yourself."

"I always tell my patients to define wrong as this—if you wouldn't do it in front of your spouse, or if you feel you have to hide it, it's wrong," I tell her plainly. "I would never let someone drink cum out of my condom in front of my wife. So it was wrong, and it was a mistake."

"But just think about it," she answers, and her voice is thin. "Where was your wife last night? You were with me because she wasn't home with you. She neglects you. You deserve someone who treats you with respect, like you're their whole world. You could be my whole world, Jude."

I'm startled now, and I'm frozen in my tracks, because all of a sudden, the way she views me clicks into place.

"I thought you were just having fun," I say slowly. "I thought you were just stroking your ego with me. Making yourself feel good. Surely you didn't think it was anything else, right? You've known all along that I'm married. I was very plain about that."

She's silent. A second ticks by, then another and another. Finally, she answers.

"Yes. I knew that. But you're an amazing guy, and you deserve better than her."

I don't even know what to say. I'm floored by this turn of events, and I have no words.

"Look, Zoe…"

"No, you look," she says sharply. "You're not thinking clearly right now. You don't want to hurt your wife, and I get that. I respect it. But she doesn't deserve you. Give it a little bit of time, and you'll see that. Just give me a chance to show you what I can do…what I can be to you. I promise, you'll be happy."

"Zoe, no," I answer, and something deep inside of me is on guard, on high alert.

"Jude, yes," she replies firmly. "Trust me, you'll be sorry if you don't."

She says it as though I'll be sorry that I missed the opportunity, but her words…something about them…raise the hair on the back of my neck.

You'll be sorry if you don't.

She hangs up, and I stand frozen in the driveway for the longest time. The cold autumn breeze chills me, blowing right through my bones. When I finally go back inside, Corinne is still curled on her side sleeping. I sit down in the chair facing her.

She's so vulnerable when she sleeps. So open and trusting.

When she's awake, she's got her guard up. With her past, with everything with her father, I understand why. I don't like it, but I understand it.

She's afraid of being hurt again by the people closest to her.

My phone burns a hole in my hand, and I want to smash it into the wall.

If Corinne knew about Zoe, it would be the biggest pain of all. It would crush her.

I'm an asshole for letting it even get this far.

I stare at the flowers on the table. They are wilting, and a dead petal falls to the table's surface. I close my eyes so I don't think of it as a metaphor for my marriage.

I'll fix this.

I have to.

23

God, I feel like shit.

I thought I was sick yesterday. Today, I'm twelve times worse. Even now, my mouth pools with saliva, and I want to vomit again. As I talk to Jacks on the phone, my words sound feathery because I feel like I'm going to faint. I lean against a wall as I talk, and I briefly consider going home.

"Yeah, Jude isn't the happiest with me right now," I admit to her. "I've been working a lot, and he's pissed about it."

"What? What in the hell?" My sister is outraged on my behalf. "You work hard so that he can piddle around in his therapist job. If he'd gone on to med school, too, you wouldn't have to work so hard."

I take a shaky breath and will the vomit to stay in my belly where it belongs. My breath even smells sick, which makes me feel sicker.

"That's not fair," I tell her firmly. "Jude never wanted to be a psychiatrist. You know that. He feels they just push pills, and he wants to actually help people. Don't be mean on my account."

"I'm not," Jackie insists. "He just shouldn't get mad at you for picking up the financial slack."

"Jesus, Jackie. He makes plenty of money. That's not an issue."

"Well, whose side do you want me to be on, anyway?" She acts bewildered. "Yours or his?"

I sigh, exhaling a sick breath. "There aren't sides. We've just been bickering about it. It's fine. Everyone fights. Everyone gets over them. He took care of me yesterday when I was sick. It was nice."

I pause and gag. I put my hand over my mouth.

"You don't sound good, Co." Jackie just now notices.

"I'm not feeling good," I admit. "Like, at all."

"I'll let you go, then." Jackie releases me. "Go get something to drink. Water will help flush out the bug, if you've got one."

"Yeah." I hang up and head for the nurses' station, where Brock looks at me in concern. "You're white as a ghost, Corinne. You should go home. I've got this here."

"Are you sure?" I ask tiredly.

He nods. "Absolutely. Go get some rest. Have Jude make you some soup."

I have to chuckle at that because Jude doesn't cook. "Good idea."

I trudge to the parking garage, and my feet feel like they weigh a hundred pounds each, and the breath coming in and out of my mouth tastes sick.

"Great," I mutter as I start my car. Wouldn't you know... the *one* time I didn't have time to get my flu shot in years.

I feel a wave of nausea well, and I barely stumble out of my car before I vomit all over the ground. Orange and pink chunks splatter, remnants of orange juice and grapefruit pieces, and the acid in my mouth is vile. I wipe my lips, and my forehead is beaded in sticky sweat.

I shiver as the breeze hits my damp skin, and there's a noise.

I startle, because I'm alone, but the loud clap came from the shadows.

"Hello?" I call out, and the darkness is ominous and huge. No one answers.

"Ed?" I call out the parking attendant's name, and he doesn't answer.

There's another clap and then a crash, like trash cans knocking together.

I suddenly feel dizzy, so so dizzy, and I lean against my car. "Dr. Cabot?"

A voice rings out through the emptiness, and I open my eyes. Lucy is walking toward me, her purse on her arm. "Are you okay, Corinne?"

My mouth pools again, and I shake my head before I vomit onto the pavement.

"Jesus," she blurts out, and she jogs to my side, holding back my hair.

"Don't get too close," I tell her, wiping my mouth. "I'm pretty sure it's the plague."

"I don't think you should be driving," she tells me, looking me up and down. "You look like you're about to fall over. Should I call Jude?"

I shake my head. "No. He stayed home with me yesterday, so he's got a packed schedule today."

"That does it. I'm taking you home. Stay right there. I'll pick you up in a second."

I don't even argue. That's how shitty I feel. She heads toward her car and comes back a few minutes later. I drop into the passenger side, my cheek resting against the cool window.

"Thank you," I murmur. "God, I feel like I'm dying."

"Don't worry. We'll get you to bed."

I close my eyes, and she drives through traffic, into the suburbs and into my driveway. My sheets have never felt so good as I slide into them.

"I'll let your dog out and bring you back some water. Can you call Jude? I don't want you to be alone."

"It's just the flu, Luce," I mumble, my face in my pillow because the coolness feels like Heaven. "I'll be fine."

"Just try to call him, okay?" Lucy disappears down the hall, and I hear the back door opening, then closing, as she takes Artie outside. I grab my phone without opening my eyes, fumbling around the nightstand.

I dial his number through slits in my eyes and wait. He doesn't answer. I leave a voice mail.

"Babe, it's me. I'm at home sick. Just letting you know. Don't worry. Lucy is here, and for some reason, she doesn't want to leave me alone. Call me when you get a chance."

I hang up and close my eyes again.

"I'm so tired I'm going to die," I moan to Lucy when she comes back in with water and aspirin.

"So your diagnosis is fatal fatigue?" She lifts a sculpted eyebrow, and if I didn't feel so crappy, I'd laugh.

"Yes."

I take the aspirin and a big drink of water. And then, just as the water hits my stomach, I have to vomit again. I lunge from the bed and race to the bathroom, barely making it. I hug the toilet afterward.

I heave and heave until there isn't anything left to throw up. And it's now, as I sit staring into the toilet, watching my orange-juice vomit float in the water, that something occurs to me.

My period is late.

"No," I breathe aloud, and I recalculate, then recalculate again.

Numbly, I go back out to my bedroom, grab my phone and look at the calendar, and it's true. It's been five weeks since my last period. I'm a week late.

But I'm on the pill.

Did I forget to take it?

It's entirely possible. Some days I'm so scatterbrained that I forget to eat.

I'm dumbfounded and motionless, and Lucy is staring at me. "What's wrong?"

I can't feel my fingers. Or my toes. Or my tongue.

"I think... I think I'm pregnant."

She stares at me wordlessly. "Are you sure?" she finally asks, and her reaction is strange.

"No, I'm not. But I think so. Maybe."

"You work so much," she says slowly. "I'm not sure a baby will fit into that life, Corinne. You'll have to change things."

"I know that," I say stiffly, because where does she get off?

But then she shrieks, out of nowhere. "Oh my gosh, you're pregnant!" And she hugs my neck and this is the reaction I was expecting.

"We should find out for sure," she chitters, like a squirrel. "There's a Walgreens down the road. I'm going to go get a test. Stay right here. I'll be right back."

She doesn't even wait for a response. Instead, she's sprinting for the door.

I don't try to stop her. I just collapse back onto the bed in wonderment, my hand on my still-flat belly.

Is it possible?

I'll find out soon enough.

Lucy comes back within twenty minutes.

"You must've broken land-speed records," I tell her wryly

as she bursts back into the room, ripping open the pregnancy test box. She doesn't even try to deny it. Instead, she thrusts the white plastic stick at me.

"Go pee on this," she demands. "Hurry up."

"You're so bossy," I mutter, but I'm dying to know, too.

It can't be.

But it might be.

Am I?

I have to know.

I have to.

I pee on the stick and pace around the bathroom, and within one minute, the second line turns pink. I'm stunned, and my fingers shake as I hold the test in my hand. I examine it. It hasn't changed.

Lucy pokes her head in.

"And?"

I hold it up.

"Two lines," I say limply. "Oh my God."

A million things are going through my head. I'm happy, I'm scared, I'm terrified that my child might be afflicted with my father's mental issues...all of it. But mostly, I can't deny it, I'm excited.

"I'm going to have a baby," I whisper, and my hand on my belly feels different now, because I know there's a baby beneath it. "I'm pregnant."

"You are," Lucy agrees, sitting next to me with her arm around my shoulders. "And do you know what else? *You're pregnant.* Your hormones are all wonky. All of the anxiety and panic you've been feeling lately...it could be attributed to your hormones, Corinne."

I stare at her, stunned. "You're right. Hormones can wreak havoc."

She nods. "Yes. So there you go. One less thing to worry about."

I smile slowly as the realization sinks in. I'm not crazy. It's my hormones.

"Congratulations, Dr. Cabot." Lucy grins. "I'm so so happy for you."

"Thanks," I say weakly, because, honestly, I'm feeling dizzy again. "I think I'll lie back down and wait for Jude to come home."

"Are you going to tell him tonight?" Lucy stands up and covers me with a blanket.

"I don't know. Probably. He'll be ecstatic." And he will. He's been wanting to start a family for as long as I can remember.

"Okay. Well, since I know you're not at death's door, I'll leave you in peace. Get some rest, and I'll see you tomorrow. You're going to have to take care of yourself now, you know," she adds. "For the baby."

I nod, and Lucy pecks me on the cheek. After she leaves, I try to call Jude again.

Still no answer.

I close my eyes and rest while I wait.

24

Michel knocks on my front door, his hands full of groceries.

"I brought cheese, beer, canned soup, frozen pizza..." he says as I let him in. "All the staples. I promised Corinne I'd make sure you ate."

"That's never been a problem for me," I tell him.

He laughs.

"That's exactly what I told her."

He takes the groceries to the kitchen and puts them away, pausing to bend down to pet Artie.

"Have you talked to Corinne today?" he asks.

I shake my head dismally. "No. Dr. Phillips still wants me to wait."

Michel scowls. "I really don't agree with that, Jude. She needs to know you care."

"She knows I care," I tell him. "She's *all* I've cared about for fifteen years. That's never changed."

"Gee, thanks, bro."

I realize what he's saying and backtrack. "You know I didn't mean it like that. Of course I care about *you*, dumbass."

"Again, gee, thanks."

I roll my eyes.

Michel stacks the soup in the pantry. "There's something I found odd, Jude. When I was there, she didn't mention the baby at all. Doesn't she remember yet?"

A pang hits my stomach. "No, she doesn't."

Michel stops moving and turns to me. "Isn't that very, very odd? I mean, I'm not a therapist like you, but it seems weird."

"It's not, given her situation," I explain. "Her dissociative tendencies have deepened over the years. It's not surprising at all, actually."

"I still can't believe that she… I mean, she wouldn't have done that."

I sigh. "Yet she did. She took the abortion pill, and then she slit her wrist. She tried to kill the baby, and herself. I can't begin to explain why, but she did it."

"But that's not the Corinne that we know," Michel insists.

"You're right," I agree. "It's not. It's a part of Corinne that she's hidden even from herself. We can't explain it. *She* can't even explain it. We can only hope that she gets better."

"I'll be praying for her," Michel tells me seriously.

"You do that."

"In the meantime, I think you should make them let you see her. She needs it," my brother tells me firmly. "She really does. She's so lost. She's floundering."

"Okay. I'll think on that, and maybe call them tomorrow."

"You do that."

"Thanks for the food."

"Yep."

He leaves, and the house is quiet. So quiet. Too quiet.

I grab a scotch and head out to the back patio, allowing

Artie to amble around the yard, sniffing this corner and that. I sit on a lounge chair, enjoying the brisk air and the cool breeze. My face is flushed from the alcohol, and the cold feels good.

I close my eyes and let my thoughts drift.

They flit away from my present, back to happier times.

The day Corinne and I closed on this house.

Ju, she'd called from out here, standing in the sun on the patio. *Come here. This backyard is better than I remembered.*

I'd joined her, and we'd held hands as Artie ran circles around the fence line, as the flowers bloomed and swayed in the spring breeze. The sun had been in her hair, and it looked like a halo.

We're going to be happy here, she'd whispered, burying her face in my neck.

I'd agreed and pulled her to me, and we'd started kissing, then ended up making love on a towel on the patio.

We hadn't even bought furniture yet.

I sigh now, the memories filling my belly with warmth.

But then I remember where I am. I'm on the same patio, but it's dark now. With the night, and from the knowledge that I'm here alone. My wife is gone.

We haven't been overly happy here.

And I'm not sure that we ever will be.

A feeling of such utter loss and sadness comes over me, so much so that I pick up my phone and dial the number for Reflections.

A charge nurse answers, and at first, she doesn't want to get Corinne for me.

"Mr. Cabot, I have notes here that say you agreed with Dr. Phillips that you shouldn't speak to Corinne this week," she says hesitantly.

"That's true," I tell her politely, yet firmly. "I did. But I've changed my mind tonight. I need to speak with my wife, and she needs to speak with me. If you could go get her, I would appreciate it."

"But," she starts, and I interrupt her.

"No buts. I can sign her out of there at any time. Please, go get her."

"Very well."

It's a few minutes before I hear my wife's voice, and when I do, it sends shock waves through my heart. I miss her more than I even realized.

"Jude?" her voice is soft and husky, familiar and warm. "Is everything all right?"

My heart clenches. She's worried about *me*. She's in a psych ward, and she's worried about me.

"Everything's fine, babe," I tell her. "I just miss you. I'm sitting out on the patio, and I was thinking about the day we bought this house, and I miss you. I know I'm not supposed to bother you this week, but I had to make sure you're okay."

She's silent, and then she takes a deep breath. "I miss you, too, Jude. God, I want to come home."

That kills me. It crushes my heart into pieces.

Her voice is small and uncertain, and it's that place that is doing it to her.

I have to physically force myself to stay in my seat and not race to my car to go pick her up.

"I know," I tell her. "Are you doing okay? Are you making any headway?"

She's quiet again.

"I don't know. I guess. I just… There's something I need to ask you."

"Anything," I say immediately. "Ask me anything."

"Is there someone else, Jude?"

Her question is hesitant, her voice thin, and it takes me a second to realize what she's asking. She knows.

She knows.

"What do you mean?" I ask stiffly, buying for time, because I have no idea what the fuck to say.

"In my sessions, I'm remembering some things from the past few weeks that just don't add up. It feels like... I mean, my gut is telling me that you're...that there is someone else, Jude. Please, tell me I'm wrong."

"You're wrong," I say immediately, because it's my gut instinct to lie to protect myself, and even to protect her. She doesn't need to know. It'll set her back, and I'm going to end things with Zoe, and everything will be fine.

Corinne never has to know.

She sighs, and it's loud and long and relieved. "Are you sure?"

"Of course," I lie to her again. "I love you, Corinne. It's only you. It's always been you. I know it's easy to get confused because of everything that's happened, but I love you. Don't ever get confused on that."

And that's the truth. I do love her. More than anything. Zoe is nothing to me.

"God, that's good to hear," she murmurs, and I think she's crying and I feel like shit.

"Babe, I'm coming on Saturday to see you. I don't care what they say. I need to see you."

"I need to see you, too. I love you, Ju."

"I love you, too. Sleep tight, and I'll see you in a couple days."

She hangs up and I stare at the black sky, and I'm a complete and utter jackass. I know that. But she never has to. I'll make sure of that.

I settle farther into the seat, and when something pokes my back, I feel around with my hand, grabbing a stiff piece of paper.

Pulling it up in front of my face, I find that it's a photo.

I peer at it and then startle.

It's a woman masturbating, her legs spread wide, her fingers inserted in her vagina. Red lace panties are pulled down and stretched to the side, and I recognize the navy striped cushion.

It's the one I'm sitting on.

It's Zoe. I recognize the blue nail polish.

I don't know when or how, but she was here, on this lounge, masturbating and photographing herself. Then she left this for me to find.

I'm not sure what I feel as I slide the picture into my pocket.

Violated because she was at my house without my permission?

Even more certain that I have to end everything with her?

Or excited because she was masturbating on my patio in broad daylight?

I'm finding myself in the same predicament with her every day—torn between the forbidden excitement and the moral compass that tells me everything about her is wrong. Every time I decide to cut all contact with her, she manages to do something to keep me from it, to keep me coming back for more.

I hate myself.

I can't stop myself.

I'm weak.

I'm pathetic.

I close my eyes and do what I do best.

Pretend it's not a problem.

If I don't acknowledge it, then it can't be real.

The irony isn't lost on me…that this exact behavior is what landed my wife in a psych ward.

25

"So after speaking with Jude last night, how do you feel?" Dr. Phillips mouth is pinched in disapproval, but I don't care.

"It was amazing to talk to him," I say almost defiantly. "He's coming on Saturday, too."

"Is he, now?" The psychologist is annoyed, but again, I don't care. "Let's worry about that on Saturday. For now, let's focus again on you."

I settle into my chair. We've been doing this every day, so it's familiar to me by now.

"You've had some concerns lately," Dr. Phillips reminds me. "About Jude, possibly. About your father and Melanie Gibson."

"Yes. I asked Jude last night if there was anyone else, and he said no."

"Let's talk about that," Dr. Phillips suggests. I'm silent. "What gives you the idea that there might be someone else?"

I exhale a shaky breath, a tool for stalling. I need time to formulate an answer.

The doctor waits.

"I guess it's just a feeling," I finally say. "I don't have anything concrete. Just a feeling. In my gut."

"And you don't give merit to gut instincts?" the doctor asks. His pen is poised above his notes. I want to snatch it out of his hand and break it, but I don't.

"I do. But in this case, they're unwarranted. Jude would never."

My stomach quivers, but I ignore it. It's just because I'm here that I'm feeling so unnerved. It's nothing other than that.

"Okay," Dr. Phillips says, scribbling a note. "I'm glad to see that your ability to trust hasn't been permanently scarred because of your father. That's very good, Dr. Cabot."

"I hope that's true," I admit. "But sometimes I worry. I mean, *am* I able to trust, or is that a lie I tell myself?"

"Go on," he urges me, his legs crossed, his pen waiting over the page. I shake my head.

"I don't know. I just… I was remembering this fight that Jude and I had. It was probably about a week ago, and it was so stupid. I'd come home early from work, something that I rarely get to do, and Jude almost seemed annoyed. And that was odd. He was always annoyed with me that I worked late."

"But that night, he was annoyed because you came home?"

I nod. "Yeah. It put a weird feeling in my stomach at the time. But I was probably reading too much into it. I was tired, I was overworked, Jude was annoyed by that. It was a pattern."

"But that night, Jude was annoyed by something opposite? So he was breaking the pattern?" Dr. Phillips asks.

I nod again. "Yeah. That's what it seemed like. It was awkward when we went to bed…tense. And when I woke up, he was already gone."

"That was unlike him?"

"Very. I went to find him, and he was at that dingy little café that he loves so much, and there was a waitress…"

My breath freezes a bit, and my words pause and my tongue sort of feels like wood.

"And there was a waitress?" The doctor prompts me. But I'm still frozen.

"When I think of her in my head, I can't remember her face. Isn't that weird?" I glance at Dr. Phillips, but I don't really see him. I'm trying to see the girl's face in my head. But all I can see is a blur.

"Well, maybe it's something of significance," the doctor suggests. "Maybe you never actually saw her face. Let's talk about it. Try to remember that day."

So I take a deep breath and focus.

26

When I come through the door, I'm exhausted. I'm still sick, but I'm also excited. I can't wait to tell Jude about the baby. I walk into the living room, and he's sitting on the edge of a chair, staring at his phone. He's frowning.

"Hey," I say softly.

His head snaps up in surprise, and he doesn't smile.

"Hey, you're home early."

I chuckle. "No, I'm home on time."

He checks his watch. "I guess so. It's been so long, I'd forgotten."

That's annoying, and his annoyed tone is annoying, and I fight back anger. It's probably my hormones, I tell myself. Calm down, girl.

"I was just heading to bed," he tells me as he stands and stretches, his muscles rippling like the surface of the ocean. "It's late."

And with that, he walks down the hallway without another word.

I'm silent as he climbs into bed and hugs his edge. After I join him, he's very careful not to touch me, and I find myself getting angry.

"I get that you're upset because of my hours," I tell his broad back. "But you're acting like a child. What is going on here? What are you really upset about?"

"I'm not upset," he tells me quickly. "I've got a rough patient. I'm just thinking about that. It's not you, Corinne."

Not sweetie, not honey. Corinne.

I'm almost stung by that.

I let it go, and he falls asleep, and in the night, he's careful not to touch me, to stay on his side of the bed.

In the night, the few times I wake, I'm careful not to touch him, and he's just as careful not to touch me.

Jude is gone when my eyes open.

He didn't leave a note, and his running shoes are still sitting by the foot of the bed.

I grab my phone and dial his number. It goes straight to voice mail. I swallow hard. He doesn't usually act like this. It's so unlike him.

I call Michel.

"Hey, big bro," I greet him. "Is Jude with you?"

There's a pause.

"No. Why? Is something wrong?"

I swallow again. "We had a fight last night," I tell him. "I don't know where he is."

"He didn't meet me for breakfast today," Michel tells me. "Do you want me to go looking for him?"

I think about that for a minute. If anyone can calm Jude down, it's Michel. But no.

"Nah. I'll do it. Thank you, though."

"If I hear from him, I'll have him call you," he promises.

"'Kay."

We hang up, and Jude still doesn't answer his phone. It's too early for work, and so I know where he'll be.

Eating.

I throw a pair of yoga pants on and a T-shirt and don't bother with makeup as I set out for the little diner that he loves.

It's been a while since I've been there, and Vilma is surprised as I walk through the door.

"Dr. Cabot," she greets me. "It's so nice to see you."

"Likewise," I tell her. "Is my husband here?"

She nods. "Right this way."

Relief floods me. *I found him.* Thank God.

When we round the corner, I see him…sitting at a little table with a waitress. She's got her back to me, and Jude looks utterly forlorn. Her long hair flows down her back, and she's patting his arm, and my guilt overwhelms me. He has to seek comfort from a complete stranger in the middle of a café because he couldn't get it from me.

"Hey," I greet him when I reach the table.

He looks up, and for a minute, he almost looks annoyed. But that can't be right. He blinks, and the annoyed look is gone, and I had to be mistaken.

The waitress slips away without saying anything, and without introducing herself. I make a point to not even look at her. I won't give her the satisfaction.

Because something about her attitude bothers me. It was almost possessive, almost agitated with me. But that also can't be right. I'm just feeling guilty.

I slide into the seat she vacated, and Jude stares at me.

"Did I wake you?" His voice is chilly.

"No," I admit. "But I'm sorry you didn't. I hate fighting with you, Jude. Tell me what's going on so we can fix it."

He looks away, his gaze stony.

"I'm not fighting," he says, staring out the window. "I'm just tired of being ignored. I get that you have issues. I get that you struggle this time of year. I know all of that. But this goes on all year, Corinne. You work all hours of the day, and you don't return my texts or phone calls, you don't come home until late at night, and I didn't sign up for that. I didn't sign up to be married to voice mail. And that's the only way I talk to you lately."

I suck in a breath. "I had no idea you were this upset about it," I say slowly. "Why didn't you tell me?"

"Because you're never home to tell," he answers, and his voice is resigned and tired. And holy shit, have I really let things slide this much?

I put my hand on his, and he doesn't move away. "Jude, I love you. I'm so sorry I've made you feel like this. I'll work on it. I swear to God. We'll fix it."

He relents now, his face softening, and I want to melt into the chair. When his sun shines on you, it's so so warm. When it doesn't, the world is cold. It makes you pray to have it back.

"It's okay," he says, even if he does sound a little stiff. "I know. I'm just… I'm not being rational. It's not your fault, Co. You're just trying to work hard. I get it."

"I feel weird lately," I tell him. "I feel like… I don't know. I feel like…you might be distracted. Like you don't like me."

I don't want to say what I really want to say. *That there might be someone else.* Because there isn't. Right? There's no way.

Jude looks away, his hand tapping anxiously on his leg. He's still upset. He's just trying to cover it.

"That's insane, Corinne," he says finally. "You're the only

person in the world besides my brother who I truly like. Honest."

"I have an idea," I tell him. "I'll take the day off work. We'll spend it together."

He hesitates, then shakes his head. "That's okay. You can't do that, and I have patients, too. But thank you for the gesture."

I stare at him. "Okay. But it's not just for you. I need to spend time with you, too. I'll take off early and meet you for dinner. We'll fix this, Jude."

"Okay." He squeezes my hand and looks over my shoulder. I follow his gaze, and the waitress has her back to us across the room. "We need our check," he tells me.

His check. I didn't get anything.

The girl comes back, and I'm determined not to look up at her. She's not important. I don't want to know if she's beautiful. And also, I don't know why, but I feel a strong urge to show her that she's not important. I keep my gaze on the table. I watch her put the check down, and her hand seems to linger next to Jude's for a second. A second too long. I grit my teeth and keep my gaze on the table, on her hand that is so so close to my husband's.

There's something something something in my gut.

Something startling.

When she walks away, I finally look up and level a gaze at my husband. "How well do you know her?"

His gaze is sharp. "Not very. Why?"

I don't know. "Something felt weird for a minute. I think she might like you more than you realize."

I can feel the girl staring at us now from across the room, and surely I'm wrong. She's just waiting to pick up his check. I steel my nerve and don't look up at her. Fuck her.

Jude is annoyed. "Seriously, Corinne? That's ridiculous. The kid is twentysomething. I think it's just your guilt talking. You're trying to displace it onto me."

It's therapist-speak for *I'm trying to distract myself from my own guilt by getting angry with Jude.*

He could be right. I *do* feel guilty.

There's nothing going on. Jude would never.

"I'm sorry," I apologize. "You're right. Of course you're right."

"Damn straight," Jude says shortly. "I'm almost offended, honestly."

He's icy cold again, and he's right. What was I thinking?

I apologize again, and he shakes his head, and I can't do anything right with him lately, it seems.

I refuse to look at her. I refuse to look at her. I refuse to look at her. Don't do it. Don't do it.

Outside, Jude turns to me.

"I'll be home for dinner. Will you?"

"Of course," I assure him, squeezing his arm. "And if you need to talk today, call me."

"Will you answer?" He's direct, and he has every right to ask.

It makes me uncomfortable and I nod. "Yes. No matter what I'm doing."

He smiles now, but it's tight and short, and when I lean up to kiss him, it's also tight and short. His cheek feels like stone, and it doesn't give. He gets into his car and drives away, and as I'm buckling myself into my own, I feel someone staring at me.

I look up, and I see the outline of the waitress through the window. I still don't see her face, but she seems like she's probably pretty. She waves. I wave back.

I'm an idiot for thinking anything was amiss. She's just a kid, and she's a waitress in a café where Jude eats every day. She likes tips, and it's her job to be nice.

Lord, I've got a vivid imagination.

With a sigh, I nose my car out of my parking spot and drive home.

27

I died a thousand internal deaths when Corinne walked into the diner and I was sitting with Zoe.

Even now, in the privacy of my own car, I feel short of breath, light-headed.

I watch Corinne's car disappear into the distance, and I try to take a deep breath.

As I do, Zoe texts.

I got a rush from that.

A pang hits my chest. God, if Corinne had walked in one second earlier when Zoe had her hand on my cheek, before I'd brushed it away, Corinne would've known.

She wouldn't even look at me, though, Zoe adds. I wonder if she's intimidated.

That makes me laugh. My wife isn't intimidated by anyone. Zoe is arrogant if she truly believes otherwise.

She was tired, I tell her. That's all.

She did look tired, Zoe agrees. She didn't even bother putting on makeup.

Corinne doesn't even need makeup, but I don't say that. Zoe is being catty now. Usually, I don't notice this kind of thing, but even I can see it now.

She's so oblivious, Zoe says.

Her words twist my gut. I hope Corinne is oblivious. I hope she *stays* oblivious. She can never know.

I don't answer. Instead, I slip my phone back into my pocket and start my car. I need to drive to work and pretend this never happened. This girl is insignificant. She's nothing to me.

Guilt overwhelms me, and I certainly feel like shit for making Corinne feel like she was the one doing something wrong. It was the first reaction I could think of when she showed up, the only plausible thing. In the therapist world, we call it "gaslighting." It's turning someone's suspicions or concerns onto themselves, like *they* are the culprit.

I'm an utter asshole.

I know that.

But I'm stuck in this terrible sticky spiderweb of deception and I have no idea how to crawl out without hurting everyone.

28

"Perhaps you're scared of intimacy," Dr. Phillips suggests. "You trusted your father, and he betrayed that trust. He hurt your mother, and he killed people. It's understandable that you would have trust issues, Corinne."

"Yeah. But… I can't explain it. It's like there's a wall in my head. And I can't get past it."

"Not even for your husband?" Dr. Phillip's eyebrow arches.

"Not for anything."

"Let's examine that."

God. Is it hot in here? My face flushes, and I fan myself. My thighs are hot enough that they're damp, and it's all so unusual for me. I'm usually cold, not hot.

"Everything is just so confusing," I murmur finally. "It feels like there is a terrible large elephant in the room, but no one is talking about it, and I don't know what it is."

Dr. Phillips closes his notebook and studies me.

"Corinne, I don't know if there are actual things going on with Jude, or if you are transferring old feelings and memories from your father and mother to your present life. Either way, you do have many suppressed memories. We can agree on that, right?"

I nod. Of course.

"I wonder if you'd be willing to let me try another form of treatment with you. It's called EMDR. Eye Movement Desensitization and Reprocessing. It's an alternative treatment for trauma. It's been successfully used in PTSD among soldiers and accident survivors. It helps allay the feelings of panic, by moving the panicky feelings from one part of your brain to another, so that they are finally processed."

I pause and then nod. He holds up a hand.

"I should warn you, though. It's not uncommon to uncover old memories during EMDR, because we're accessing old emotions. Are you still willing?"

I swallow, and swallow hard. I don't want to.

But I think I need to.

Finally, I nod. "Yeah. I guess."

He smiles. "Good."

He digs around in a little black bag and pulls out two nodules. "Hold one of these in each of your hands. You will feel an alternating vibration, but no pain."

He turns it on. I feel the buzz. First in my right hand, then in my left.

"Now, let's talk about that night with your father. What is something you feel when you think about that night?"

"Fear," I whisper, my eyes closed.

"Let's examine that," he suggests. "When did that fear begin?"

I think about that, prepared to say that it began when my

father arrived. But I can't remember when my father actually arrived, and I felt fear before that point.

"Earlier in the night," I say, without even meaning to. The hand sensors buzz, to and fro. To and fro.

"Focus on that emotion," he tells me. "Let it go wherever it takes you."

I keep my eyes closed and focus on the feeling in my belly, the feeling of tightness and anxiety, of anxiety and panic. It spreads into my chest and then into my hands. I flex my fingers around the vibrating sensors.

"I wasn't alone in the house," I remember out of nowhere. Someone had stepped out of the laundry room after I'd put the kids to bed.

"He cupped his hand over my mouth and dragged me to the bedroom," I whisper, and I can smell him still. His aftershave, tart and strong, and his skin. It smelled like sweat, and it was damp. His fingers cut into my lip, bruising it. I scratched at him, and he shook me.

"Who was it?" Dr. Phillips asks calmly. "Remember, you're safe here, Corinne."

I focus, but I can't see the face. It's dark and blurred, and I can see only a shadow above me, moving in the night.

"I can't see," I whisper. My hands are tightly clasped, and Dr. Phillips notices.

"Corinne, you're here. This is a safe place. You aren't there."

I open my eyes. "I wasn't alone that night."

I extend my fingers, and my palms have half-moons carved into them from my fingernails.

Dr. Phillips nods. "Okay. That's a place to start. I think we've done enough for today, Dr. Cabot."

He's pleased, and we're finished, and I rush outside to the common area, into the sunlight. I take a deep breath, then hunch over on my knees and vomit onto the pavement.

29

Four days until Halloween
Corinne

Jackie squeals and jumps out of her chair, almost spilling her coffee.

"You're sure? How far along?" She hugs me and almost knocks me over.

"I'm sure, and not very far," I answer, removing her arm from my windpipe. "You're going to be an aunt."

"It's about time," she tells me, settling back into the chair across from me. We're in the sunroom, and Artie is in the backyard. Frost etches the edges of the windows, but I can still see through them. The dog roots around by the fence, trying to get at something. The chill seeps through the tile, into my socks.

Winter is coming.

"I think I need to see Dad," I tell Jackie as casually as I can.

"What?" She sits up straighter. "All of a sudden? Why?"

I sip my hot chocolate and ignore my pounding heart. I can't even speak about any of this without the panic welling up in me. It's getting ridiculous. My hand flutters over my belly, but that's also ridiculous. I can't protect it from me, from my emotions. It will feel the adrenaline, too. Everything I feel will course through its veins as well as my own.

I fight to calm myself.

"Because I need to know what happened."

I don't have to explain what I'm talking about.

Jackie stares at me. "Why? Why can't you just leave it alone, Corinne? You've got a new life now. None of that matters."

"It does matter," I argue. "It affects me in ways I don't even understand. I don't remember everything that happened, and until I do… Until I do, I worry I might go crazy like Dad."

"Dad didn't go crazy," Jackie says adamantly, like she always does. "It was a crime of passion. He… It was a bad situation. Love triangles and all that."

She's uncomfortable now. She hates to talk about what Dad did. What he did to our mother.

"Yeah. But…" I trail off, uncertain how much I should say…about myself.

"What?"

"I feel like I'm going crazy, Jacks. I hear things. Whispers. I see words written on things that aren't there. I don't know what's happening, but I feel this overwhelming feeling that I need to run away. That I'm not safe. That I might be crazy."

"You're not," Jackie says quickly, reaching over to grab my hand. She squeezes my fingers tight. "You're not. You're the sanest person I know."

"I don't feel like it right now. I keep having weird feelings about Jude, too."

Jackie watches me. "Like what? You don't feel attracted to him? Because that would be normal. You're pregnant."

I shake my head. "No, not that. I feel like he… I'm scared he is… I mean, what if he's cheating on me?"

My sister bursts out laughing, then after a moment, she stops and looks at me. "You're not kidding?"

I shake my head, and I feel silly.

She smiles. "Your hormones are twisting you all up," she says. "Jude would never cheat on you, Corinne. That man loves you more than anyone I've ever seen."

"Yeah. I know," I murmur.

I lay my head back on the chair, and Jackie examines me.

"You're pale," she tells me. "Paler than normal."

"I know."

"I think you're losing weight, too."

"I'm sicker than a dog. That's why."

"I bet your hormones are just making you feel weird," she finally says. "You're not crazy. Hormones are powerful things, Corinne. They can wreak havoc on a person."

"Yeah, I know."

This isn't hormones. I don't tell her, though. She doesn't want to worry, and I don't want to burden her.

We chat for another hour or so, and then Jackie takes her leave, hugging me at the front door. She smells like Chanel, and it turns my stomach. I gulp in fresh air.

"Let me know if you need anything," she says, staring into my eyes. "I mean it."

"Of course."

"You've got the baby to think of now. You've got to take care of yourself."

"I know. Hey, Jackie, don't tell Jude yet. I'm going to tell him as a surprise. I'm just waiting for the perfect time."

She grins. "My lips are sealed. He's going to be ecstatic."

She hugs me again and waves as she trips down the steps.

I watch her drive down the road, and the dead leaves flutter on the road behind her. I close the front door, closing out October's cold air with the thick iron of the door. My house is a fortress. I made it that way on purpose. It might've been subconscious, but my house is no less safe because of it.

I head back into the kitchen, stopping first at the fireplace to turn the flames on. The wood and the tiles are cold this time of year.

I let Artie in, and I'm pouring another cup of hot chocolate when my phone rings.

I glance at it, and it's Jude's name flashing at me.

"Hey, babe," I answer, balancing my cup and my phone as I head to my chair.

"Just checking on you," he says, the huskiness of his voice rasping in my ear. "You doing okay?"

"Yep," I tell him. "I'm feeling better."

"Good. Do I need to bring you something home for lunch?"

"No, don't drive all that way," I tell him. "I'm not that hungry."

"Okay. I'm coming home early this evening," he answers. "Get some rest."

"Will do, boss."

"If only," he says wryly.

I laugh.

We hang up, and Artie whines at the door. Ready to go again already.

"You have a bladder the size of a peanut," I tell her, letting her out. She races past me with intention, bounding down the back porch and out to the fence. She lunges at it, barking loudly, trying with all her might to get through.

Alarmed, I go out, wrapping my sweater tightly around me.

"Artie, stop!" I call out as I get closer. "Stop."

She doesn't even look up, her paws scratching at the fence, barking and growling.

"Hush, girl." I grab her collar and try to peer through the slats. There's nothing there. "There's nothing here."

I pull her toward the house, and when I reach the back steps, I swear I hear someone laughing.

A weird giggle, carried on the cold wind.

A woman.

I whirl around, but just like I suspected, there's no one there.

30

Two days, fourteen hours until Halloween
Jude

Are you coming to the diner for breakfast?

I answer Zoe's text quickly. I'm running behind today.

You've been running late a lot lately.

She seems accusatory, suspicious.

Suddenly, it occurs to me that Zoe knows everything about me. My wife's name, my name, my address. If things end badly, she could blow my entire life up.

I can't let that happen. So I have to make sure they don't end "badly."

Maybe I can make it.

Try! she answers, then adds a winky face.

I finish lacing up my shoes, then pause. I'm actually running a bit late. If I go jogging, I won't have time for breakfast.

Sighing, I take my shoes back off.

I text her back.

I'll be there.

"Hey, who are you talking to so early?"

I turn, and Corinne is in the door of my closet, watching me sleepily.

I slide my phone into my pocket quickly. "Just Michel. He wants to have breakfast."

Corinne glances at the time. "You'd better hurry, then. You'll be late for work."

"Yeah, I know. I'll have to skip my run."

I strip off my clothes, and Corinne pecks me on the cheek. "I still feel yuck. I'm going back to bed."

"Have a good day, babe."

I put on slacks and a shirt and head to my truck.

Somehow, the drive to the diner feels more like a prison sentence than anything else. This whole thing with Zoe has become tedious, a tricky balancing act.

I'm not sure it's worth the thrill anymore.

In fact, as I make my way through the café and see Zoe's flushed face, and the way she looks at me so possessively, I know it's not.

It's not worth it.

Not anymore.

In fact, it wasn't ever.

31

"How you feeling?" Jackie asks when I answer the phone.

I take stock as I make tea. "Okay, I guess," I tell her. "I haven't thrown up yet."

"Good," she tells me. "That's progress."

"I guess," I say, holding my hot cup in my hands, warming my fingers. "How are you?"

"I'm good," she says brightly. "Teddy is going to take me on a last-minute getaway. I'm so excited I can't see straight."

"Where to?" I ask, more to make conversation than anything else.

"Sonoma and Napa. I'll bring you back some wine. You can have it after the baby's born."

I smile. "Thank you. I'm sure I'll need it."

She giggles. "I leave tomorrow, and I'll be gone for a week. Do you need anything before I go?"

"Nope. But thanks for checking."

"Okay. Well, I've gotta go do laundry and pack."

"Talk to you later."

I hang up and turn the fireplace on, and as I do, I see Michel's truck pulling into the drive. He and Jude must've cut breakfast short.

He doesn't even knock. Like usual, he just pokes his head in and calls to me.

"Come in, goofball," I tell him. "I'm right here."

He has two cups of coffee in his hands, and a sack.

"I came to bring my brother breakfast," he says. "Am I too late to catch him?"

I pause, startled, and my chest feels weird. Tight.

"Um, weren't you meeting him at the café?"

He blinks, staring at me.

One beat passes.

Then two.

"Uhhh, yeah. We were. But then I ran late, and I'm not sure if he got my text."

His tone is off and he's uncomfortable. He even pulls at his collar.

"Michel," I remind him, "lying is a sin. Is everything okay?"

He nods slowly. "Yeah, of course. Why would I lie?"

"I don't know." I eye him. "Why would you?"

He loosens, rolling his eyes. "You're worrying too much, Co. We just crossed signals. No big deal. And the bright side? You get a free breakfast."

He thrusts the sack at me, and I take a cup of coffee, even though I know I won't drink it. Now that I'm pregnant, I have to give up caffeine.

"Thanks, bro," I tell him.

He grins. "Anytime. You need anything else?"

"Nope. I'm just going to eat my newly acquired breakfast and then maybe shower."

He pats my back, and before he's even pulled out of the drive, I've texted Jude.

How was Michel this morning?

Because something isn't right.
I feel it.
I feel it.
Jude doesn't answer until I'm throwing my breakfast trash away.

Fine, why?

My heart pounds and pounds. Because why would he lie to me?
No reason, I answer. Have a good day.
I try to enjoy my own, but it's almost impossible…because something something something niggles at me.
Something tells me that everything is wrong.
I consider digging around, and trying to find things out on my own, but decide a direct approach is best.
I call Michel.
"Hey!" he answers. "Don't blame me if the breakfast was crappy. I didn't make it myself."
I roll my eyes even though he can't see. "No, it's not that. Can I ask you a question?"
"Of course." His answer is immediate.
"It's about Jude," I warn him. "I don't want to believe it, but I feel like something might be going on."
"What do you mean?" Michel is cautious, his words slow. I know I have to tread lightly here. Michel is a priest, and he loves me, but Jude is still his twin brother. I know his allegiance will always lie with him.

"There was something weird about this morning. He told me that he was meeting you for breakfast, but he didn't. And when I asked him how you were, he said fine."

Michel is silent.

My brother-in-law is still silent, for one beat, then another.

"Michel?"

He sighs. "Yeah. I...I don't exactly know, Corinne. But I do know this. He's been very worried about you lately. And you know him. When he's worried or upset, he withdraws. He probably thought it would hurt your feelings to tell you that he just wanted some alone time."

"You really think nothing is going on?"

"What do you think would be going on?" he asks, and he's still careful.

I feel sillier by the minute. "I...worry that he might be seeing someone."

"Oh. Don't worry about that, Co. No way. I know my brother, and he wouldn't. He loves you. He's always talking about you, always worrying about you. I swear—it's just this time of year. He's always worried that he's going to say something that will trigger you."

I consider that.

"Well, if he wasn't with you, where was he this morning?"

Michel's answer is immediate. "Probably taking some alone time. Running or eating. It's all he ever does. And when he's upset, he likes to be alone. He hasn't been calling me much lately, so I know he's troubled."

I'm troubling him.

That thought makes me feel guilty and troubled myself.

"Thanks, big brother," I tell him softly. "I'll talk to him. I don't want him to tiptoe around me. I'm not made of glass."

"I know you're not," he answers. "I'll talk to him, too."

"You don't have to," I start to say, but he interrupts.

"I want to. You know I love both of you."

"I know."

32

My thumb taps my desk, and I stare out my office window, into the street.

Halloween is just in a couple of days, and it's a good thing. The jack-o'-lanterns are starting to shrivel. I notice that some-one's scarecrow has lost its head in the wind. It rests in the dead grass twenty feet from the rest of the straw body. For some reason, it seems eerie.

I stare at it, watching it tumble and roll, and I push away my growing concern about my wife. It's while I'm staring at it that I notice a beat-up truck idling down the street, with my brother's familiar face inside.

I greet him at my office door. "Hey! What are you doing here?"

Michel brings the cold October air in with him as he breezes past me.

"Be my guest," I offer wryly, closing the door after he enters. I trail behind him and wait for him to get to his point.

"Are you okay?" I ask as he takes a seat across from my desk.

He shakes his head. "No."

I'm startled, then concerned. "What's wrong?"

I sit down and Michel shakes his head.

"I was at your house earlier," he mentions. "And you weren't."

He stares, and I pause. "So?"

"So, your wife was under the assumption that you were with me. But you weren't."

Fuck.

"Um, I…"

"I told her that our signals must've gotten crossed. But I know something is up, Jude. I feel it, and she does, too. Tell me what it is."

My shoulders drop, because I'm sure he does feel it. He knows me too well for me to lie.

"I don't want to talk about it," I try to tell him. But as I knew he would, he doesn't let that fly.

"Jude," he says sternly. "Tell me. I mean it. I have a really bad feeling. What's going on?"

One look at his face, and I know that stalling isn't going to work. Or lying. Or excuses.

"I don't know," I tell him honestly. "I have no clue what I'm doing, or what I've gotten myself into. I only know that I wish I hadn't."

"This has to do with the girl at the diner? Zoe?" Michel's question is plain and knowing.

"Yeah." I don't even ask how he knows.

"Son of a bitch," he swears, staring out the window, away from me. "You have to end it."

"That's not necessary. I mean, yeah. I have to get away from her, but I haven't actually done anything with her. Not really."

Michel sighs and situates himself in his chair. His white collar is stark in the room, a glaring reminder that he's everything that's good in the world, and right now, I'm everything shitty.

"Do you know how many times I hear that in the confessional?" he asks. "Countless times. *But, Father, I haven't acted on it. But, Father, it was just emails. Or texts. I haven't really sinned.* I hear it all the time. I never thought I'd hear it from you, though. Jude, any time or attention that you place on someone other than your wife is infidelity. You're being unfaithful to your wife right now. Do you realize that?"

"I'm not," I protest, but his words slam into my heart.

"You are," he argues. "Don't try to tell me you haven't done things. Phone calls or texts or lunches or whatever. I already know. I don't know everything, but I know you, and I can see it on your face. You've got to put a stop to it. If you don't, there will be severe consequences. Do you love your wife?"

"Of course I do." My answer is immediate.

"Then end whatever this is with Zoe. She's nothing to you, Jude. She might be lovely, but you've got a beautiful wife and a life you've worked hard for. Whatever you're seeing in Zoe… it's just because she's new. That is all. End it immediately before it gets out of hand. I'm saying this as your brother, and I'm advising you as a priest."

I stare at the floor. "I don't even know how it got this far," I finally admit. "She's really into me and pays me attention, and, Jesus, it sounds so pathetic."

Michel doesn't argue. He's simply silent.

"She started texting me, and I… It hasn't gone very far," I tell him. "I would never."

"You think you would never," Michel points out. "But these things get out of hand. I've seen it happen a hundred times. End it. You're a better man than this. Corinne deserves better, and so do you. If there's a problem in your marriage, put in the time to fix it. Don't occupy yourself with distractions."

I nod, because he's right. Because I've been pathetic, and my brother knows it. My cheeks flush because I'm humiliated.

"Please, don't say anything to Corinne," I say, staring him down. "I'm asking this as your brother. I'll end it."

"I'm always your brother," he assures me. "This is yours to handle. But I love you, and, bro, this is a dangerous path. I just had to tell you that. I love Corinne, too. I don't want either of you to get hurt."

"We won't," I assure him. "Let's just chalk it up to *something else dumb that Jude did* and move on."

"Corinne called me this morning," he says. "She has a feeling something is off. You need to handle things, Jude."

"I will," I promise. Somehow.

"We don't have to speak of it again," Michel confirms. "I just had to say something."

"I appreciate that. Now, I've got to get to work," I tell him, and I feel like I have to be careful now. He's going to watch everything I do to make sure I'm coloring inside the lines.

He rolls his eyes. "Stop. I trust you."

He gets up, and then he's gone. I watch his truck rumble out of the neighborhood, and I slump against the wall, and my knees literally feel weak.

Fuck.

Me.

33

"Let's talk about Michel," Dr. Phillips suggests. "Just for a moment."

I nod. Because that won't be hard.

"They're twins," I tell him. "Identical. Michel is three minutes older, and he always holds it over Jude's head. When they were little, they dressed alike to trick people. Typical twin stuff."

"You get along well with him?"

I nod. "Yeah. He's easy to get along with. Plus, I'm married to his twin. So I feel like I know him very well. They're very similar."

"Except that Michel is a priest." Dr. Phillips states the obvious.

"Yeah, except for that."

"So you do get along with him."

"Yes. He's funny, he's sincere. He's not uptight or stuffy like you'd think a priest would be. He's real."

"Do you trust him?"

"Yeah. Of course. He's never lied to me."

"So when he told you that Jude wasn't doing anything wrong, you believed him?"

I nod. "Yeah. Aside from me, Michel knows Jude better than anyone. In fact, at times, I think he might know parts of Jude better than me. I'm sure Jude confides in him about me. And I don't mind. Everyone needs a confidant."

"True." The doctor nods. "Everyone does. Who would you say is yours? Besides Jude, I mean."

"My sister, Jackie. And my friend Lucy. I don't open up to people easily, but my sister has always been my best friend. She knows me, you know? She was there for...well, back then. And Lucy... She's worked side by side with me at work, day in and day out. The things we have to do, it brings people together, you know?"

He nods. "Yes. I can imagine."

"But back to Michel... I trust him," I say, because I feel that I need to emphasize that. "I trust him right now to take care of Jude while I'm gone. He's taken care of Jude his whole life. He's not going to stop now."

"Why do you say it that way?" Dr. Phillips asks curiously. "Do you feel that Jude needs to be taken care of?"

I pause, reflecting on that.

"No. He just forgets to do stuff, like shop for groceries. Michel will make sure he does."

"Michel is more responsible?"

I shake my head. "It's not like that. It's just the difference in their personalities. They might be twins, but Michel has always played the role of older brother, and Jude has played the younger brother. I think that's normal, right?"

The doctor nods. "Yes, it's very typical of twins. And of human beings in general. There has to be a pecking order. It makes people comfortable. Everyone has a role."

I agree, and I've seen Michel and Jude play out that relationship throughout the years, ever since I've known them, and far before that, I'm sure.

"They take care of each other, though," I add. "Jude takes care of Michel, too. There's nothing they wouldn't do for each other."

"Would you say that they'd protect each other no matter the consequence?"

His question is odd, and I tell him that.

"Humor me." He smiles. "Would they lie for each other?"

I think on that. "I'm not sure. Probably."

It's something I ponder long after our session ends, and that makes me uneasy even as I try to sleep.

It's almost as though Dr. Phillips knows something I don't.

But that's crazy.

Isn't it?

34

Our bedroom is dark, and Corinne is sleeping.

Her hand hangs over the bed, her blond hair spread across her pillow. A strand of it tickles my nose, and I brush it away. She doesn't stir.

My phone lights up on the nightstand again, as it has every few minutes for the past hour.

I see the picture of Zoe from here, nude, provocative, racy.

I reach out and grab the phone, pulling it to me, shielding it in case Corinne opens her eyes.

Why aren't you sleeping? I ask Zoe.

Because I'm thinking about you, she answers.

A knot forms in my belly.

I don't know what to do.

I don't know how to handle this.

It's gone so far. Too far.

Jude? I feel like you're slipping away from me.

What the fuck is she talking about? I'm not hers. I never have been.

You know I'm married, I tell her.

Yes. But I mean, aside from her. I feel like you're not interested anymore.

Corinne rolls over in her sleep, turning her back to me, and I stick the phone under the covers, just in case she wakes. I wait for a few minutes, waiting for her breathing to deepen and even out again.

When it does, I pull my phone back out.

Zoe has texted again.

I'm going to bed. But know this, I'm not ready to let you go yet. I'll compete for you, Ash. And you'll like it.

I don't bother answering.

This isn't going to end well. There is no competition. I'm married, and I have no plans to change that. Why Zoe thinks otherwise, I don't know.

I stare at the ceiling for a long time, before I text my brother.

Hey, I know you're sleeping, but I've got a problem. I need your advice. Can we meet for dinner tomorrow?

I delete Zoe's texts and am just putting my phone on the nightstand again when my brother answers.

Of course. I'll see you tomorrow night. Don't worry. Everything will be fine.

His words do calm me.

Because he's right.

Everything will be fine. I'm in control of this. I started it, and I can end it. It's up to me.

"Grow a pair," I mumble to myself, staring at my phone yet again on the way to work. I'm at a stoplight, and it's broad daylight, and I'm watching a video from Zoe, when I should throw my phone out the window.

She's fingering herself, moaning my name, and I shouldn't watch it because I don't even like her, but yet I am. And I'm hard.

There's something seriously wrong with me.

She texts me an hour later.

Well, did you like that?

I don't know what to say.

So I don't say anything.

I focus on work, and when Zoe texts at the end of the afternoon, I finally reply.

I'm sorry—busy with patients all day!

She answers immediately. When am I going to see you again?

I don't know, I reply, and that's the truth.

She responds with a frowny face.

I call my brother, and it goes straight to voice mail.

He texts a little bit later.

Sorry, bro. Someone died. I'm with their family. I can't make dinner tonight. We'll catch up soon. You ok?

I sigh. No, I'm not. Of course I'm not. But I don't say that to him. I lie.

Yeah, I'm fine.

35

Now
Jude

I'm resting on the couch when the doorbell rings.

My eyes pop open in the dark, because who is coming at this hour?

Michel, I decide as I head to the door. Artie isn't even growling.

But it's not my brother standing on the porch with a take-out bag.

It's Zoe.

She's dressed in a tiny miniskirt and a low-cut peasant blouse, and her eye makeup is painted on thick. She smiles.

"I hope you don't mind," she says almost shyly. "But I wanted to make sure you ate dinner."

I hesitate, and she notices.

"Jude," she says softly. "Your wife isn't home yet, right? You shouldn't be sitting around in the dark alone." She glances over my shoulder into the dark house. "You don't even have a light turned on."

She pushes past me, and I allow it, for whatever reason, I don't even know.

"Come on," she calls over her shoulder, inviting me into my own home. "I hope you like Chinese."

"I do," I tell her, watching her arrange it on the table. She opens the kitchen cabinets, hunting for dishes, as though she belongs here. "You didn't need to do this."

"I know," she tells me, sitting down at the table. Incidentally, she's sitting in Corinne's chair. I swallow hard and take a seat. I've got to get out of this. I've got to get out of this. I've got to get out of this.

Her perfume is cloying and cheap, and it fills the kitchen with the scent. It emphasizes the fact that this is wrong. Corinne's scent is soft and refined, understated. She and Zoe are as different as night and day.

"Jude?"

Zoe lifts an eyebrow, and her hand is frozen in the air, a spoonful of beef broccoli dripping into the white container.

"I'm sorry. Yes?"

"How much do you want, love?"

Love. I'm not her love. A heaviness settles in my gut, and I blink, then shake my head. "Not much. I'm not hungry."

She ignores that and heaps a plate with rice and beef and slides it to me. "Trust me, you're going to need your strength." She winks, and my heart pumps hard harder harder.

I've got to get out of this.

I take a bite, and it's good, and I find myself eating the entire plate because I haven't eaten since breakfast.

"You didn't come to the diner today," Zoe comments as she chews. "Why?"

"I was running late," I lie. I picked up breakfast at McDonald's instead.

She nods. "Your schedule must be all turned around, you poor thing."

She's sympathetic and I'm a liar. I don't say anything. Instead, I clear away the dishes, and she comes up behind me, wrapping her arms around my waist. She feels foreign to me, not like Corinne. Her arms are too tight, her body too short.

"I'm here for you, you know," she murmurs into my back, and I stand tightly wound at the sink.

"I know."

I'm just trying to figure out what to say to her when she speaks.

"I'll be right back. I've gotta use the powder room."

I nod and she's gone, and I let Artie out while I wait. I watch the dog disappear into the darkness, and I take a seat in an armchair in the living room. I purposely don't sit on the couch so that there's no room to sit next to me.

It's quite a few more minutes until Zoe shows up in the living room door, and when she does, I startle.

She's wearing one of my shirts. A button-up that Corinne likes to wear from time to time.

"Hey," Zoe says softly, and the bottom of the shirt reaches her knees. It reached only midthigh on Corinne. "I hope you don't mind. This was lying in your bedroom. I thought I'd get more comfortable."

"Uh…" I don't even know what to say.

"I like making you speechless," she practically purrs, crossing the living room toward me. I start to get up, but she pushes me back in my seat and straddles my lap.

Her hands are on my shoulders, her breath on my neck.

"I want you so much," she breathes against my skin. "I've always wanted you, Jude."

My own breath hitches, and my heart races because this isn't good.

"Zoe," I begin, and my hands are on her arms, and her crotch is grazing my own. She's not wearing panties, and she leaves a damp spot on my pants.

Jesus.

"Yes?" her voice is sweet and sinful at once, and she slides her hand on my chest.

"I can't do this."

"Yes, you can." Her answer is immediate. "We're the only two people who will ever know, Jude. You can."

It's true. We are the only ones who would ever know.

The house is quiet but for Zoe's whispers, and the night is dark outside. We're alone.

Her arm snakes behind my head, pulling my face toward hers, and for a scant second, I almost let it happen. I almost do the easy thing and kiss her.

But...

I can't.

I pull away.

"I can't, Zoe."

Her head snaps back, and a flush stains her cheeks. "Why not?" she demands. "I know you want me. Here's proof."

Her hand cups my dick, and it *is* hard, but it's a physical reaction. My penis doesn't have rational thought.

"Zoe," I begin again, but the doorbell rings, and it interrupts any thought I might've had because it means one terrible thing.

We're not alone anymore, and there is a clear view of my living room from the porch.

I push Zoe back, and her feathers are ruffled, but she steps to the side, and the door opens before I can think of what to do.

Michel stands before me, looking from Zoe to me. He examines her lack of clothing, and the fact that she's wearing one of my shirts, and the look on his face is one of utter and complete disappointment. I see it in his eyes, I see it in the grim way his mouth is set... I know that expression. It's exactly like my own.

"I'd ask what's going on, but it's obvious," he says gruffly. "Jesus, Jude." He turns to Zoe. "Go get your clothes on, Zoe. I'll take you home."

"My car is here," she says, and the flush is deeper on her cheeks and has spread to her chest. She's embarrassed and looks to me. I nod. She scurries away down the hall, into what I assume is my bedroom.

Michel looks at me. "We talked about this last week," he says pointedly. "You said you were going to take care of it. What the hell, man?"

"It's not what it looks like," I tell him limply. "She went to the bathroom and came back with her clothes off. I haven't done anything."

"She shouldn't even be here," he snaps. "Your wife is in the hospital, or have you forgotten?"

"Of course I haven't," I snap back. "You don't understand the situation. I wasn't doing anything. I just hadn't figured out how to end it."

"It's not that hard," he tells me. "You say, *This is over.* It's pretty simple."

"It's not that simple," I answer.

The sound of a throat clearing snaps our heads up, and Zoe is back on the periphery of the room.

"I'm ready," she says quietly.

Michel looks at her grimly. "Would you mind following me back to the church? I'd like to talk to you for a while, if you don't mind."

"I really should go home," she says hesitantly. "I have work early in the morning."

"I won't keep you long," Michel says firmly. She nods reluctantly and steps past me, pausing.

"Call me later?"

I'm silent because Michel is staring me down.

Zoe sighs and walks to the door.

"I'll talk to you later," she calls over her shoulder.

The door closes behind them, and I watch their taillights disappear down the road.

Within seconds, I receive a text from Zoe.

You aren't going to listen to him, are you?

I stare at the words, and the letters bleed into each other.

Jude? Are you?
You'll always regret it if you do.
I'll make you regret it.

Her words are sobering because I know she means them.

Artie scratches at the back door, and I lay my phone down and go let her in. She's dirty, her muzzle covered in mud, and I sigh. This is the last thing I need.

"What the hell, girl?" I shake my head and she walks in, after dropping something onto the patio. Bending, I examine what she's dragged up here, and I stiffen up, my feet frozen on the floor.

An address stares up at me from a plaque, 131 All Hallows Lane, in muddy bronze letters.

36

One day, sixteen hours before Halloween
Jude

Hey. You didn't come for breakfast.
Hello?
Jude?
Are you ignoring me?
Jude??
You aren't talking to me now??

I lean against the granite counter and try to decide what to do. My wife is sleeping in the other room, and this girl... whatever she is to me...is blowing up my phone. My palms feel sweaty, my heart is racing.

I do the only thing I think I can to de-escalate what seems to be a ridiculous situation.

I answer.

My wife is still sick.

Three bubbles.

So you're playing nurse to the doctor?

Is she being snotty or not? I'm trying to decide when another text comes in.

Lol

I guess not.

You said you were going to call and then didn't, so I got worried.

I somehow know that's bullshit, but I play along.

Thanks for your concern! But there's no need. Just holed up at home.

Three bubbles.

With your wife?

Didn't I just say that? I'm annoyed as I answer.

Yes. Gotta go. I need to figure out what to make for dinner. I don't cook.

I wait for just a second, but there are no bubbles, and then I get annoyed. I don't have to wait for her answer.

I return to the living room and sit on the couch with my wife. Corinne doesn't wake up, and I channel surf, finally coming to a rest on the History channel. My hand rests on her calf, and I listen to her even breathing as I watch a documentary on a tribe in Africa.

It's warm and cozy here with my wife, and little by little, I find my eyelids closing.

I've just dozed off when the doorbell rings.

I startle awake, and it takes me a minute to realize what woke me. Then Artie barks, heaving herself to a standing position and limping to the door.

I hurriedly extricate myself from Corinne's legs and rush to answer the door. I don't want them to wake her. She hasn't rested like this in months.

I throw open the door, expecting to see a neighbor, but instead, Zoe stands in front of me, with a disposable container in her hands.

My heart drops, then ricochets against my ribs.

I glance back inside at the couch, and Corinne is still there, although she looks to be stirring a little. I step outside and close the door behind me.

"What are you doing here?" My words are sharper than I intended. Zoe looks wounded, her eyes widening. She shoves the disposable bowl into my hands.

"I came to help you," she offers. "You said you couldn't cook. I was just leaving Vilma's, so I thought I'd bring some soup for your wife on my way home. That way, you can look like a superhero. I was just trying to help."

She sincerely sounds offended, although I'm pretty sure her top is unbuttoned more than usual. I can see the top of her red lace bra peeking out. I look away, focusing on her face.

"Thank you," I say formally. "This was very kind. I'll make sure to tell her you were thinking of her."

Zoe giggles. "No, you won't. You shouldn't mention me to her at all. You don't want to incriminate yourself."

"I haven't done anything wrong!" I say, and I'm not sure who I'm trying to convince. Zoe or me.

She raises her eyebrows. "Okay. Calm down."

"You should go," I tell her, lowering my voice. "Corinne is asleep, and I don't want her to wake up."

"Of course you don't." Zoe nods. "Put the soup inside and come for a drive with me."

I shake my head. "No, I need to be here."

"Come on…" she cajoles. "Just come for a drive. You need some fresh air, and I'll make it worth your while." She raises her skirt so that I can see the top of her thigh. I grit my teeth because OH MY GOD. This can't be happening. My wife is twenty feet away, and my heart is pounding.

"No. I'll see you at Vilma's."

I step back inside and close the door, congratulating myself on my deft handling of the situation, and Corinne is standing in front of me. I startle, and she raises an eyebrow.

"Who was that, babe?" She eyes the container in my hands. "Food?"

My heart pounds, but I nod because it's not a lie. It *is* food.

"Soup. For the sickly."

"You're too good to me." She kisses my cheek and I feel like an utter ass. How am I going to get myself out of this situation?

"Let me go dish it up for you," I tell her. "Go back and lie down again. You still look awful."

"Gee, thanks," she says wryly, but she does as I suggest, shuffling back to the couch and collapsing onto it. She really does look bad. Dark circles, pale skin. Her exhaustion is finally catching up to her.

In the kitchen, I dish out soup into a bowl, plating it with a few crackers on the side. I hold the serving spoon out for Artie to lick.

"Don't tell Mom," I instruct her. Human food gives her gas. She wags her tail.

I take the food to Corinne and sit at the other end of the couch while she sips at it. She leaves the crackers on the plate.

"I'm feeling better," she announces when she's finished. "I'm still tired, but a thousand sleepless hours is hard to recover from."

"I still don't want you up and about," I tell her. "You need to rest some more."

"But I'm bored."

"I'll get out the chessboard," I decide. "We haven't played in forever."

"Not in years," she agrees. "Do you remember how we used to leave a game running on the coffee table in college?"

I nod, chuckling. "Yeah. Because sometimes that was the only way we could interact with our busy schedules. I'd come home and move a piece, and then you'd come home and move a piece."

"I felt like I was with you even when you weren't there," she says with a slight smile. "Maybe we should start that again."

"We can keep the game running," I tell her as I get the game from the sideboard. "But I don't want it to be the only way we interact, Co."

She shakes her head quickly. "It won't be. I told you, Ju. I'm going to concentrate more on us. You deserve it."

"*We* deserve it," I correct her as I set up the board. She slides down to sit at the coffee table, a blanket around her shoulders and Artie's head in her lap. She strokes Artie's head absently.

"I love you. Do you believe me?"

She stares at me with such a soft look in her eyes, making them seem as light as the sky.

"Yes, I believe you," I answer quickly. "Why wouldn't I?"

"Because I've been so absent lately. I'm sorry. I'm fighting demons that I shouldn't fight. My marriage comes first."

"Sometimes demons are insistent," I muse as I move a chess piece.

She nods. "Yeah. Mine certainly are."

"Can you talk about them?" I'm hesitant to ask. She doesn't like talking about it, and she never has. That's not going to change.

"Maybe. I'm starting to realize that the way I've handled it all of these years hasn't been healthy. Ignoring it doesn't work. I have to address it."

"Seems to me like a really good therapist told you that once." I stare at her pointedly. She refuses to look up, studying the board intently instead.

"Yeah. He was a smart one."

We're quiet for a while. Corinne reaches out a finger and pushes her first piece, moving one square.

"I hate Halloween," she says quietly, needlessly.

"I know."

"I'll always hate Halloween," she adds.

"I know. That's okay."

"There was blood caked under my fingernails." Her voice is low, and she stares away from me, at nothing. "I couldn't get it out. It was there for days and days."

I sit back, waiting. She's never told me this before.

"That night...the cops came and wrapped a blanket around me and took me out to a car. But I was there to babysit the kids. And I forgot about them. Their parents were in the house, in pools of blood, and I forgot about them. I forgot about them, Jude."

Her voice cracks, and I grab her, pulling her to my chest. I stroke her hair, and she cries.

"Corinne, they couldn't have been there long," I tell her

rationally. "The cops were there. I'm sure they got them out, just like they led you out."

She sniffs, her hand balled into a fist against me. "Yeah. But still. I was there to protect them. And I couldn't."

"You were their babysitter," I tell her helplessly. "You were an eighteen-year-old kid who was there to feed them dinner and put them to bed. You weren't there to protect their lives. It's not your fault. Surely this isn't what you've been carrying around all of these years."

I pause, because maybe it is. Guilt is sometimes irrational. As a therapist, I've seen that a million times. But she shakes her head.

"Surely not. I do feel awful about it, though. I didn't see the cops take them away. The state came and got them. They were put into separate foster homes. The scandal probably followed them everywhere."

"Well, you know how that is." I sigh. "You suffered from the scandal, too."

"Yeah. But my father did it. Theirs was just an innocent bystander. It's not fair."

"Life isn't fair sometimes." I stroke her back. "You know that. But you know what else? You'll get past this, Co. You're the strongest person I know."

She closes her eyes and curls up more tightly, and I'm practically holding her like a baby now. It feels good. I feel like I'm guarding her.

"No one will ever hurt you again," I promise. "I won't let them."

"But don't forget—" she looks up at me, her eyes watery "—the queen is the most powerful piece on the board, Ju. I think I have to protect myself."

I chuckle at her effort to lighten things up. "Maybe. But the game is over when the king is taken. So whoever wants to hurt you will have to come through me. It's not gonna happen, because I refuse to be taken without a fight."

She cuddles into me. "Promise?"

I squeeze her tight. "I promise."

Guilt tightens around my stomach like a vise, and I ignore it, pushing it away farther down until it disappears. If I ignore it long enough, then it isn't there.

That's my logic, anyway.

37

I slice through the water like a knife, allowing it to flow over my back as I breaststroke my way down the pool.

I don't take the time to swim much these days, but I love it here.

The physical therapy pool here at Mercy is always quiet, and this morning, it is completely empty except for me. It is still and peaceful, with only the sounds of the water breaking the silence. The reflection of the water glints on the ceiling, shimmering blue and turquoise from the corner of my eye.

I kick off the wall and flip around, heading back to the other side.

The cold water is a welcome treat on my face. My belly rolls and rolls, the nausea welling up in me. It flushes my face, and overheats me until I feel like I might pass out. I'd thought about calling off to work, but there's no one to cover.

Cold water seemed to be the next best thing. A brisk swim before my shift.

I kick hard off the opposite wall, sucking in a breath before diving under again. Opening my eyes beneath the surface, the water is clear and blue, and so so silent. I love it under here. There are no problems here...no bad memories, no strained marriage, no panic. It is utterly peaceful. I should do this more often.

One stroke, two strokes, three strokes, four.

I find myself down the pool yet again.

Then again.

Then again.

Physical exercise empties the stress from my body, wringing it out like water from a dishrag. I'm almost too tired to feel sick. But not quite.

As I heft myself up onto the side of the pool, the water drips around me, and I take a shaky breath. My mouth still feels sick, a bit like vomit, a bit like pooled saliva. I swallow hard.

I will not puke in this pool.

I resolve to take some Phenergan when I get to the ER. I can't work a shift like this today. Hell, no.

Sitting on the side, I towel my hair and enjoy the silence for a scant minute more. In a few minutes, I'll be immersed in the chaos of Emergency, so I'm going to enjoy this while I can.

It is as I'm standing up that the music starts to blare, suddenly and loudly, from the overhead speakers.

Lyrics from "American Pie" again.

I'm frozen as the notes and words swirl around me, into the chlorinated air, and my stomach seems to hit the tiled floor like a brick.

This song.

This song.

I swallow, and my heart is banging in my ears, the roar drowning out the sounds, and I look around, but no one is here, and there's no reason why the music is playing, and I'm alone.

But I'm not alone.

Because the music triggers me into panic, and I'm clutching at the air and struggling to breathe as the memories stand around me, like sentinels waiting to drag me to prison.

The bloody bodies. The pumpkins and the full moon. My father's eyes, staring at me in accusation. *In accusation?*

I sink to my knees and I relive it all...and something new pops up in my head. The kids' crying from their bedrooms. "Help, help. Mommy?"

Their voices.

So helpless, so small.

And I hadn't done anything...but stand there like a statue.

I can't breathe.

I can't breathe.

I can't breathe.

"Dr. Cabot?"

My eyes open, and my hand stops scratching at the ground.

A physical therapist stands in front of me, concern in her eyes. "Are you okay?"

Am I?

"I'm not feeling well," I finally manage to say, and my voice is weak and small. The PT reaches out and steadies my elbow.

"Let's get you over here to a seat."

I allow her to help me and to wrap a towel around my shoulders. She even sits next to me for a minute, rubbing my shoulder.

"Can I get you a drink?" she asks.

I shake my head.

"No, I'll be fine in a second. I'm fighting a bug."

And seventeen-year-old memories.

After a few more minutes, I'm able to stand and to breathe,

and so I thank her and head to the ER locker room, where I throw on my scrubs. I feel dizzy, and in fact, the lounge spins for a minute. I lean my head against the cool metal of my locker. I can't seem to gather myself or gain my bearings.

Brock comes in, pulling off his stethoscope. When he sees me, he puts it back on.

"Go back home," he announces, without greeting. "You look awful."

"Thanks."

"No, I'm serious." He puts a hand on my forehead. "You don't have a fever, but you look like crap. You've run yourself down. You've got to get some rest, and you don't want to give the rest of us whatever you've got."

I nod, because I know he's right.

"Okay."

"I'll go call someone else in. You go home."

I nod again. "Thanks."

As I trudge to my car, I consider the bright side.

I can spend the evening with my husband.

I don't bother texting him. After he's complained so much about my not being home, I'd rather surprise him. In fact, I decide to surprise him with food. I stop by Vilma's on the way home.

The little café is bustling, but Vilma greets me with a smile.

"Dr. Cabot, it's so nice to see you!"

The little old lady offers me a hug.

"It was so nice of you to send soup to me yesterday," I tell her warmly. "I felt like I was at death's door."

"Glad we could help. Did we send you beef stock or chicken noodle?" She seems a bit confused, but it's no wonder. I doubt she personally dished it up.

"The chicken. And it was delicious. I've got to pick up

dinner for tonight," I tell her. "Do you know what Jude gets when he's here?"

She scrunches her nose. "It's been a while since I've taken his order. Let me ask one of the girls."

She scans the busy room, then picks up the phone, calling the kitchen.

"Zoe, what does Jude Cabot usually order?"

She nods, then hangs up.

"She said he loves the steak, but that's not good for take-out. So he'd probably settle for a salad."

"My husband is eating salad?" This surprises me. He usually runs so that he can eat whatever he wants. And then I instantly feel dumb, because I'm his wife and I should know these things.

I shrug. "All right, then, we'll take a chicken Caesar, and I'll take a big cup of soup with crackers."

"You've got it," Vilma tells me. She walks into the dining room, and a minute later, I see her talking with a girl. I can see the girl only from the back, but I know it's Zoe.

Her skirt is short, her top is tight, and she's definitely young. I swallow hard. As Vilma starts to walk back toward me, Zoe talks to a customer. She laughs and it rings out like a bell, and she's flirtatious.

I remember when I was, too. It seems like a thousand years ago now, though.

I crane my neck to see her face, but she moves, and I don't want to seem too obvious.

I pick up a magazine.

"She's a good waitress," I say aloud to Vilma. The old woman looks like she swallowed a bug.

"Maybe. The male customers seem to like her."

Her meaning is clear. With the short skirt and tight top, I'm sure that's the case. Men are easy to please.

"Does she wait on my husband a lot?" I try to sound casual.

Vilma pats my arm. "You don't have anything to worry about, my dear. Mr. Cabot is a good man. It's some of these other yokels that I worry about."

I glance to the guy Zoe is waiting on now. He's middle-aged and doughy, and he's flirting right in front of his wife. Dick.

"You're right," I agree with the elderly woman.

I return my attention to the magazine, but out of nowhere, my stomach starts rolling. I rub it and close my eyes because the wave of nausea is intense and sudden. I know I'm going to vomit again.

I run for the bathroom, through the smells of cooking food and meat and perfume. All of it combines to make me retch even harder, and I barely make it to the bathroom. I can't even lock the door behind me.

I drop onto the scuffed floor and puke my guts up into a dingy public toilet.

I heave and heave until there isn't anything left to throw up.

That's when the bathroom door opens and someone steps into the stall next to me.

I gulp at some air and heave again.

"Are you okay, Dr. Cabot?"

It must be Zoe. My foot is under the wall, sprawled into her stall, and I pull it back.

"I'm…" My voice is shaky. "Yeah. I'm pregnant."

There's a pause. Then, "Oh my gosh, congratulations!"

"Thanks." I put my hand on the wall, trying to stop the stall from spinning. The nausea is making me dizzy.

"Will your husband be happy?"

I swallow the pool of saliva in my mouth, fighting the urge to vomit again. "Yes. He's been wanting a baby for a while now. Don't mention this to him, okay? I'm going to surprise him."

"Of course." She flushes her toilet. "This bathroom is gross," she points out. "You might not want to stay on the floor."

I hear her wash her hands, and when I come out, she's gone. A little part of me is disappointed. I *need* to see what she looks like. I need to see if she's prettier than me.

But then again, that's dumb. It's not like she's competition.

I rinse my mouth out, pick up my food from Vilma, and the crisp air outside feels so good on my flushed face.

I drive home, wait for the garage door to open and walk into the kitchen entrance of my house. I call for Jude, but there's no answer. I find him in his office, staring at his phone.

"Hey," I greet him. He startles and shoves his phone into his pocket.

"Hey," he answers, and he's clearly surprised. "What are you doing home?"

"I'm still sick. I'm going to take a couple days off."

Only now I know—I'll be sick for a few months. I'm still trying to process it.

I glance at my husband, assessing his mood. He seems to be tired, antsy even. Now is not the time to tell him.

"I came bearing gifts," I tell him. "Dinner. It's in the kitchen."

He's appreciative and tired, and I kiss him on the cheek. "I'm just going to change, and then I'll be right there."

I head to the bedroom, and on a whim, and I don't know why, I decide to put on one of his shirts instead of my pajamas. He's always loved it when I wear his shirts, and I guess I'm hopeful it will make him smile. He seems so distracted lately. Work must be bombarding him. I certainly know the feeling.

I wear only a pair of panties underneath his shirt and unbutton the top few buttons so that the swell of my breasts shows when I move.

I run my hands over my silhouette in the mirror.

It's going to change very soon. My breasts will engorge, my belly will swell.

I swallow hard. I don't know if I'm ready.

But I guess I have to be.

I join my husband in the kitchen, and his gaze flickers over me from top to bottom. I know he must be tired when he doesn't react much.

"Well, well," he says quietly as he serves our food. "Look at you."

I grin. "It's just a little something I picked up."

He smiles back. "I like it."

But his eyes don't have the spark in them that I thought they would.

"You're tired," I observe.

He nods. "So tired."

"Me, too."

Now is definitely not the time to tell him.

I eat my soup, he eats his salad, and afterward, we sit staring at each other.

"Want to continue our game?"

"Sure."

We walk into the living room together, and as I sink to the floor, I notice something out of the corner of my eye. Something on the porch. I can't see what it is from here, but it's small and dark.

"Did you order something?" I ask Jude, climbing back to my feet.

"Nope," he answers, studying the board, already plotting his next move.

"Don't cheat while I'm gone," I warn him as I head to the door.

He chuckles. "I can't promise."

I'm snorting when I reach the porch.

And then I'm frozen.

The address stares up at me. *The* address. Tarnished bronze numbers and letters stare up at me, and this can't be happening.

131 All Hallows Lane.

My eyes flit around the lawn, at the dark, at the shadows, and there is no one there.

Yet someone was.

I'm not imagining this.

It's real.

My breath is caught and I'm floating, and I'm falling, and I can't decide what I'm doing. Floating or falling? My thoughts come in slow motion and blurs, and the old metal burns a hole in my brain, and Jude's voice cuts through it all.

"Co. Corinne. Corinne."

His hands are around me, then his arms, then he's carrying me to the couch. I can't breathe and he's rubbing my back, and his voice is soothing.

"It's okay. Take a breath. Relax. Relax. Tell me what you see in the room. Open your eyes, babe. Open your eyes."

I feel like I need a crowbar to do it, but I open them, and the light comes in, and my breath still won't come. The room spins, and I try to focus.

Jude sits down next to me again and holds my hand.

"Tell me what you see, Corinne."

"There's a fireplace."

"What color is the flame?"

"Orange."

I take a breath. It's short and stilted, but it still feeds my lungs.

"What color is the clock on the mantel?"

"Bronze." Almost the same color as the address plaque. "Why is that on our porch?"

I pant now, and fear floods through me, and I don't know why. What is there to be afraid of?

"I don't know what you mean," Jude answers calmly. "But don't focus on that right now. Focus on me. Focus on breathing. Focus on my voice."

He starts singing to me, giving me something to focus on. A dumb song that I know he hates from the radio. He hates it and I love it.

I focus and focus and focus.

And after a few minutes, my throat relaxes. My heart slows. I can breathe again.

I rest my forehead on Jude's shoulder and try to stay calm.

"Are you okay now?" Jude asks me. He strokes my fingers. I nod.

"How long have you been having panic attacks?"

He's not accusing, just concerned. His mouth is drawn, his eyes are guarded.

"Not very. My hormones… I…" I almost tell him, but now isn't the time, so I trail off, and Jude waits. I begin again.

"The address plaque on the porch," I say. "It's the address from…that night. It's the same address plaque."

Jude looks at me in concern and then gets up. He walks to the door, opens it and looks outside. He looks one way and then the other. He's there for a minute, and when he comes back, I'm terrified of what he is going to say.

His face is a blank blank mask, and he looks at me oh so carefully.

"Corinne," he says softly. "There's nothing there."

38

Now
Corinne
Reflections Mental Facility

"So the address plaque wasn't there?" Dr. Phillips asks, and his pen is ever ready on his page. I shake my head painfully, acknowledging the truth.

"No."

My face sinks into my hands, and I stay like that, my eyes hidden, for minutes and minutes. It's humiliating to admit. It's devastating to realize.

"Dr. Cabot?"

I don't respond.

"Dr. Cabot?" I finally lift my face, and Dr. Phillips is watching me.

"Don't hide from it now," he advises. "That's the last thing you should do. Let's face reality together, shall we?"

I have to laugh, a bitter-laced laugh, and he raises an eyebrow.

"You don't think I know your reality?" he asks. "I assure you, my dear, I do."

My head snaps up. "You know what it's like to be unsure of reality? To not know what is real and what's not? I doubt that."

He smiles, a bit wry. "Not firsthand, but I've had a practice for a long time. I've treated dozens of patients that this has happened to in some capacity. Trust me, I get it."

"But you don't," I tell him firmly. "Until you have holes in your brain, until you personally think you remember something, but it turns out that you don't at all, then you don't know, Dr. Phillips. With all due respect."

He nods slightly. "Okay. Point taken. Your case is exclusively yours. Your situation is unique to you, and so you are correct. I do not know. I do not know personally. But I'm still here to help. Will you let me?"

"I really just want to go home," I tell him simply. "I want to forget everything that's happened and get on with my life."

He's sympathetic, but resolute. "Yeah, but that's not possible, is it?"

I sigh. "No."

"Let's revisit your memory from last time. You said you weren't alone. Have you remembered anything else?"

I stare at the floor. "I had a nightmare once, before I came here. I'm not sure if it was just a nightmare or if it was part of the memory."

Dr. Phillips waits.

"Someone called me a cunt. Kept saying it in my ear. A man. I've been seeing and hearing that word...in a lot of places lately."

"The same man you remember seeing in the house that night?" His pen scratches on the page.

"I'm not sure, but that would make sense."

"Who else would be at the house?" He looks at me. "Melanie and Joe were out for dinner, right? It was Halloween. Why weren't they out trick-or-treating with their kids?"

"Well, Joey was just a baby. And the two older girls… Joe didn't want them going out for some reason. I guess I never asked why. But it *is* very strange, isn't it?"

"I agree," he says. "Unless it's for religious reasons. Were they religious?"

I shake my head. "Catholic, but not devout."

"Hmm. Okay. Well, let's go back to that night. When you walked through the door, what did you feel?"

I close my eyes, trying to focus on my memories. "I was nervous. I knew about Melanie and my father, and it made me uncomfortable. I didn't know what to say."

"What did Melanie say to you?"

I picture the way she'd been at the sink and had turned to me, wiping her hands on a towel and her shirt.

Hi, hon, she'd said. *Glad to see you. Joey has missed you.*

"The baby loved me," I remember. "That's why Melanie liked for me to babysit."

"And the girls?"

I focus on them. They had blond pigtails and serious eyes.

"They were very quiet."

"What are you feeling right now?" he asks quietly, and I focus on my belly. It's heavy and knotted.

"Fear."

"Why?"

"I don't know," I murmur. "I feel this…foreboding. Something bad is going to happen."

"Did you put the kids to bed?" the doctor asks me.

I nod. "Yeah. We watched television for a while first. I bathed the baby, and the water was still in the tub when…"

I pause. A memory has dropped itself into my head… Shoes. A hand over my mouth. The taste of dirt on his hands.

"I was going to go clean up the bathroom when he grabbed

me. I tried to scream, but his hand was big. I couldn't make a sound."

"Can you see who it was?"

I'm looking through the eyes of eighteen-year-old Corinne, and I see the bedroom, the dark shadows and the unmade bed. I smell the fall leaves coming in from the open window, and I feel the sheets as they're pressed into my face.

"He holds me down and pushes my face into the bed," I whisper, and my hands are knotted together. "He keeps telling me that I'm a cunt. I tempted him, and I'm a cunt."

"Who is it?"

I focus and focus and focus.

The face blurs into black and then comes back into focus. I blink.

"Joe Gibson."

39

I text my husband.

Want to come home for lunch? I'll make it worth your while.

My stomach is queasy, but I need to be up and about. I need to tell my husband our news. He's going to be floored. Thrilled. Ecstatic.

He doesn't answer for a while, and that's fine because I know he had patients all morning.

Sure. Should I bring lunch?

I think about that for a minute, and about our bare cupboards.

Sure, lol. You might need sustenance, I suppose. Can I get some soup?

He answers right away. Chicken? From Vilma's?

Yes, please, I answer.

K. I'll be there around noon-ish.

Despite my nausea, I make myself take a shower and get ready. I put on makeup and lip gloss and blow-dry my hair. I vomit in the middle there somewhere, but it's not a big deal. I'm growing used to that.

I nibble on saltine crackers while I wait, and when the clock hands hit noon exactly, Jude's Land Rover turns into the drive.

I feel ridiculously nervous.

This is Jude. *My Jude.* There's no reason to be anxious. This is what he wants. My hands flutter to my belly, shielding the life within. Our baby will be beautiful.

Jude opens the front door, and his smile is radiant, the hazel in his eyes warm, like liquid gold.

"Hey, babe," he greets me, kissing my cheek. I grab him, inhaling the cold air in his clothes, and kiss him on the mouth instead.

He's surprised but holds me for a minute.

"What's wrong?" he asks quickly, and I laugh, taking the bag from him.

"Nothing at all. I just have something to tell you."

His mouth curls up at the edges anxiously, and I put a hand on his arm. "It's not bad," I tell him. "In fact, sit down."

He sits, and I put our food on the coffee table, taking a deep breath as I turn to him. I grab his hand.

"I'm pregnant," I tell him simply.

He stares at me for a minute, uncomprehending. Then his entire face lights up, and he grins.

"You're...pregnant."

I smile. "Yes. You're going to be a daddy."

He grabs me and hugs me and doesn't let go. "So, you didn't have the flu."

I shake my head. "No."

"I'm stunned," he admits finally, pulling back. "How did it happen? I know you didn't plan it. You weren't ready. Oh my God, you weren't ready. Are you okay?"

He's worried now, worried about me, and that pulls on my heart.

I squeeze his hand. "It's ours, Ju. Maybe it'll be a little boy with hazel eyes like you."

He smiles at the thought, looking out the window. "Or a blonde girl with blue eyes like you."

I push away that thought—because I don't want our child to be like me. Or worse, like my father. I push push push the thought away.

Jude stares at me, and I think he can read my mind. "It will be okay," he assures me. "It will."

I nod and swallow, and he hugs me again, just as happy as I thought he would be.

"Is it wrong that I want to make love to you right now?" he asks thoughtfully.

I laugh, reaching for him.

"Please do. I miss you, Ju," I whisper into his ear.

He makes love to me on the couch, and for a few blessed minutes, we feel close again, like the same person. All of my worries and fears fade away as we rock together, my ankles on his shoulders.

"I love you," I whisper afterward.

"Not as much as I love you."

40

My phone buzzes with texts, and while they used to make me feel good, they only make me disgusted now.

Hey, how are you?
Where are you?
Can I see you soon?

Zoe's words make me a monster. My actions have made me a monster. I have to end it.

And I will.

But not via text. That would be a total dick thing to do. It's not this girl's fault that I was using her to make myself feel better. And I know that's what I've been doing.

I felt neglected, I felt insufficient for my wife, and I used this girl, this girl who has clear daddy issues, to boost my ego.

It was a total dick thing to do.

But I'm getting everything I want now. Corinne will be home more often, we're having a baby. Everything will be fine.

I'll break it off with Zoe gently.

I haven't even had sex with her.

No blood, no foul.

I text her back, finally. How about now? Meet me in the park? 20 minutes?

She answers immediately. Yesssssss!

Corinne is at the grocery store, so I feed Artie, then slip out the door. I'll make this fast and be home by the time she gets back.

The cold air bites at my cheeks, and I drive rather than jog.

When I arrive, Zoe is already there.

"Hey, handsome," she greets me. She's wearing jeans this time, but her shirt is unbuttoned practically down to her navel. "I've missed you."

She reaches for me, but I step back.

"Zoe, we need to talk."

Her face goes dark. "What do you mean?"

I pause. "I mean, I can't keep doing this. It's wrong."

"You haven't had a problem before now," she points out, and she's confused. "I don't understand. I'm not asking you for anything, Jude. I just want your time now and then. I know you're married."

"That's the thing. I'm married. I'm not the kind of person to do this type of thing."

"But you've been doing it already," she mentions, and the guilt builds up in me again.

"Yeah, I know. But I haven't crossed the line yet, and I don't intend to. You're a beautiful girl, and you'll make someone else very lucky."

"But not you."

"No, not me."

She thinks on that and stares at me and reaches for me, but I take another step back.

"I mean it, Zoe. I just can't. I hope you understand."

"Oh, I do. I understand that you're missing out on the best thing that's ever happened to you. It's a mistake, Jude."

Her eyes are sharp, her tone is sharper.

"I'll have to take that chance. Think about it, Zoe. You deserve better than being the other woman. You deserve someone who is free to marry you. You deserve to be someone's first priority."

"And I'll never be yours?"

I shake my head, my eyes on her face.

"No. I'm afraid not. I'm already married, Zoe. That's not going to change."

"This is a mistake," she tells me.

I don't say anything.

"Fuck you," she mutters.

She stalks away and roars out of the parking lot.

I feel lighter than I have in weeks.

41

So many things go through my head.

The plaque that my wife thought she saw, that we thought was imaginary.

Was real.

My wife is in a psych ward, and I don't know if she should be. When I'm in the car, I try to call, but the receptionist tells me that Dr. Phillips is in session with her currently.

"They'll be out in an hour or so," she tells me helpfully. "They just began."

Then a text from Zoe comes in.

I need you, she says. Before I do something I regret.

My heart starts to pound, and the bad feeling in my gut spreads to my chest.

Why? I ask her.

There's no answer.

Zoe?

Still no reply.

I have no way of knowing if she's going to hurt herself, or if she's planning on telling the world about us.

And even though I know I'm playing straight into her hands, there is only one way to find out.

I head for Vilma's.

Vilma smiles at me when I walk through the door.

"Hey, Mr. Cabot." She reaches up to hug me. She smells like cinnamon and something akin to lilacs. "How is your wife feeling?"

I pause. *Does she know where Corinne is?*

"She's fine," I tell her. Vilma smiles.

"Good. I have to tell you, I was uncomfortable letting Zoe medicate her for you, but I'd do anything for you and Dr. Cabot. You're such good people."

I almost don't hear her, because I'm focused on looking for Zoe, but those last words slam into me, and I grasp them, and I'm still.

"What?" I ask slowly.

Vilma looks at me. "I was surprised to hear that a doctor was so adverse to taking medication that it needed to be dissolved in her soup. But I think you're sweet for arranging it."

"I don't know what you mean," I tell her slowly. "What medication? And what soup?"

My thoughts start to whirl, and Vilma starts to stammer.

"The chicken soup for Dr. Cabot. Zoe showed me a text from you, telling her that Dr. Cabot was pregnant and that the prenatal vitamins made her sick. You asked her to dissolve them into the soup. It's unorthodox, but like I said, we love you both around here."

I'm stunned and I stare at her, and she stares back. I see the thoughts moving in her head, and her lips move.

"You didn't ask her to do anything of the sort, did you?"

I shake my head. "No. I would never do that. Is she here?"

"No. She's not in today."

"Can I have her address?"

Vilma hesitates. "I'm not supposed to give out that information."

I start to argue but then remember Michel. He probably knows.

"It's okay," I tell her over my shoulder. "Thanks."

I jump into my truck and call my brother as I head down the road. He doesn't pick up, so I leave a voice mail.

"Bro, I need you to call me ASAP. I need Zoe's address. Some fucked-up shit is going on. I don't know even exactly what yet. Call me."

He's probably in confession or something. It's frustrating because I haven't been able to reach him since he left my house. I head toward Immaculate Conception anyway, determined to be there when he comes out.

Something isn't right.

At all.

I feel on the edge of something terrible, and I'm afraid I'll only make things worse.

But Michel will help me sort it out, he always does. He can come with me to Reflections, he can help figure out things with Zoe.

He always knows how to keep me grounded.

I pull into the church parking lot twenty minutes later and see his truck parked in front of the rectory. I park next to it and jump out. His front door is open, and so I walk on in to the little stone cottage.

The smell greets me first.

It's acrid, thick and horrible. A heavy heavy feeling settles in my chest and my belly and my heart. Something is wrong.

Very wrong.

I don't allow myself to think or feel as I move through the rectory toward Michel's study.

"Michel?" I call out. There's no answer.

I cover my nose with my shirt, and an odd noise enters my consciousness. It sounds almost like bees.

"Michel?" I call out again. The silence is thick, and he still doesn't answer.

I take a step inside of his study, and I see his shoe.

His legs are sprawled on the floor, and he's lying in a giant pool of black blood.

My heart pounds and my blood is ice, and I discover what the odd noise is.

Flies.

42

Halloween
Corinne

Someone is chasing me.

I race through the house, knocking photos off the walls, and slam a door behind me.

He's there, though, pounding pounding pounding, his fists heavy and strong.

"Come out," he sneers. "I know where you are."

I'm silent, and my hands are clenched so tightly that my fingernails cut into my palms.

"Come out," the man says again. "Or I'm coming in."

I try to open a window, but I can't. My fingers scratch at the pane, and the lock is painted closed.

"Please," I beg God. But no one answers.

I'm alone.

"I'm here," the voice says in my ear, and a hand clasps over my mouth.

I wake with a start, sitting straight up in bed, my hands curled in the blanket.

I try to slow my breathing, try not to need Xanax.

It was a dream. A horrible dream.

It wasn't real.

"Artie!" I call. I hear her nails clicking on the floor, and she comes to me. "Come up here, girl," I tell her, patting the bed. She looks at me questioningly, because normally it isn't allowed.

But I need comfort today.

I need to feel safe.

Obligingly, she hefts herself onto the bed and stretches out next to me. I bury my face into her fur, and before I know it, Artie's warmth is lulling me to sleep.

I don't know how long I nap, but I sleep heavily, until at some point, the doorbell wakes me.

Lucy waits on the porch, her hands full of bags.

I answer the door groggily, still half asleep.

"Hey, Luce," I greet her. "What's up?"

"You haven't answered your phone, that's what," she says grumpily, stalking past me. "I've been trying to call you for days."

"I'm sorry. I've been busy puking my guts up." I close the door and then follow her. "Come on in. Make yourself at home."

She gives me the side-eye.

"I finally asked Jude what was happening. He told me you were just sick and resting and asked me to bring you some lunch."

"He loves me," I tell her, my belly tingly with warmth.

"I know." She hands me a disposable container. "Eat up. I'm going to do your nails when you're finished."

"I don't really need my—"

But she interrupts. "Pish-posh. Pregnant women need to look good, too."

I head to the kitchen and she follows. "Should I take the dog out?"

I glance at Artie. "Sure. She hasn't been out in a while. Thank you."

I sit in a chair and grab a spoon, digging into the soup, and Lucy lets Artie out onto the patio. I hear her nails clicking as she trots off.

"If you really want to be helpful," I tell her, "you could do Artie's nails."

She rolls her eyes. "Um, no."

I laugh and take a bite.

"Jude said he brought you dinner last night," she mentions. "Did you eat?"

I shake my head. "No. We got…er…distracted. I told him about the baby."

"You did?" Lucy grins. "And I assume he was…happy?"

I nod. "Ecstatic." I take another bite, then another.

"You're sickening," she says. "You had it all, and now you get a baby, too."

It's weird, but her tone is a little off.

"Pardon me?" I ask, rolling my eyes. "I've worked myself into the ground for this. It wasn't just handed to me." I smile like I'm joking, but I'm kind of not. "Seriously."

She nods. "Oh, yes. Little Corinne Friess. She had to work for everything, didn't she?"

Her tone is acerbic now, and how did she know my maiden name?

The air between us has changed, somehow. I feel it. It's tangible.

I swallow my bite and stare at her. "Luce? Is something wrong?"

Her eyes seem black as night, and somehow familiar, and when her mouth finally moves, it says the ugliest things.

"You're a fucking cunt, just like my father said."

She moves, lightning fast, and there's a sharp pain in the back of my head.

43

Now
Jude

I'm frozen.
  Because Michel.
  He's still.
  He's bloody.
  He's silent.
  I know it's him.
  It's him.
  And my heart.
  My heart.
  Stutters and stops.
  And I kneel next to my brother's body and I pick up his
hand, his hand that is so identical to my own, and his eyes are
lifeless and his head is bloody.
  I check.
  I check I check I check.
  My fingers at his neck.
  And his blood is cold.

And my brother cannot cannot cannot be dead.

But he is.

He's dead.

I'm numb.

I can't feel.

I can't think.

I can't be without Michel.

We're one half of a whole.

That's how it's always been.

He's not breathing and he's cold.

He's cold.

He hates to be cold.

And then I'm yelling and everything is unfocused and blurry and fragmented, coming together and then pulling apart.

I sprawl on top of him, covering him up because he hates to be cold.

My brother is cold.

His blood covers me, and it's cold, and he's cold.

I dial 911 with a bloody hand, and I can't understand what she's saying because my brain is shutting down.

I hold my brother's hand, and nothing matters anymore but this.

I lie down with my brother, and his blood soaks into my clothes, and together, we wait for the ambulance.

There will be no need for the sirens.

I close my eyes.

44

Halloween
Corinne

I'm dreaming again. Damn, but pregnancy gives a person vivid dreams.

Even though I know it's a dream, it's so amazing that I don't want to wake up.

I'm in a nursery, and the morning sunlight is flooding the room, and it's so bright, so airy, so cheerful. I'm rocking a swaddled baby dressed in pink and white, and her face is just as pink. She smiles up at me, and then she suckles, nursing from me, and I gave her life. She's mine, and the warm feelings flood me as I rock her and sing, rock her and sing.

She grasps my skin with a tiny hand, and when her eyes open, I see that they're the exact color of Jude's. I smile into them and hold her close, and I've never felt so warm and good before in my life.

The warmth spreads from my belly into my chest, spreading through my body, into my fingers and toes, into my legs and arms.

I'm consumed with it.

And then I wake up from it, and when I do, I realize that it isn't warmth, it's pain.

It's in the back of my head, in my belly, and spreads around to my spine.

I open my eyes. It's four thirty, and I'm not alone.

Lucy waits, perched on the couch, and I'm sprawled on the floor.

How did I get in here from the kitchen?

"You're heavier than you look," Lucy points out, and the expression on her face is ugly.

"I... What is happening?"

I feel like I'm on my period, and I stagger to the bathroom. Yanking down my pants, I find drops of blood, red and bright. I feel sick instantly and reach for my phone.

My fingers come up empty.

The room spins.

"Looking for this?" Lucy has my phone in her hands. I reach for it. She laughs. "Uh, no."

The room spins again.

I put a hand to my head. "What the hell is happening?"

"Don't you know?" Lucy asks. "Can't you tell? You are a doctor, after all. A big, important doctor. I'm just a little nurse."

She's derisive, and I'm confused. I see two of her, then they merge into one.

"You're losing the baby," she tells me. "Any idiot could see that."

"What did you give me?" I ask, trying to stay calm. Blood is gushing down my legs.

"What do you think?" she spits. "Mifepristone and miso-prostol."

My stomach contracts. "The abortion pill."

She smiles. "Now you're getting it."

I think about the soup. I didn't finish it. I don't know how much I imbibed. Maybe there's still time.

I try to reach the door.

"But of course, that's not all," Lucy tells me, and her outline wavers in and out. "You didn't think that was all, did you?"

I stare at her. Or try to stare at her. The dizziness is overwhelming. Lucy laughs.

"It's a roofie, Corinne. Not all medicine is prescribed."

I take a breath. "Why?"

"Because I need you compliant, you whore."

I feel my uterus contract, pulling and pushing at itself, the muscles surrounding it contracting and contracting.

Dear Lord.

This can't be happening.

I feel more warmth between my legs, and I squeeze my eyes closed, waiting waiting waiting.

My eyelids are too heavy to open now, and I'm pushed and pulled, my legs moving like rubber. I feel the room spinning, but I can't look. It's all too much. Even the pain fades away. I can't feel it even though I know it's there.

I'm pushed, and I think I'm on the ground. Yes, I'm on the ground. The bathroom floor? I feel the cool tile under my legs, and I feel the moisture, and I know it's blood. My cheek is wet. Am I crying?

"Please," I whisper.

"It's too late for that," she tells me, and her mouth is so close to my ear. "You fucking cunt."

The room spins again, and something about her mouth, her voice. How did I not see it before?

I whirl and freeze, and her face is contorted grotesquely, her mouth a slant.

She grins. "You recognize me, don't you, Corinne?"

Her mouth.

Her eyes.

Her nose.

Her face.

They all flash in the streetlight, one by one by one, and in that moment, I…

Do.

I'm back on All Hallows Lane, and the night is dark, flickering with jack-o'-lanterns.

Lucy was there, but she was different. She was younger.

"You're Jessica," I whisper, and she nods, and in my head, she's the little girl she used to be, with long pigtails and pink sneakers, and how did I not recognize her before?

She was playing with teacups in her room, pouring tea with a pot, as her father was raping me in the bedroom.

"I heard the screams," she tells me now. "Only, I didn't come. Because it was better you than me, Corinne."

Everything flashes, the memories the memories the memories, and they all come together in a picture, then break apart, then fit together again.

I focus.

And it hurts.

I squeeze my eyes closed tighter, remembering what it had been like…his meaty hands all over me. He'd held me down, and I struggled so hard that I bit through my lip, but he had raped me anyway. He was stronger, bigger, more determined.

He'd entered me violently, taking my virginity in one terrible thrust. His onion breath was in my face, warm and hot. His fingers pinched my nipple hard, so hard. I screamed, but no one cared.

You cunt, he'd whispered in my ear as he raped me. *You fucking cunt. You fucking cunt.*

He'd kept repeating it, as though he was angry at me, as though I was getting what I deserved.

"He kept us at home so that he could 'play' with us whenever he wanted," Lucy says. "You had to ruin everything. If you'd just shut up and played with him, he would've left you alone."

"It wasn't *playing*," I say, and my words are slurred now. "It was *raping*."

"Whatever you'd like to call it." She shrugs.

"I didn't do anything," I whisper.

"That's right," she hisses. "You didn't do anything. *Until you killed him*. And my mother came home with your father, and...well, you know what happened next."

"I don't," I whisper. "I can't remember." I hold my hand to my head, and everything hurts.

"I think you truly don't," Lucy says, examining me. "You really *are* crazy. Your father killed my mother protecting you, you fucking cunt. Your pussy wasn't worth it."

"Oh my god," I murmur, and the world caves in, and my memories flood me, weighing me down. I rock back and forth and fight to stay conscious.

I feel like I'm swimming through memories, and the water is murky and thick.

"Lucy," I try to say, but she laughs again.

"Don't even try. I'm not helping you."

The craziness whirls and twirls, and I can't focus anymore. I...I...I can't.

I drop to the ground, and my legs won't hold me. My hand is outstretched, and I can't move it. My fingers feel like splinters of wood. My body feels like concrete. Then something cold is sliced across my wrist. It doesn't hurt. I just feel the warmth pouring over my hand.

The blood.

I can't feel.

I can't feel.

I can't feel.

"Lucy?" I think I say.

Nothing.

I hear Artie yelp sharply, then there's silence.

Nothing.

My fingers are sticky and it's my blood.

I feel cold, and I know I'm dying.

I'm dying.

This is what it's like to die.

I fight onto my elbows and muster up every ounce of strength I have. I don't know how I do it, but I pull myself over the bathroom threshold and into the bedroom. I feel for the phone on the nightstand, and the lamp falls on top of me.

But my fingers...they close around the phone. I dial 911.

I drop the phone.

I...

I...

I don't know anything anymore.

Time doesn't exist.

I wait and time runs into itself.

I'm on the floor.

I'm in the sky.

I'm floating.

Floating.

My hands and feet turn cold and faint, and my vision starts to fade. I think someone touches me.

Voices.

Sounds.

I babble something.

Does my tongue work?

It's so black.

Black.

Black as night.

Brock is a shape beside me, with spots of light swirling around his head. I can't see his face. I think he's touching me, but I don't know where. It's like I'm behind a veil of fog and the only thing keeping me grounded is the pain.

"It's a hemorrhage," he tells someone. I don't care who. Not anymore. I close my eyes because the lights are too much to bear.

The pain carries me on a wave. It goes higher, higher, higher…then crashes down, and I can't take it. I can't take it.

"Jude, I love you," I say out loud. I think I say it out loud. But it's not Jude's voice that answers. It's Brock.

"I'll tell him, Corinne. He's right outside."

My belly rips apart from pain, and I cry out, and I'm moving, and my eyes are closed, squeezed tight.

That's all I know.

45

Corrine

When I open my eyes, it's bright, blindingly bright.

The pain is gone.

I look around the room.

Jude is sitting next to my hospital bed, and there is an IV in my arm.

"What…"

I'm confused because I'm not usually in hospital beds. I'm usually standing over them. I can't remember.

I can't remember anything.

I finger the gauze circling my wrist, concealing stitches. How did it get there?

"What happened?" I ask, and my voice is scratchy. "Why am I here?"

Jude's face is grim. There is pain in his eyes, true deep pain, and I'm puzzled. I've never felt so disoriented. I was in my house, and now I'm not.

Now I'm here, and my husband is hesitant to tell me why.

"Jude?"

"You…" He clears his throat. "You tried to kill yourself, Co."

My heart pounds, and I stare at my wrist, then at him.

"No," I argue. "I didn't." I shake my head, but he's so very grim, and I'm dizzy still.

"You did," he says limply. "I got there just as the ambulance did, and you were in a pool of blood. Corinne, God. Why?"

He drops his head into his hands, and I'm stunned.

"I don't… I don't remember," I say, and my words are wooden, and my heart is still. "I don't think I would ever do that."

But there are holes in my brain. More holes. Just like from that night so long ago, and I can't remember what happened. I can't remember then, and I can't remember now. I'm so damaged, so very damaged.

"Oh my God," I moan, and I feel sick. "I'm so broken, Jude. I'm so sorry."

Jude swallows, and he's got a shadow of stubble on his jaw, and his eyes are red and tired.

"If you didn't want to have the baby, you could've told me. You didn't have to…" He closes his eyes. "You didn't have to attempt an abortion yourself. At home."

My eyes fly back open. "Attempt an abortion? Jude, what are you saying?"

He sighs, and he grasps my hand, and I don't know why he even wants to touch me. Not if what he's saying is true.

"You took the abortion pill, Corinne. They found it in your bloodstream. You took it all at once."

He keeps his eyes closed, and I try to breathe.

"No. I wouldn't." I shake my head, and Jude nods.

"You did."

I'm stunned. I'm speechless. I don't even… I can't… I can't form a cohesive thought.

I…

I...

"I wouldn't," I say again. "Jude, that doesn't make sense. Why would I give myself an abortion and then try to kill myself? Why wouldn't I just kill myself and save a step?"

The words are harsh and painful, but they are logical. Why in the world would I do that?

Jude shakes his head. "You weren't thinking clearly," he says, and he's so sad. He looks so forlorn and alone, and where is Michel? Surely he didn't leave Jude here to deal with this alone. "There's more," he adds.

I'm still, utterly frozen. "How can there be more?"

I'm afraid to ask, afraid to know.

"You...you hurt Artie. Could have killed her."

The room spins.

"I..." I can't even speak. I can't.

I would never.

Jude stares out the window. "Michel is at our house right now. Cleaning. It's...it's a mess there, Co."

Oh my God.

"That isn't me!" I know myself, don't I? Don't I? "I wouldn't."

"You had a mental break of some sort," my husband tells me, and his voice is clinical now. "It was likely a result of this time of year and your hormones combined. They were a trigger and you..."

"And I hurt our dog, gave myself an abortion, then tried to kill myself."

Jude nods.

I can't even think.

Everything comes in fragments, and I try to remember what I did, and I can't. It's all a blur.

"I was in the bedroom," I tell him. "I remember that. I was sleeping with Artie. And then...something happened."

I strain hard, trying to think…but it's just gone.

"It's not there," I tell him. "It's like it was just extracted from my head. I can't…" But then something something something is there. A shadow. A figure. Standing over me. Shoes, maybe.

"I wasn't alone," I blurt out, and Jude lifts an eyebrow.

"Then who was there?"

I focus and focus and think and think, and I can't remember.

"It's a fog," I tell him. "It's maddening. I can't remember. I just know someone was."

He sighs, and I know he doesn't believe me.

"Corinne, you tried to kill yourself. We need to put you into a treatment program to figure this out. We have to figure out why you'd do it."

I'm silent, and Jude stares at me.

"Will you? Will you go?"

I…I…

"If you want me to," I finally say. None of this feels right. None of this feels like me. I'm crazy like my father. I'm crazy like my father.

"I do," he says simply. "Thank you, Corinne."

I close my eyes to block it out, but something occurs to me, and my eyes fly open.

"Wait!" I say suddenly. "The baby. You said I *attempted* an abortion. What about the baby?"

Something moves in Jude's eyes, something in the depths, and he takes a deep breath.

"It survived. You're still pregnant, Corinne. It's a miracle."

46

Corinne

"Where is he, Michel?" I ask my brother-in-law.

Michel turns to me, and in that moment, in the light from the window, he looks so much like my husband that he takes my breath away.

"He'll be here, Corinne. He just went home to change his clothes and shower. How are you feeling?"

He sits in the chair next to the bed, grasping my hand in his. The machines beep around us, and he's so very concerned.

I shrug. "I'll be better when Jude gets here."

"He's coming," Michel says, and there's something wrong. I see it on his face. He's unsettled, disturbed. Restless.

"What is it?"

But he shakes his head, protecting his brother the way they always do. "Nothing at all. I'm just worried about you."

I let it go, and my fingers rest on my belly, hovering beneath my navel. There is life there, however faint.

"It's all going to be okay," Michel tells me, reading my face. "Everything."

"I hope so."

"Trust me."

He holds my hand and I close my eyes, because I'm exhausted. But I can't...I won't...sleep until my husband gets here, until it's all been worked out.

A bit later, Lucy pokes her head into my room. Her hair isn't pulled into a ponytail today—it's hanging down, and she seems different to me, somehow.

"How are you feeling?" she asks softly, slipping into the chair next to me. Her hand pats mine, and it scrapes my IV tube.

"You need to do your nails," I point out.

She smiles. "Yeah. I guess I got distracted. You know, with worrying about you and all." She pauses. "They say you don't remember anything."

I stare at her. Her eyes. They seem so...something. Sad?

I look away. "It's embarrassing. I...wouldn't do this." I glance at my wrist, at the bandage. Lucy does, too. She's uncomfortable, and she won't meet my gaze now.

"It's okay," she tells me, her voice hollow. "Sometimes we all do things we regret. You're going to be okay."

She's so sad, and I feel awful for making everyone worry. I close my eyes.

"Just sleep, Corinne," she tells me. "I'll check on you later."

The next time I open my eyes, the room is dark, immersed in shadows. It takes a minute to acclimate to the dark, and then I see him.

Jude.

Sitting next to me where Michel had been.

"Hi," I say, because I can't think of anything else through my sleep-addled brain. My voice seems loud in this quiet room. Jude's eyes pop open, relief in them.

"Hey," he answers. "God, you scared me, Co."

"The baby is okay," I tell him. "For now."

"That's not what I meant," he answers. "I thought I'd lost you."

His shoulders slump, and I don't know what to say.

"I'm sorry, Jude." My words aren't enough. I know that.

"I should've seen that you were in distress, and all I did was ride you about coming home early every night. God, I'm sorry." Even in the dark, I can see the angst in his hazel eyes, and his hand grasps mine more tightly. "I'm sorry. Please forgive me."

"Already done," I tell him, and my heart is warm and full. I thought we were done, and now we're not, and it's like the end of a happy chapter in a book. I didn't lose the baby. Jude and I are fine.

"Brock saved you," he tells me. "He saved you, Corinne. He did an emergency aspiration for the hemorrhage. You've got to be on bed rest for now, so you'll have to slow down, but the baby is fine. You're fine, too."

He's so happy, so genuine and warm, so full of wonder, and all I want to do is sleep curled up with him.

"Get in bed with me," I tell him. He's surprised for a second, but then he does as I ask, folding himself into the hospital bed with me, holding me from behind, his forehead pressed to my back.

"I love you," I whisper.

"I love you," he answers. "Rest now. I'm here."

Tears run down my cheeks, and I'm not sad. Everything is going to be fine. Michel was right.

I close my eyes and let the darkness overtake me because the exhaustion is immense.

Buzzing from the machines wakes me later, when the

morning light penetrates my eyelids. I don't open my eyes, and I realize that the buzzing is Jude's phone.

There's a rustle as he gets to his feet, and I hear his voice hiss, hiss, hissing as he closes the door behind him.

It sounds like he says, "Don't call me," but that can't be right. He's rarely rude to anyone. I focus on waking up, and when Jude comes back in, my eyes are open.

"You're awake." His relief is evident on his face, and I try to smile.

His smile is warm and reassuring, and it's mine. It's always been mine… Our priorities were just skewed.

"You're still here," I say weakly, and he squeezes my hand.

"Of course. I haven't left."

I'm happy about that, until I remember the dog.

"Artie…" I say, and I try to remember what happened with the dog. I remember hearing her yelp, and I try to focus on that, to remember what I did to hurt her, but I can't. "What did I do to Artie?"

Jude is still. "There's no reason to dwell on this, Corinne."

"I have to know," I insist. "I have to, Jude. I want to remember."

"You… It seems…that you struck her in the head with something."

My heart sinks. "I don't remember… I couldn't have, Jude. I wouldn't have…"

"We'll get through this, Co," he assures me, even though I injured our dog. "We'll get you some help, and you're going to be okay."

The IV in my hand stings.

"God, poor Artie. She must've been so afraid. She trusted me, and…"

"Corinne, don't. She's okay now. And I'm here, and I'm not leaving, and everything is okay."

I want to ask him why that little muscle in his jaw is ticking, the one that ticks only when he's upset. But I know why.

I'm some sort of monster.

47

"Joe Gibson raped you," Dr. Phillips repeats. I nod, and the movement is painful.

"Yes," I whisper.

"Did your father save you?"

I focus focus focus.

"No," I say, surprised as I remember. "He didn't. My father told the police that he killed Joe Gibson. But he didn't."

I did.

I stare at my hands, the hands that have saved so many lives in the ER, but they are hands that took a man's life.

"What happened?"

"I... There was a heavy crystal owl on the nightstand next to the lamp. I didn't even think... I was just trying to get away. I grabbed it and bashed it into the back of his head. He collapsed on top of me, and he was dead. I couldn't get out from under him. He was too heavy."

The shock, the memories, the horror...it all encompasses me like a blanket made from stone. I can't lift my shoulders, I can't breathe.

"Take a deep breath," the doctor instructs me. "In, then out. Fill your lungs, then push it all out."

I do that a few times.

"Better?"

I nod.

"What happened next?"

"My father burst into the room. With Melanie. I don't know why they came to the house. I don't know. But they came in just as I was shoving Joe off. He rolled onto the bed, and his eyes were wide-open."

I squint my eyes, trying to see the past, trying to see through the murkiness of my brain. My heart pounds pounds pounds, and the adrenaline pulses, and my feet want to run run run.

Melanie's screams...they're in my head, just like it was yesterday, and I can't un-hear them. So shrill, so anguished.

"Melanie...she came flying at me. She didn't understand. She was hysterical. She was scratching at me. Her thumbnail scratched my hand."

I finger my hand where it was cut that night.

"So that's how you got the cut on your hand?"

I nod. "Yeah. She tried to come at me, and she was hysterical. My father grabbed her..."

"Yes?"

"He shoved her away from me, and her head hit the corner of the dresser. It was sharp. And...she...just... She died," I say limply. "I think it was instantaneous. She just died."

"How did your father react?"

"He was in shock. He...he dropped to his knees and gathered her into his arms, and he held her for a few minutes. He just stared at me, and I think… I think he hated me in that instant. I saw it in his eyes."

"But it wasn't your fault," Dr. Phillips says, ever calm. "Surely he didn't hate you. He was probably in shock."

"I was, too," I tell him. "I lost my virginity and killed a man in the same night. I was raped. And I killed someone." I'm numb as I try to wrap my mind around that fact. "I wonder how much trouble I'll be in."

Dr. Phillips shakes his head. "It was self-defense. You were eighteen years old. You had repressed memories, something that I can attest to in court, if need be. I don't think you'll need to worry about it. And certainly, I don't want you worrying about it in this moment. Let's just process it, shall we?"

I don't know if I can. It's too much. It's so much. But I don't want to voice that.

"The human brain is an amazing thing," I say instead. "All of these years, my own brain has been protecting me."

Dr. Phillips nods. "It *is* an incredible thing. But now we have to finally come to terms with it. So that you can finally be free, Dr. Cabot."

I swallow. It's true. It's affected me for yours, even if I didn't know the cause.

"I don't know if I *can* be free," I admit. "It's a lot to carry."

His eyes are sympathetic, and it almost makes me feel worse, that my situation is so bad that a cold person like Dr. Phillips feels sympathy.

"Would you like to stop our session early?"

I grit my teeth. I'd like to stop it and never come back. I'd like to unsee my memories. I'd like to undo the past. But those things aren't possible. And I need to know everything.

"No," I say almost defiantly. "I'm almost there. I can feel it. I've almost remembered everything. Let's finish."

"I'm going to call your husband so that he can be here when we're finished."

I nod quickly. "Yes, please."

I wait while he dials, and it's quickly clear that Jude isn't answering. The doctor leaves a message. When he's finished, he looks up.

"Is there anyone else you'd like for me to call? I really don't want you to be alone this evening. You need a friendly face."

I think about that. I'd like for Jackie to be here, but she's gone with Teddy to Napa.

Since Jude didn't answer, he was probably with Michel, so Michel won't answer, either.

There's only one other person I can think of.

"My friend Lucy."

48

Now
Jude

Through the window, I stare as the coroner's van loads up my brother.

They zip him into a black bag and take him away, slamming the van doors behind him, and now he's gone.

I'm in shock.

I can't feel my feet.

I can't feel my heart.

I can't feel.

I'm in complete and utter shock.

"Mr. Cabot?" The detective stares at me, waiting. "Do you have any idea who might want to hurt your brother?"

"No, I don't. Everyone loves him. *Loved* him. He's a priest, for God's sake."

Was a priest.

Oh my God, my brother is dead.

This can't be real.

But then something…something…something jumps into my mind, and I can't breathe. Zoe's text from last night.

You'll always regret it if you do.

I'll make you regret it.

She basically was saying she'd make me pay if I listened to my brother.

I stare at the bloodstain on the floor, and at the stone crucifix that is splattered in his blood.

"Could a small person have done this?" I ask hesitantly. The detective looks at me.

"Yeah. If he was caught by surprise, anyone could've done it."

I feel sick to my stomach as I examine that possibility. It can't be. It can't…

"What are you thinking?" he asks me, waiting.

I hesitate and then tell him of my involvement with Zoe, and of how she threatened to blow everything out of the water if I didn't stay with her, and how Michel took her from my house last night.

His expression changes, and am I imagining that he's looking at me differently now?

"So he was upset with you last night?"

I nod. "Yeah. But not as upset as I was with myself."

The detective's face is expressionless.

"Did you argue?"

Shock slams into me. "Jesus, man. I didn't hurt my brother. I love my brother. He's my twin, my other half. I'm going to be lost without him. What the hell?"

The detective is calm. "I'm just doing my job, Mr. Cabot. We'll look into Zoe. And I hope you'll be around for further questions if we have them."

"Of course I will," I snap. "I want whoever did this to pay."

He leaves, and I walk to my truck, and I'm limp as I slump behind the wheel.

What am I supposed to do now?

My phone is in my pocket, and it buzzes with a voice mail, and I listen to Dr. Phillips's voice.

"Corinne is having a rough session. It would be nice if you could come be here for her when she's finished. Give me a call."

I don't bother calling. I just head for Reflections. I drive down the road, and when I'm passing my neighborhood, I'm so overcome by anger and rage and grief that I can't even see straight. Red billows in from the corners of my eyes, and I can't think one coherent thought. That's why it takes a while for me to notice the car behind me is gaining on me, and flashing its lights.

I startle, my first thought being that it's Zoe, but it's not a Hyundai.

I pull over, and Chelsie bounds out of her car at me.

"You've got to listen to me. Zoe has lost her damned mind."

Blood is staining her clothes, and she's got scratches on her face, red angry welts that will stay with her for days.

"What happened?" I ask her quickly.

She limps toward me and I see that even her ankle has a welt. She stumbles into me, and I steady her arm.

"Zoe happened," she snaps angrily. "I've known that girl for a long time, but I've never seen her like this. I don't know what you did, but she's out for blood."

"I didn't do anything but tell her that I can't see her anymore," I say tiredly, flinching as the headlights from cars passing by shine into my eyes. "She was a mistake. She's had her claws in me for weeks, and this might sound crazy, but I think she might've killed my brother."

Chelsie looks at me, and pity hides in the depths of her eyes.

"It doesn't sound crazy," she tells me. "She attacked me to-night. I went to her house and found a bunch of stuff on her table. Stuff she didn't want me to see. A ton of articles about your wife, and you, and a bunch of her notes. Zoe has planned everything down to the tiniest detail. She wanted you, and she worked hard to get you. She's not going to give up now."

I'm still and quiet. "Why?"

"Revenge of some sort. She had lots of photos of your wife, with her face scratched out, and one with her belly cut out."

Her belly.

"Did she give my wife abortion pills?"

"I think she did. She knows your wife somehow. And I don't know what else she's going to do. She said she's just get-ting started. I swear to you, I didn't know about any of this."

Chelsie is ominous and covered in blood, and my wife is at Reflections alone, unsuspecting and helpless.

"Fuck."

I try to call Dr. Phillips, but there's no answer. So I try again. Still no answer.

I call the reception desk and ask to be connected to him. After a minute, the receptionist comes back.

"I'm sorry, sir, he's not answering right now. He must be with a patient. Would you like to leave a message?"

"Motherfuck."

I hang up and turn to Chelsie. "You need to call the police and tell them what she's done and then go to the hospital."

She nods and I get into my car and head for my wife.

49

Jude

I tuck my wife's feet into the car, ensuring that she is buckled up before I close the door after her.

"You're a good man, Mr. Cabot," Corinne tells me tiredly.

I flash back to everything that's happened with Zoe, and I flinch.

Not so good.

But I'll be better now.

I drive toward home, and Corinne leans her head on my shoulder.

"I am going to hate Reflections," she confides. "I don't even know what to pack."

"Well, take your time. We don't have to be there until this afternoon."

She nods.

"Yeah."

"When you come home, I'm going to hire someone to come in to help. I'm serious. I don't want you up. If you need to go to the bathroom, tell me. I'll carry you."

She chuckles and rolls her eyes. "Let's not get crazy, Jude. The bathroom is my personal space. You're not allowed. But I'll go straight back to bed."

I'm satisfied with that, and she's quiet, her hand on my leg for the rest of the ride home. When I turn the car off, she's snoring lightly, and I smile.

I walk around to her side, unfasten her seat belt and slide her into my arms. She stirs only as I'm lifting her from the car.

"I'm too heavy," she protests, and I carry her up the steps.

"You're not," I answer, pushing the door open.

Carrying her in, we're greeted with music.

"What the…"

"Put me down," Corinne says, and her voice is stilted and sharp. I glance at her, and her face is drained of all color, and she walks straight to the stereo, turning it off.

"Who would do this?" she asks, turning to me. Her breathing is short and heavy, her hands are shaking. She looks like she's seen a ghost, and I'm suddenly very afraid for her.

"Corinne, are you okay?" I ask her, keeping my voice low. "Tell me what's wrong."

"That song…" She closes her eyes. "That song was playing the night my father killed those people. That night on All Hallows Lane. Someone played it in the pool the other day at the hospital, too. Someone was in here, Jude."

I look around. Artie looks up from her place by the sofa. "There's no sign of a break-in, Co."

I'm concerned because my wife's panicked. And she seems irrational. Suddenly, the stay at Reflections doesn't seem like such a stretch.

"Someone was here," she insists. "Please, Jude. Please, believe me."

I take a shaky breath because it's devastating to watch

someone as strong as Corinne turned into an anxious mess. It's almost unfathomable.

"Let's just stay calm," I tell her. "You go pack a bag, and I'll look around."

She studies me, checking to see if I really believe she's serious. I make a point of seeming sincere.

"Okay." She nods and heads down the hall.

I look at Artie, and my gut clenches as I remember what Corinne did to her. I still can't believe it.

I give it a few minutes before I join Corinne in the bedroom, where she's placing items into a bag.

"What can I do to help?" I ask her.

"You can grab my toothbrush and stuff," she answers, folding a nightshirt.

"Okay."

I am distracted as I enter the bathroom, but when I look up, my feet freeze to the floor.

Twenty or thirty text messages between Zoe and me are taped to the mirror. All of our sordid words. Dirty words directed to each other.

All of it.

Taped to the glass in front of me, and panic wells in my chest and spreads into my head. I can barely think as I stride toward the mirror. The only thing I can think is *I've got to get rid of this before Corinne sees it.*

But her voice comes from behind me, icy and sharp, and it's too late.

"What the fuck, Jude?"

50

Corinne

Oh my God.
　Oh my God.
　No.
　Utter shock comes over me in waves, and I can't think.
　This can't be.
　This can't be happening.
　It's not real.
　But I stare at the text messages taped to my mirror, and through my numb haze, I see that it's real.

I want to suck you.
Your cum tastes delicious.
Please let me touch you.

Do you like my hard cock?
I'm going to tie you up and cum in your mouth.

　My husband is having an affair.

I sink to the floor, and I want to melt into the tile. My ears roar and I can't hear and I can't feel. The room spins and spins and spins, and I'm stunned, shocked, appalled, devastated, shredded, annihilated and more. A thousand feelings swirl around me, sucking me down, and I can't breathe.

I can't breathe.

Jude.

My husband. I never in a thousand years would have thought he would do this.

We're Corinne and Jude. Jude and Corinne. I've always been enough for him. Until...apparently, I wasn't.

My heart.

It's constricting...crushing me. I thought I was in pain earlier. That was just the tip of the enormous, ugly iceberg. It's nothing compared to how I feel now.

Absolutely *nothing*.

"Corinne." His voice comes from nowhere, yet everywhere, like I'm in a cloud. "Corinne, open your eyes."

I do. I open them and stare into his, and I want to punch him in the face.

"Who is she?" I manage to ask. *"Who?"*

He hesitates, which infuriates me further, and I find myself screeching.

"Who is it? Ginny?"

He shakes his head immediately. "God, no. I didn't... We didn't... I haven't had sex with anyone, Corinne."

He sinks to his knees next to me, and I flinch away from his touch.

"She's tasted your cum," I point out, reading the words. "You're talking with her in an intimate way—a way that should only be used with me. Get the fuck out, Jude. Leave me the fuck alone."

"Corinne, please," Jude pleads. "It isn't what you think. I

felt all alone, and Zoe tried very hard to be something to me. It got out of hand, but I don't love her, I love you. I ended things with her before they went even further. I swear."

But all I can focus on is the name.

"Zoe? The girl from the diner? I asked you once about her, and you made me feel stupid—like I was crazy for thinking anything was amiss."

I stare at him, and he drops his gaze, ashamed.

"Fuck you, Jude. Get out."

"Can you at least lie down before I go?" he asks simply. "I'll stay in the kitchen until Michel gets here. I'll have him take you to the clinic. Please."

"Call Michel and then Get. Out."

My words are like ice pellets, and they are shaved from my heart.

Without a word, Jude stands up and walks away.

I wait until I hear the bedroom door close, and then I sob.

51

Jude

I don't even remember driving to the park after I leave the house. I know Michel is probably already on his way to Reflections with Corinne, and I am so furious that I can't even see.

My thoughts come in red waves, like ink or blood or pain.

When I arrive, Zoe is already in the gazebo, wearing a short skirt and a white lace bustier. If the look she's going for is virginal, she failed. She's anything but. She knows it, and I know it.

"Hey," she greets me with a smile, but it dies on her lips as she looks at my face. "What's wrong?"

"You are," I growl, standing over her. "And you know why."

Her eyes widen, and she tries to feign surprise, but then she gives up.

"You mean…my gift for Corinne? Knowledge is power, Jude. She deserved to know."

"The joke is on you, then," I tell her, and I can't help but get a little satisfaction from this. "She doesn't remember. She's blocked it out."

"Jesus, your wife is a head case," Zoe says, shaking her head. "God damn. What a freak."

"You're a fucking bitch," I tell her. "Don't speak about my wife. Don't even say her name." My hands clench and unclench. She eyes my hands, and she smiles.

"Do you want to hurt me, Jude?" she asks, her voice velvety smooth. She takes a step toward me. "Do you want to wrap those hands around my neck and squeeze?"

God help me, I do.

"You'd like that too much," I answer.

She smiles again. "Oh, how you know me."

"I wish I didn't," I tell her, and I grab her arm, and my fingers sink into her flesh, and she flinches, and I like it. I like knowing it hurts her. If I could kill her and get away with it, I think I would. In this moment, I would.

I've never hated someone so much.

"I like that," she tells me, and I think she probably does.

"You're such a twisted bitch, you probably do."

"Such language." She clucks, and I want to throw her on the ground.

The fury is all I can see.

The next few minutes pass in snippets, because my anger takes over, and my rational thought disappears. It's gone, like it never existed, and in its place is rage like I've never felt before.

Zoe takes a step and laughs.

I grab her arm again and shove her backward onto the picnic table.

Her eyes widen, and then she smiles that strange smile.

"Have you ever fury-fucked someone?" she whispers, and then she spreads her legs, and she's not wearing underwear.

"I hate you," I say through my teeth.

She throws her head back and laughs.

She stands up and slaps me across the face, as hard as she can. I don't even feel the pain. I just feel white-hot light pass across my eyes, clouding my vision.

I grab her and shake her. My fingers cutting into her flesh, and God that feels so good.

"How could you fuck with Corinne?" I growl at her. I shake her again, and her teeth snap together. I've never put my hands on a woman in such a way, never never never, and I don't care now. All I want to do is hurt her like she's hurt me, like she's hurt my wife.

"You wanted me so much?" I ask, shoving her backward, and my fingers cut into her waist as I spin her around and push her against the table. Her thighs are pushed against the wood and she bends, shoving her skirt up to her waist.

"Yes…" she moans. "Do it. Fuck me. Make it hurt. Make me hurt."

I do want to make it hurt. I want to punish her.

It's about punishing now. And I want to.

She has to know.

She has to know she's wrong.

I grab her neck and push her face into the wooden table, pushing it into the wood, hard harder harder.

I don't feel sexual.

I feel vengeful.

In this moment, I feel powerful, like I'm inflicting punishment or revenge. I push against her, pondering for one moment, the idea of fury-fucking her. Of making her hurt. Of pounding into her until she begs me to stop.

I push against her hard, through our clothing, harder, harder, and then, from the haze of my anger, from the rage, I realize she's moaning.

The sick bitch likes it.

I stop moving.

I'm still.

I'm frozen.

She looks over her shoulder, up at me, and blood streams from her lip, from being forced against the table. Her cheekbones are red and scraped, and her lipstick is smeared all over her face, making her look grotesque.

"Fuck me," she says, breathless. "Do it, Jude. More. Slap me across the face. I like it hard."

"You don't deserve to like it," I tell her, and I'm coming to my senses now.

But then she slaps me again, hard.

And I slap her back.

God help me, I slap her back.

Her head snaps to the side, and her hair is askew. A patch of blond shows through against the brown. It shouldn't surprise me that her long hair was a wig all along. She smiles slowly, a grin that makes its way across her clown mouth.

"Again," she whispers.

And I don't know what happens or why, but I do.

I slap her again, harder this time.

Her cheekbone is red, and it will bruise, and I like it. I like knowing that.

It's when she asks for it yet again that I catch hold of myself.

I take a breath.

I let it out.

I'm out of control.

I'm out of control.

I don't want to be here.

I don't want my dick anywhere near this girl.

Not anymore.

She smiles, and she looks more fucked up than ever, her red

lipstick a slash across her chin, her hair crooked and mussed from my fist, her cheekbone starting to swell.

"Fuck my mouth, Jude," she breathes, and she shoves her face into my crotch. Her mouth seeks me out, warm and hot and needy, and tries to suck me, tries to lap at me, to pull me into her mouth, but I stagger backward, trying to clear my head.

I suck in a cold breath.

"Stop," I snap at her as she tries to touch me. "Don't fucking touch me."

"Fuck my mouth, Jude. Punish me. You know I've been terrible. I'm a terrible, awful person, and I deserve to be humiliated. Show me how pathetic I am. Do it."

She grabs at me again and tries once again to pull me into her mouth, her mouth warm on my pants as she scrambles for my zipper.

"You're fucking pathetic," I tell her, and I'm so so angry. I'm so sick to my stomach. "Never come near me or my wife again."

I whirl around to leave, but her next words leave me cold.

"I own you, Jude Cabot."

I turn back around, slowly, slowly.

She's watching me, waiting, satisfied.

"You will do what I want. I own you. I have bruises on my face, scratches on my arms. You have my skin under your fingernails, I'm sure. One wrong move from you, and I'll call the police. And tell them you attacked me. I barely fought you off."

I can't wrap my mind around that.

I'm stunned.

I'm so fucked.

She sees it when I realize. I open my mouth and then close it.

"I'm not a rapist," I tell her, and I'm so numb.

"I know that, and you know that. But that's not what it looks like," she says, and she's so smug that I want to slap the expression off her face.

"I'll have a bruise on my face from you, too," I tell her. "How will you explain that?"

She shrugs, not concerned. "Defense injuries. I was trying to fight you off."

"You're a cunt," I tell her.

She smiles. "I've heard that before."

"What the hell do you want from me?" I ask her. "Why would you want me, when I don't want you?"

"I don't have to explain myself to you," she answers pleasantly. "Just know that I do. I want you. And if you know what is best for you, you won't argue."

My options fly through my head with lightning speed, and I quickly come to one conclusion.

I don't have any.

"You can do whatever you want to do," I tell her. "You're an unbalanced bitch, and I can't control that. Just know this, *I don't want you*. I'll never want you. You're pathetic, and you're nothing. I feel sorry for you."

I ignore her shrieks of outrage as I walk away.

52

Corinne

I stare at my phone and wait for Michel to come.

I've never in my life felt such pain. It's like my insides are being ripped out through my mouth, and I can feel every agonizing inch of the gutting process.

I collapse into Michel, crying when he arrives. The whole story comes out, as much of it as I know, and Michel stares at me in horror.

"He wouldn't do this," he says softly. "He wouldn't."

"He did," I insist, twisting my hands. "I feel like he stabbed me in the heart, Michel. He might as well have."

My husband.

My love.

The beautiful man I fell in love with.

I see him in my head when we got married…when he smiled at me from the end of the aisle, when he smiled at me from our bed on our honeymoon. His eyes were like gold, like caramel, and his arms were strong and mine, and he loved me, he loved me, and he'd never have hurt me. He'd have died first.

But it changed.

Over the years, it changed.

"We grew apart somehow," I whisper to Michel. "I don't even know how it happened. My schedule, and he got distant, and then he... I guess he sought out solace from someone else. She stroked his ego probably. He was flattered, and he wasn't getting that from me."

I choke on my words and Michel grabs me into a hug. "It's okay. It's going to be okay."

"It can't be okay," I whisper. "It will never be okay."

Michel hugs me, and he smells good and he's strong, and he's so very much like Jude. I close my eyes.

The pain slices me like a knife.

"Jude screwed up," Michel tells me. "No matter what issues your marriage had, he chose to cheat. This is on him, not you."

"I know," I all but whimper. "But God, it hurts. How could he do this to me?"

"He was making a selfish choice," Michel answers, patting my back. "I doubt it had anything to do with you, and everything to do with himself."

"But we're married," I tell him. "That means that everything he does affects me. He had to know what it would do to me. And he didn't care. Look, I don't want to bash your brother to you. I just don't want to be alone, and..."

"Hush with that," Michel replies, looking at me sternly. "You're my sister. I'm here for you. We'll work through this. Let me get Jude on the phone and—"

"No," I interrupt sharply. "I don't want to talk to him."

Michel holds up his hands. "Okay. Don't worry. It's just you and me here."

I slump into him and he holds me, and we stay like that for a very long time.

"Fuck you, Jude," I eventually growl.

"Let's go to Reflections," Michel suggests. "Let's take care of you now. I'll go talk with Jude, and Zoe, too. She's a member of my church. I'll get this sorted."

"It's not yours to sort," I point out.

"Hush," he tells me. "Just get your purse. I'll go get your bag."

I nod, and I can't swallow because of the pain, and within a minute, Michel is back with my bag.

"Let's go, sis," he says. "I'll call Jackie and explain everything. You don't have to worry."

I climb into his old truck, and he buckles me in, and then he drives silently to the clinic. When we arrive, he does the paperwork and gives me a kiss on the cheek.

"It'll be okay," he tells me again. "I promise. You go rest. I'll go knock some sense into your husband."

I don't answer. I just let the nurse lead me down the hall so I can take a nap.

I'm so tired.

So so tired.

When I get up, maybe none of this will have happened.

Maybe it will have just been a nightmare.

53

I open my eyes.

"Oh my God." My words are a whisper, and Dr. Phillips studies me again. "Jude was having an affair."

He nods and looks away.

"You've known all along," I say, remembering. "When did I... When did I block it out?"

He clears his throat. "Michel brought you and checked you in, and you were lucid in the beginning. But we gave you a sedative to help calm you, and you took a nap. When you woke, you had no recollection of anything. Not of the affair, not of trying to kill yourself, and not of still being pregnant."

My hand flies to my belly. "I'm still pregnant."

The doctor nods. "Yes. Part of our job here was to ensure the safety of your baby. We thought seeing Jude might jog your memories of...his affair, and might make it overwhelming for you when you actually did remember. We weren't even sure if you would. Your brain has become very efficient at disassociating."

"When I do something, I do it," I say weakly. And my knees are weak. My hands are shaking. I can't think. "How long have I been here?" I ask, trying to think.

"Five days," he answers quietly. That hits me hard. It doesn't seem like it's been that long.

"Is Lucy here yet?" I ask him.

"I'll check." He picks up his phone and calls the receptionist.

I need someone.

Anyone familiar.

Anyone familiar to tell me that everything is going to be okay.

This is all too much.

"I'll go get her," he tells me. He gets up, and he leaves, and I stare at my hands, at my wedding ring. I want to take it off and throw it against the wall. How could Jude do this to me?

My Jude.

My beautiful Jude.

I twist the ring and twist it.

A few minutes later, Lucy comes in with Dr. Phillips.

Her face is dark and she knows.

"He told you?"

She nods. "That fucking prick."

I close my eyes and she sits next to me, her arm around my shoulders.

"Thank you for being here," I murmur as I bury my face in her sweater. "I don't know what to think."

"You think of a good divorce attorney," she advises. She pats my back, and my mind is empty, and it's nice to have one person I can count on.

54

Now
Jude

I slam my car door and stride for the entrance, and when I walk into Dr. Phillips's area, his receptionist startles.

"I'll tell him you're here," she stammers. I shake my head.

"Don't bother."

I open his door without hesitation.

He's in front of me, his leg crossed, his notepad on his lap. And Corinne is on the couch with Zoe.

Zoe's arms are around her shoulders, and her face is buried in Zoe's shirt. Zoe looks different... She's wearing a baggy shirt and her hair is shorter and darker...but it's definitely Zoe.

I stop.

My mouth falls open.

Shock and utter horror pounds through my veins.

"What the hell is going on here?"

55

Corinne

"What the hell is going on here?"

My husband stands in the doorway, stunned, disheveled and covered in blood. He looks from Lucy to me, and back to Lucy.

I sit up.

"I think I'm the one who should be asking that," I say icily. "I remember, Jude. I remember everything."

He's stunned and astounded, and we all wait for him to speak.

"If that's true, then why are you sitting there with *her*? *This* is Zoe."

I pause, and I look at him, and I look at Lucy, and as I do, all of it falls into place.

The holes are filled.

With *Zoe's* face.

I inhale sharply and yank away from Zoe's arms. And I'm not crazy. I'm not crazy. I've never been crazy.

It was her all along.

She made sure I never saw her face at the diner. She's been angling for my husband. To hurt me.

Jessica. Lucy. Zoe.

They're all the same.

She looks up at me now, and she bursts into tears.

"I'm so sorry," she sobs. "I'm so sorry. I… Jude…he fooled me. I got sucked in, and I can't believe I fell for it, and I'm so awful. I'm terrible."

"Why have you done this?" I demand, ignoring everything else she said. "I never did anything to you. What happened wasn't my fault. Why have you done this?"

She's silent and then whimpers.

"He…kept saying he wanted to leave you and wanted to have a baby with me, and I thought he was using protection, but he wasn't. And God, Corinne, I'm so sorry. I don't know what to say."

"That's a lie," Jude snaps, and I hold up my hand.

"He never slept with you," I tell her, and the mere words stab my heart.

"Is that what he told you?"

"Yes. And I believe him."

"He's lying. I want to apologize. I didn't mean for any of this to happen," she protests. "He said he was tired of waiting for you to have a family. I had no idea that he was going to go this far. You don't know what he's really like, Corinne."

"Fuck you," I tell her, because I've been married to him for fifteen years. "You don't know anything."

That's when her expression changes, and her eyes narrow and they turn stormy and dark, and she spits her next words.

"That's where you're wrong. I know everything. I know everything about you, and what you did, and what you deserve."

I'm stunned and quiet, and she laughs in my face.

"Did you really think I liked you all of these months? It was all I could do to pretend. You're such a pathetic person, Corinne. God, I could barely stand being around you. Do you want to know something?"

I'm silent and she stares at me, studying me.

"I loved hurting your dog. Why? Because I knew everyone would think you did it. How did that feel, Corinne? Did it feel like shit? Because that's only a small taste of what you deserve."

She's maniacal, and I can't imagine why the men in the room haven't rushed to subdue her, until I see the answer for myself.

A flash of silver in her hand, and I see it only as she grabs for me, and then I feel the cold metal against my throat.

It happens so fast, and I had no idea she was so strong.

"Don't," she tells Jude as he reaches out for me, "move."

He looks from her to me, and he's as helpless as I am, because one small move on my part, and the knife will be buried in my throat. I'll bleed to death and no one can help me.

"Don't hurt her," Jude says cautiously, his hands in the air. "Put the knife down, Zoe. I'm the one you're mad at. Not her."

Zoe laughs and her teeth glint, and she's insane.

"You silly boy. Don't flatter yourself. This has never been about you. It's been her all along."

56

Jude

There's nothing I can do as Zoe pushes past me, a knife held at my wife's throat. I outweigh her by a hundred pounds, but if I misjudge a single thing, Corinne would be dead in an instant. I can't risk it.

I can't risk it. I fight to stay calm, and I have to force myself to let them go. Corinne looks over her shoulder at me as they disappear down the hall, and the look in her eyes is haunting and raw, and, Jesus, I have to do something.

Dr. Phillips is already calling the police, and I chase behind the two women, sprinting through the hall and emerging into the parking lot just in time to see them get into Zoe's car.

I get into my own truck, and the engine roars to life. I stay close on Zoe's tail. The rain falls so hard that I can barely see her lights, even at a close distance.

It all feels surreal as I drive, as I watch their heads in the car in front of me. It feels like a dream or a nightmare. Not something that is truly happening. My phone rings, and Zoe's name flashes on the screen.

"What are you doing?" I demand as I pick up. "Don't hurt my wife."

"Tell your wife how you wanted to fuck me," Zoe instructs, her voice icy but a bit hysterical. "Tell her how you always wished she was me."

"That's not true," I tell her slowly. "You know that. You pursued me, Zoe. You pursued me all along."

"I didn't force your dick from your pants and into my mouth. I didn't force you to fuck me."

I hear Corinne gasp, and I realize that I'm on speakerphone.

"Corinne, don't listen to her. I'm so so sorry. I didn't have sex with her. I never wanted her. I got sucked in and..."

Zoe laughs. "Don't you mean, sucked *on*?"

I flinch. "It didn't get that far and you know it."

Corinne is silent.

"Corinne, she baited me. I swear to God. I wanted to hurt her. I... She blackmailed me, and I..." I don't know what to say. I can hear Zoe laughing at my helplessness and at Corinne's pain, and my blood threatens to boil right out of my veins.

Their car swerves sharply, and then Zoe overcorrects, bringing it back too hard over the center line.

"Zoe, pull over," I implore her. "Please. It's raining too hard to go this fast."

The road flashes beneath us, wet and slick. Her tires swerve again and then swerve back. She's driving like a crazy person.

"Don't tell me what to do." And her voice is so spiteful. "You don't get to anymore."

"I never did," I insist. "I never wanted anything from you."

"I wanted everything from you," she finally says. "And I'm finally going to get it."

57

Corinne

Zoe's mascara is smeared, and her eyes pierce into mine. She has her phone to her ear, and she's talking to my husband.

"He's mine." She turns to me, and her voice is so odd. It's almost like she's suspended from reality. "I'm carrying his child, you whore. I'm the one he wants. He doesn't think so right now, but it's true. When I touch him, he comes to life. I'm everything he'll ever need. You're old, Corinne. You're old and used up, and he doesn't want you."

"Don't listen to her," Jude tells me urgently over the speaker. "We never had sex. She's not pregnant, Corinne. I never wanted her. Not really."

Pain jabs me in the heart, and our car weaves to and fro in the rain.

"You're lying, Jude," Zoe interrupts. "You did want me. Remember all of those texts you sent me? How you sent me your pictures and wanted me to see you naked? You did want me. You wanted to be inside of me. Admit it."

"You pulled all the strings, Zoe," Jude says, and his voice

is so strange. Like he's not the person I knew, and I guess he never was. "You pulled my strings, you played Corinne. You pulled off whatever you were trying to do. And you're a crazy bitch."

"Oh, I haven't finished yet," Zoe says, and her voice makes a chill run down my spine, and it freezes the blood in my veins.

"What do you still want to do?" I ask her, and my voice is too quiet. It's hard to hear in the rain. "Slow down," I speak louder, more firmly.

For a minute, I see her as the little girl she used to be, with the long pigtails, the one who always wanted to have tea parties with me and asked me to braid her doll's hair. I almost almost almost soften. But then her eyes glint in the moonlight, and it's clear how crazy she's become.

She's a monster now, and I have no idea how much I am to blame for that.

I'm living in a cage of lies, and that's all I can see in front of me.

"She's crazy," Jude tells me. "She's crazy, Corinne. She put the abortion pill in your soup."

My head snaps back and I stare at her, and she laughs, a grotesque sound that ricochets through the car.

"What?" she demands. "You're surprised? I'm going to take everything from you, Corinne. Just like you took from me."

In the background, from somewhere, I can hear sirens. But all I can focus on is Zoe and what she's done, and what she still has planned.

"Zoe, pull over," I tell her, trying to be firm.

But she laughs again. She knows full well that I can't make her do anything. I eye the door handle. I could maybe jump out. But we're going too fast. I'd die. The baby could die.

We're so close to town. If I can just hold on…

We curve around the next bend, and I feel the tires hydroplane a bit. But then they catch and I exhale in relief.

But my relief is short-lived.

It happens in a blur...fragments.

Our car is in control, and then it isn't.

It spins and tumbles, and the water engulfs it in the ditch. The tires spin and spin in the air, the water flecking off them, as the roof of the car sinks into the mud.

Steam rises.

Zoe gasps.

I scream, I think.

We skid and skid.

I'm half in and half out of the car, and I'm conscious and I'm wet.

The rain is pelting me.

I pull myself out and I stand, and I'm wobbly. I slip and slide down the soaked grass and through the ditch and the smell. The smell of burned oil and wet rubber, and hot water is in my eyes and I can't see.

I hear Jude calling for help, and then I hear her. A gurgle. A whimper.

I drop to my knees and she's halfway out of the car, the glass is shattered and blood runs down her arms, streaming into the ground, and her eyes are open.

They cut me, into my heart.

"You." Her voice is raspy. "You did this."

Blood bubbles from her nose and her words are so short, so jagged, like broken bits of glass.

"I didn't," I tell her. "*You* did this. Breathe deep, Zoe. Hang on. Help is coming."

"You don't care," she whispers, "if I live or die. It's nothing to you." Her bottom half is crumpled in the car seat, and she wasn't wearing a seat belt. Her pelvis is smashed to bits, and

I know, that if she'd actually been pregnant, that there's no way her child could still be living. There's no way it could've survived. *Jude's child.*

Anger swells in me, and I see red, and the pain the pain the pain grows bigger than my logic, bigger than my compassion, and that's all I see. White-hot pain and it's mine and I own it.

"It's nothing to *him*," I tell her coldly, steeling my heart. "*You're* nothing to him."

She smiles, and her teeth are red and grotesque and broken.

"But I'm a nothing who took your husband. Just like you took everything that mattered to me."

My heart pounds and twists, because she did take my husband.

She was young and lovely, and I thought she held so much power over me, and I thought she was my friend, but here she is on the ground, and she's bleeding and broken and she's nothing to me.

"You're dying," I tell her.

"You're a bitch," she manages to say, her last words with her last breaths. All of my instincts and experiences feel it. She gurgles now, and she can't talk anymore, and her chest heaves up and down raggedly.

"It didn't have to be this way," I say quietly, and the wind steals my words and carries them away. Zoe watches me, her eyes already beginning to cloud.

I hear the sirens, I see the red lights flashing around us in circles, and when the EMTs shove their way through the rain, I step to the side, and her eyes still follow me, dark as night.

They pull her out, sliding her easily onto the wet ground. I can see her weaken, and her breathing slow. She's going. She's slipping away and I don't feel anything.

And then Jude is here, wet in the rain.

And he's all I've ever wanted, and he's broken my heart.

58

Jude

"Corinne!" I yell through the rain. I'm desperate and terrified, and if something has happened to her, I'll never forgive myself.

I scramble down the wet hill to the crumpled car, and she is standing, and I can't believe it. She's soaking wet, her blond hair plastered to her head, but she doesn't appear to have a scratch on her.

Her eyes meet mine, and there is so much pain in hers that I can't stand it.

"Corinne," I whisper. Red and blue lights flash against everything eerily in the night, and chaos is everywhere.

And then I hear the EMTs.

"Her pulse is thready. We're gonna need epinephrine," one calls out, talking about Zoe, and I startle because I know they shouldn't.

I'm allergic to epinephrine and bee stings, she'd told me once, and it seems like so long ago.

She's allergic.

She's allergic.

Zoe hears him, too, and her eyes widen and she tries to say something, she tries to call out, but she can't because her lungs are collapsing, and blood is streaming from her mouth. Her eyes connect with mine, and she knows that I remember.

She wants me to help, I can see it, I can see it. But I don't. My heart is cold and steel and in shock, and I don't say a word. Because if I say nothing, this all ends. It will end now.

She killed my brother.

She tried to kill my wife.

She tried to kill my baby.

She's insane. She'll never stop. I know it. I know it.

Our gaze is still connected when her eyelids freeze. She can no longer move and her heart is slowing slowing slowing. I see it, and deep down, in the hidden part of my heart, in the place where I feel such dark things, I know she's still there. Her eyes still have life, and she still sees me.

I bend next to her head. "I know you killed my brother."

Blood bubbles from her nose. "Had to," she manages to say, her mouth filling with blood.

"And I have to do this. For my brother."

Her eyes widen.

"Good night," I whisper.

I step away and I don't stop them as they jam a needle of epi into her chest and the plunger goes down and it's done.

Years ago, when my wife took her Hippocratic oath, I vowed to do the same, to never do harm, but in this case... in this case...it was necessary, wasn't it? I could've stopped them. I could've.

But I didn't.

I see the moment the life drains from her, the moment her eyes go empty.

She's gone and she can never hurt me or my wife again.

A human being is dead, and I didn't intervene, and I don't care.

I stand limply in the dark, and then…out of the chaos, I hear Corinne's voice, calling for me, pushing through the bodies standing in the rain.

She reaches me, and she doesn't look at Zoe, not even for a second.

It doesn't matter what comes next. In this horrific moment, we're together. I'm all she has, and she's mine and I'm hers. My arms fold around her, and her head rests against my chest.

"God, Corinne, are you all right?" My voice is cracked and terrified, and she nods against my shirt.

I don't speak the unspeakable. I don't tell her that I could've helped Zoe and I didn't. I don't say any of those words, and I never will.

I close my eyes.

59

Jude

I wait for hours in the ER waiting room as Corinne is checked out.

The fluorescent lights shine on me, turning my skin a pale green, and I'm numb.

I'm numb.

My brother is dead and my wife is traumatized and I'm alone.

When she finally emerges from the swinging double doors, Brock walks her out and hands her off to me.

"She's okay," he tells me, his voice low. "She's in shock, and obviously, she's upset. But physically, she's okay. And the baby is okay."

I feel like hugging him, but I shake his hand instead.

"Thanks, man," I tell him, and my voice cracks. He nods, sympathy in his eyes, compassion in his voice.

"No problem. Take care of her."

Corinne won't even look at me, and the ride home is quiet

as she sobs in the passenger seat, her forehead pressed to the glass.

I've never seen her so broken, not even after mass deaths in the ER, and I don't know what to do. So I stay silent.

Everything is broken. My marriage, my wife. My brother is dead. I don't even know which way is up anymore.

I help Corinne into the house, and she yanks away from me and stalks to the shower. She's in there a long time, and when I finally feel like it's safe to check on her, she's curled up in bed on her side.

"Corinne?"

She blinks but doesn't answer.

I sit on the end of the bed, hesitant to speak, hesitant to breathe. I know I've wronged her, I've devastated her. What I don't know…is how to fix it.

"How could you do this to me?" she finally asks, her voice so quiet in the dark. I have to strain to hear her.

"I don't know," I answer simply. "It didn't start out this way. It evolved into more than I could handle. It honestly started out at the diner."

Corinne looks away. "I thought you were just hungry. I guess you *were* hungry. For something. Just not for me."

"Christ," I mutter. "Corinne, I'm so sorry. I love you. I've always loved you. I felt alone and neglected, and she paid me so much attention. I…guess I got carried away. It's no excuse. I have no excuse."

"No, you don't," Corinne says icily, her back still to me. "She may have been targeting you to get to me, but our marriage should've been rock solid. You should have said no, Jude."

"She meant nothing!" I'm exasperated now. "I swear to God, Corinne. You're all that matters. She was nothing… She was a *mistake!*"

"Jesus, Jude," she snaps. "A mistake is tripping and falling into her with your dick. You didn't do that. You purposely created a relationship with her. You gave her bits of you, and that kills me, Jude. *It kills me.* Out of everything that's happened, this is the worst."

Her voice cracks, and tears fill her eyes and tumble over, hot and wet.

"God, Co," I croak, and I rush to put my arms around her. She doesn't resist. "I didn't give her anything. She was an incident. She was a fucking incident. An error in judgment born out of desperation and a bad situation. I put myself in that situation and I know it and I'm so fucking sorry. If I could change it, I would. I swear to God I would."

She cries into my shoulder and her fists flail against my back and I let her. I let her hit me hit me hit me until she doesn't have any strength left. I deserve it.

Finally, she falls into me, and her tears are gone, and her eyes are a void, a void free of her love.

"She wasn't a relationship," I tell her again. "I gave her just enough to carry out the charade, to keep her giving me what I wanted. All I wanted was the fantasy of it, Co. I wanted the thrill, the dopamine. She filled that need."

"She was a girl, damaged by a terrible event," Corinne tells me, like I don't already know. I'm a therapist, for God's sake. "She was molested as a child, and Lord only knows what else. She targeted her rage on me because I'm still alive. When I think of you...with her... I...I just can't right now, Jude."

She closes her eyes, and her sobbing racks her body. I want to hold her, but I know she'd push me away. I sit helplessly next to her instead.

"You're my life," I tell her when her sobs finally lighten. "I'll do anything you want me to do to prove it to you. If you let me stay with you, I swear to God, I'll never hurt you again. I swear it."

She's silent and her hand shakes as it curls around the edge of the sheet.

I place my own over it, stilling it, and she closes her eyes.

"God, I wish I could hate you."

"But you don't."

I don't know if I'm hopeful or if it's a fact, and it's a couple of minutes before she answers.

"I don't know what I feel. I'm overwhelmed...by everything." Her voice cuts off and she swallows hard.

"I don't want to live without you," I answer, and I'm resolute. "I'll do anything you want. Can I sleep here? I'll even sleep on the floor. I just want to watch over you and make sure you're safe. Please, Corinne."

She nods and hides her face and then cries herself to sleep.

True to my word, I stay on the floor with a pillow and blanket. I watch her sleep, listen to her even breaths and replay the events of the past month in my head. I don't know how we even got here, how it got so far.

My brother is dead, and I can't tell her yet. It would devastate her.

Like it's devastated me.

Corinne is on a precarious ledge, and one more thing would push her off, and she might break.

I grieve alone, in the night, the darkness concealing my pain.

Corinne wakes in the night once and calls my name.

I'm up in a second, holding her hand as I kneel next to the bed.

"Was it a nightmare, Jude?" Her voice is small and hopeful. "It wasn't, was it?"

"No," I answer regretfully. "It wasn't. But it's going to be all right, Co."

She pulls her hand away and turns over.

"Is it?" Her words are painful and hopeless.

I return to the floor.

I stay there until morning, finally falling asleep, and when I wake, Corinne is watching me, perched on the side of the bed.

I sit up and rub the sleep out of my eyes.

"It happened," she says darkly, her words heavy. "It was real."

I nod.

"Can we ever get past it?"

"I don't know," I answer. "I can. Can you?"

"I feel like I never knew you at all," she says, her voice cracking. "The Jude I knew...he wouldn't have done any of this."

I sit next to her and gather her into my arms and rub her back as she cries. "The Jude you know is flawed," I tell her. "He's a mess. But he's going to get help, and he loves you more than life itself. If you give him another chance, he swears he won't hurt you again."

"Why is he speaking in the third person?" She sniffs.

"Because he can't comprehend that he did this," I admit. "It feels like someone else. I can't believe it. I just can't. If I admit it happened, then it's real. I don't want it to be real."

"We have to admit it and figure it out, if we're ever going to heal," she points out.

"I'm the therapist here," I tell her, attempting to lighten the mood, but it's too soon for that. She looks away.

A lump forms in my throat, and I can't seem to swallow it.

"It's my fault," I admit. "It's all my fault. I was supposed to protect our marriage and I failed. But if you give me another chance, I swear to you...I won't fail you again."

"I don't know if I can," she answers quietly. "I offered my-self to you, and you took my heart and annihilated it. You know I have issues because of my father. You know, and you still destroyed me...my heart. I don't know if I can ever trust you with it again."

"You're safe with me now, Corinne," I tell her, and in this moment, I mean it. "You're safe. I'll protect your heart. I'll never hurt you again. I swear it."

"I need some time," she says woodenly, and now she won't look at me.

"Take all the time you need," I tell her. She nods, and I'm at a loss. I don't know what to do with myself, so I resolve to put one foot in front of the other, and go through the motions of my life, and keep my head above water.

It's all I can do.

60

Jude

Nothing is better when I wake.

In fact, everything is worse.

The shock has worn off, and the first thing I think when my eyes open is *My life is fucked.*

Michel is gone.

I can't even fathom it.

He's been with me my whole life—even before I was born. And now he's not.

And not only that, but Zoe took his life. I brought her into our lives, and now my brother is dead because of it. I don't know if I can bear it. But I sure as hell can't bear it if Corinne is gone, too.

I take a shaky breath.

Corinne stirs at the sound, her face pale. Her hand drops over the side of the bed, and her wedding ring glints in the light. I'm surprised she's still wearing it.

"Jude?"

I look up and she's watching me.

"Yeah?"

"I don't know what's going to happen, or what I'm going to decide to do, but you have to promise that you won't ever lie to me again."

She's solemn and her mouth is drawn and her eyes are tired. I nod. "Yes. I promise."

"I mean it, Jude. I can't take any more lies."

"I hear you. I understand. I…" My voice trails off, and my heart is broken, and she watches me. I can't tell her. It will kill her. But if I lie…

I swallow, and there's a lump that won't budge in my throat.

"There's something I have to tell you. I don't want to, because you've been through enough, but you deserve the truth."

Her face drains of what little color it had, and her eyes look so dark.

"What is it?"

I close my eyes and my hands shake, and I exhale, counting to five.

"Jude? You're scaring me."

Her voice is thin, and I have to just do it.

"Michel is gone."

She blinks, not comprehending.

"Where did he go?" Her words are slow, and her eyes are guarded.

"He's…dead, Co. He's dead. Zoe killed him."

Corinne blinks again, and she's frozen, and my heart is broken. "What do you mean? That's impossible."

I shake my head and it's hard to speak, and my eyes burn. "She surprised him. It looks like she came up behind him and hit him in the head with a crucifix. Blunt force trauma, the paramedics said."

"No." Corinne's single word is sharp, and she's shaking her

head because she doesn't want to believe me. I wish to God I was lying. *If only*.

"If only she could've taken me instead," I say, and I've never been so honest in my life. "I would rather die than have anything happen to you or my brother."

I look away, because it's too late to protect Michel from her, and the tears start to fall. *My* tears.

Finally.

I've been so numb until now. I couldn't cry. I couldn't think.

But now... The dam breaks and I think of my brother, and the hot tears well in my eyes, and I can't stop them.

My shoulders shake and my eyes close and I turn away.

I sob for several minutes before I feel cool hands on my shoulders, and Corinne draws me into her arms, her hands stroking my hair.

"Shhhh," she soothes. "Don't ever say that. It's okay. It's okay. Michel is with God now, Jude. He doesn't feel pain. He's with God."

It doesn't help, but her presence does. Her arms wrapped around me do.

I turn to her and hold on to her like I'm drowning.

Because I am.

61

Corinne

Michel's funeral is attended by everyone in the local Catholic community.

The sanctuary is a sea of black as everyone mourns.

My husband sits next to me, and he's careful not to touch me, careful to respect the space that I asked for. Our legs are an inch apart, his hands are in his lap, his shoulders are stiff and straight, and we are separate entities.

But God, he's in so much pain. His face is a stone mask as he tries to hide it, but the torment is there. It's in his eyes, in the way he holds his mouth. He and Michel were closer than anything, and the idea that Michel is just gone...

I swallow hard.

I blink back the tears, and I utter a prayer. I watch Jude's hands, folded in his lap, and I watch them shake as the priest speaks.

Then, even though my heart is still broken because of him, I reach over and grasp my husband's fingers within my own. His curl into mine, and he relaxes ever so slightly.

He broke my heart, but his is broken, too.

No matter what he's done, I love this man, and I took a vow to have and to hold, for better and for worse—and he needs me now. He needs me to get through this. He doesn't have anyone else. Not anymore.

We'll sort our mess out afterward.

For now, we're grieving someone we loved.

Jude is a pallbearer, and at the end of the service, when he carefully carries his brother down the long aisle and out of the church, my heart has never known such pain.

My husband's torment guts me. His brother is dead, and he's dead because of a mistake that Jude made. Jude knows it. I can see it on his face, in his eyes, in the way he carries his brother.

He shoulders the weight of the casket easily and handles the polished mahogany with such reverence and care. He runs his hand along the wood gently as he slides it into the hearse, and he never once falters. No matter his grief or his tears, he'd never drop his brother. He didn't in life, and he certainly wouldn't in death.

He stands still and watches the hearse pull away from the curb, and he's in a trancelike state as we drive to the cemetery. He never says a word. Jude has paid a heavy heavy price for his transgressions. Even if I wanted to punish him, I'd never be able to punish him more than *this*.

The priest blesses the grave, sprinkling holy water on top of the casket. Jude and I both cry as they lower Michel into the ground, and it's a sight that will haunt me forever.

The finality of it is staggering.

It's our last act for Michel. The very last thing we can do for him.

It feels wrong to leave him here, and it feels wrong to cover him up with dirt. He was alive just the other day. He hugged me and told me everything was okay, and it's not. Not for me, and not for him.

The priest speaks the final words of interment. "May his soul and the souls of all the faithful, departed through the mercy of God, rest in peace."

Jude weeps openly, kneeling next to the gaping hole.

I grasp his shoulder hard, because I know if it's killing me, it's unbearable for him.

His shoulders quake from sobs.

Time passes, seconds, then minutes.

Funeral-goers leave, and we're alone, and the cemetery workers respectfully wait a small distance from the grave, waiting for Jude to back away. Waiting for him to be ready.

I know he'll never be *ready*.

He sits still for the longest time, staring into the grave, his eyes open, but unseeing.

He's overcome. He doesn't know what to do.

He's never in his life been without Michel.

I fold into a nearby chair, my heart breaking as I watch. As I wait. I don't rush him. I don't prompt him. I don't interfere. This is between him and Michel, a last private moment.

I hear Jude murmuring to his brother, but I can't hear the words. I recognize only the sadness, the pain, the desperation. He's barely holding it together. I can hear that.

I can see that.

It kills me. No matter what he's done to me, I love him so much that his pain is still *my* pain.

Finally, finally, Jude stands up, and we walk silently to the car.

His hands shake on the steering wheel, but he doesn't say a word.

When we get home, Jude disappears into his study, and he doesn't come out.

I don't know what to do.

I'm grieving our marriage, I'm grieving Michel. I'm grieving everything.

And so is Jude.

I curl up on the couch and sleep.

I wake in the night, and Jude is beside me, watching me sleep. His eyes are red.

"Can I get you anything?" he asks quietly. I shake my head.

"Are you all right?" I ask him. He shakes his head.

"No."

"Me, either."

He sits with me on the couch until morning.

62

Jude

How can I fix my life, when all I can feel is pain?

It's unending.

Today, I sit on the floor of my study, sorting through boxes of pictures.

Michel and me...from the time we were infants to the last photo we'd taken together. A cookout this past summer. We were as alike on the outside as we were on the inside.

Only now, my heart beats and his doesn't.

It's hard to think of him in the past tense. I constantly find myself thinking...Michel *is*, and it is such a jolt when I have to remind myself that Michel *was*.

The bitch of it is...he was the better brother. He was the better person. He would never hurt anyone. He was trying to help me straighten up my life and fix things with my wife, and he got sucked into a fucked-up situation of *my* making. It should've been me who died. Not him.

It isn't fair.

Life isn't fair.

And this is a guilt that I'll always carry.

There's a knock on the door, then Corinne's voice.

"Jude? Are you okay?"

"Yes!" I call out, lying yet again. She knows I'm not. But it's the only thing anyone knows to do when someone is hurting. To ask if you're okay. It's human decency.

I've hurt my wife beyond comprehension, and I know she still cares about me.

It still kills her that *I'm* hurting.

My wife is a better person than me, too. I don't deserve her.

With a sigh, I shuffle the pictures together and put them on my desk. Right now, they're too painful to look at.

I haven't looked at my email in days and days. I haven't been able to focus. So in an effort to distract myself, I open it up.

I scan and delete, scan and delete.

Until the name Michel Cabot shows up in the list.

Sucking in my breath, I open his message.

Hey, Asshole.

I'm going to come talk to you. But just in case you don't let me finish talking, I'm sending this, too.

You're a good person. You've always been a good person.

I don't know how it started with Zoe or why, but what I do know is that Corinne is your better half. She makes you a better person, and I know you love her.

I don't care what you have to do to disentangle yourself from Zoe, but for the love of God, do it, man.

I only want the best for you. And for Corinne.

We're a family, and we'll always be a family, no matter what. So I'm not judging you. To be honest, you're the best man I know. But men, by design, are fallible.

You've made a mistake. Own it. Confess it.

Then make it up to her.

She loves you, too. Every bit as much as you love her. What you have is rare, so don't be a dumbass. Fix it.

And also, I don't say it enough, but I love you. I don't want you to think that I'm anything other than disappointed. Everyone falls sometimes, bro.

You just have to get back up.

Make it right.
I love you.

Tears fill my eyes until the words blur together. My last correspondence with my brother had to be about Zoe. This devastates me.

But Michel's very last words to me were that he loved me. God, I hope he knows how much I loved him, too.

63

Corinne

"You've been through more trauma in your life than most people can even imagine," Dr. Phillips summarizes, sitting in the chair next to my bed. Given the circumstances, he made a house call.

I nod.

"I know."

My sister sits next to me, holding my hand, even though her face is stony. She hasn't said much, but she's judging me. I know she's judging me.

I stare out the window, at the rain, at the dead leaves plastered against the window, at the oranges and reds and the gray sky.

"You were raped, Corinne. You killed someone to protect yourself. Your father killed someone to protect you, and he's in prison. I'm sure you have latent guilt that you weren't processing."

I do have guilt. I think of my father in that prison jumpsuit and behind the glass with the hardened eyes and the graying hair, and I do feel guilt.

"He didn't have to kill anyone for me," I say limply. "I didn't ask for that."

"You didn't *have* to ask," Jackie interrupts, her mouth twisted in torment. "Jesus, Corinne. He's our father. He loves you. He did it without asking."

Dr. Phillips interjects. "Of course you didn't ask him. But as a father, walking in and seeing someone violate his daughter, his rage clouded his judgment. It's not your fault. You need to realize that. None of it was your fault. You didn't ask to be raped. You didn't ask for your innocence to be stripped away or for anyone to die or for your life to be irrevocably changed. Do you realize that?"

"Logically, I realize that," I agree. "But my heart... I think it's going to take some time to convince. It feels like I could've stopped it."

"You couldn't have," Dr. Phillips argues. "But we'll work on that."

Jackie watches me, her fingers like a steel birdcage around my own. "I don't in any way think you could've stopped what happened," she tells me, trying to clarify. "What I'm upset with you for...is that our father has been sitting in jail for years, and you wouldn't even visit him. I know right now isn't the best time to address this, but I'm pissed about that, Corinne."

A lump is in my throat, and I can't swallow it.

It's the story of my life lately.

"I know," I tell her softly. "I'm pissed about it, too. There's a lot I'm pissed about. I don't even know how to process all of the things I'm pissed about."

For a minute, her gaze softens, and I see sympathy in her eyes and I hate that.

"Don't feel sorry for me," I tell her. "Don't."

She squeezes my fingers. "My emotions are confusing, Co. I'm mad at you, and I love you. Don't ever forget that part. I love you."

Dr. Phillips glances at Jackie. "Your feelings are normal," he observes. "You've been affected by this trauma, too. Be gentle with yourself. You've got to process this, too. Everything we're dealing with here…it's a lot. But I know you love each other, you and Corinne. It's apparent to everyone who knows you."

She nods and I nod because it's true.

The knot tightens again in my throat, and I stare out the window again, and I find myself humming the stupid song. "Bye, Bye, Miss American Pie…"

I tell Dr. Phillips the significance of it.

"Jessica had been playing her mom's cassette tape. She kept rewinding this song, over and over. It was her favorite. It was playing when her dad raped me. And then as her parents died."

"Sound is a very significant memory trigger," he answers thoughtfully. "Try to avoid the song for now. Avoid anything that might trigger panic. We're going to use some EMDR in the next few weeks to try to stabilize your memories and make them more tolerable. In the meantime, would you like to try to call your father? We can do it here so that I'm able to facilitate."

I'm startled, then afraid, but Jackie is squeezing my hand so so tightly.

"Please, Co. Please," she begs me. "It would mean so much to him. You have to. Please."

Dr. Phillips pats my hand. "It'll be okay," he tells me. "It's up to you. But I think you need to do this to start your healing."

I nod wordlessly, and he calls the prison. While they get my father, Dr. Phillips puts the call on speaker and I wait, fidgeting with Jackie's fingers. I twirl her wedding ring round and round. It's minutes before my dad's voice comes on the line.

"Hello?"

"Mr. Friess, this is Dr. Phillips, your daughter Corinne's therapist. I've got Corinne and Jackie both here. We're here to talk about that Halloween night seventeen years ago."

"I don't want to talk about that," my father says abruptly. "Anything else?"

"Daddy?" my voice sounds small, like it did when I was eighteen.

My father pauses.

When he speaks, his voice is gentler. "Yeah?"

"I remember what happened."

He's silent again for a very long time.

"Are you still there, Mr. Friess?"

"Yeah. Baby, you okay?"

My father is my dad now, familiar and loving. I start to cry, and my shoulders shake, and my father reassures me.

"Don't cry, baby. It's okay. It's not bad here. I'd do it all over again, I swear it."

I cry until I'm cried out.

"It wasn't your fault," my father finally says gently, and I hear tears in his voice, too. "Your mother never wanted you to remember. That's why she didn't take you to a therapist. I hope you forgive us. We only wanted to protect you."

I nod, even though he can't see me, and I wipe at my wet eyes.

"Daddy," Jackie says, and her voice is thin. "Corinne is sorry she hasn't come to see you."

I feel a pang of resentment that she's speaking for me, but she's doing what she feels she has to do, what she has to do in order to deal with all of this. I remain silent, and my dad immediately answers.

"Don't hold it against her, Jacks," he says, and he's almost stern. "I don't. She didn't know. What she went through that night…" His voice is jagged like glass, and it breaks. Jackie's eyes fill up with tears because we've never heard our father cry. Not ever.

"I'm pregnant," I tell him through my tears.

"Lord, that's good news," he says. "I've been waiting to hear that for years. You deserve a family, Corinne. Make a family with that man of yours, and be happy for me. That's all I want. That's all I've ever wanted."

My heart breaks because of Jude, and I don't know what's going to happen with him. But I don't tell my father. Instead, I tell him, "I'm on bed rest right now, but when they let me up, I'll come see you. I'll try to make this right. We'll get a lawyer and get you out of there."

"That'd be real good, Cori-kid."

My heart constricts at the old nickname.

"I love you, Daddy."

Jackie echoes my words, and our father's voice is gruff.

"I love you, too. Both of you."

Dr. Phillips disconnects the call and stares at us.

"How do you feel?"

Jackie nods slowly. "I feel better. I'm sorry, Corinne. I know you couldn't help it. I'm just… It's all so…"

"I know," I interrupt. "I know."

Dr. Phillips looks at me. "And how do *you* feel?"

"I feel better, too, I guess. I meant what I said. I'm going to hire an attorney and get him out of there."

The doctor nods.

"And about Jude?"

I look away. "I don't know. He's grieving so much, and my heart is breaking for him. But at the same time, he hurt me. So much. He'll never understand how much. I don't even know if I can process it."

"You can," Dr. Phillips says. "And you will. Don't retreat into your head. Don't disassociate. Stay in the present. Face the pain, and face the past. We'll get you through this."

"But what about my marriage?" My voice breaks.

"We'll figure that out."

64

Corinne

Crying doesn't help.

If it did, I'd be healed by now.

Seven straights days of sobbing should've done it. But it didn't.

It's been seven days of questioning everything I've ever known to be true.

I've thought and thought about All Hallows Lane, and I've thought and thought about Jude and Zoe. I've thought so much about it that it's all starting to run together.

Was Jude attracted to Zoe because she was younger than me, prettier than me, better than me? My brain knows the answer is no, but my heart struggles.

The fact remains that I'm thirty-five, and my husband had an affair with a twenty-four-year-old woman. That stings. That wounds. That scars. Even though he tells me over and over that it was never about her, it was about a deficiency *in him*, it hurts. It makes me insecure. It makes me someone I'm not.

I hate it.

Worse, because Michel just died, it's hard to discuss this devastation with him. It feels selfish somehow, as though I can't focus on my pain, because he's got so much of his own to carry.

But it all needs to be dealt with.

Decisions have to be made.

Right now, I'm curled on the couch with Dr. Phillips on speakerphone as we discuss my marriage.

"Stay with me," Jude urges me fervently, his eyes so so sincere and warm. "Please, Corinne. We're so much more than this. Our time can't be up. We have so much left to do."

"You should've thought of that before." I'm hesitant, but God, Jude is my rock. He's my life. He was the target of a psychopath. We were on shaky ground. I swallow hard.

"You have to decide if you think you can ever trust him again," the therapist advises, and I kind of want to punch him in the teeth. "I know it isn't fair, but it's on your shoulders now."

"So, he gets to fuck around, and then I get to clean up the pieces?"

The therapist says, "Yeah. But he has to work hard, too. He has to earn back your trust by being transparent and trustworthy. Jude, can you do that?"

"I'm an open book," my husband tells me. "You can look at my phone, my computer, anything. I'll earn back your trust. I'll earn back your love."

"I've never stopped loving you," I tell him honestly, and the honesty hurts my throat. "It would be easier if I could."

His head snaps up. "Don't say that," he tells me, and he's got bags under his eyes. He's not sleeping.

"It's true," I answer limply. "If I didn't love you, this would be so easy."

I'd just snip the ribbon of Fate. I'd cut ties, I'd run far away. But I can't.

I love him.

"I've loved you since I met you," I tell him. "From the very moment I met you. I could leave you. I know that. I could start all over with someone else, someone who might make the very same mistakes as you did. And then what? I'd be right back where I started."

"No one will ever hurt you again," Jude growls, and I know he means it.

"You can't stop the world from hurting me," I tell him, although it warms my belly just a little that he wants to try. "I don't know if I can forgive you. I want to, but...all I can see is you with *her*, and God, Jude, you've got to try to earn back my trust. It's shattered right now, Jude."

"I know." His eyes are hopeful. "But if you give me a chance, that's all I need, Co. One chance."

My Jude is in front of me now, *my Jude*. The sunlight hits his eyes and they turn gold, and I want to lose myself in them. He's the man I've loved for years. I don't think I can love anyone else. I don't think I'm capable.

"If you hurt me again..." My voice trails off, and his jaw twitches as he clenches it.

"I won't."

His fingers clench and unclench around the curve of his chair arms, and he looks at me again, his gaze liquid.

"Can I hug you?"

I haven't let him touch me in days. I couldn't...because he touched *her* with those hands.

I nod now, though, because I need him. It's so strange that the one person I need more than anyone, the one person who can help heal me, is the one person who injured me in the first place.

But it doesn't change the fact that I need him to breathe. I need to feel how much he loves me.

He scoops me up and pulls me against him, and I can hear his heart against my ear. It beats fast and faster, and I clutch him, my fingers curled into his back, and I try to avoid wondering if *she'd* ever clutched him in exactly the same way.

God, it hurts.

Is it always going to hurt like this?

"I'm yours and you're mine," he murmurs into my ear. "That's how it's always going to be."

The therapist clears his throat and we break apart, but Jude keeps my hand tucked in his. I let him, because I need to absorb his strength. I need to feel that everything is going to be okay…even if it's not.

Truly, for the first time in my life, I know I'm in a situation where it might not be okay. Jude and I might be over. I don't know if I can fix this.

For the millionth time this week, I cry.

Hours later, I call someone and order an entire household of new furniture, arranging to have all of the old taken to Goodwill. *She* was in here, and I don't know what she touched.

I'd light the house on fire if I could.

65

Corinne

The pain is the first thing I think of when I wake, when I'm brushing my teeth, when I'm getting a drink, when I'm breathing. It's the last thing I think of before I sleep. I think of it always.

I don't know if I can keep living like this.

I tell Jude that one night as we sit on the sofa, staring at each other over Chinese.

"What are you saying?" he asks quietly, and there's panic in his eyes.

I swallow. "I don't know. I'm just saying that I can't keep obsessing over it. I look in the mirror, and I worry that you don't find me sexy, I worry that you wanted her because I'm too old for you now, I worry that..."

"Corinne," he interrupts, and he's firm and stout. "You are everything to me. I never wanted her. I swear to God. I wanted the idea of her. I wanted the words and the texting and the pictures. I've always wanted you. You're who I love.

You're who makes me laugh and makes me cry and shares dinners with me."

"You shared dinners with her, too," I remind him painfully, and he clenches his jaw.

"I wish I hadn't," he tells me. "That's the God's honest truth, Co. I'd give anything to undo all of it."

My rib cage hurts when I breathe, and the panic sets in, overwhelming me. I've been fighting panic attacks all week.

I try to focus on the things in the room, to bring myself back to the present, to center myself. I close my eyes, and the pain the pain the pain.

"It hurts," I tell my husband. "It hurts so much more than I ever thought possible."

His face is anguished, a tiny muscle flexing in his cheek. I breathe in, I breathe out. I breathe in, I breathe out.

He looks at me, something flickering in his eyes.

"Let's start over," he tells me. "We can move away, away from the memories. I'll start a new practice and you can, too. A new house...a new life."

I pause, and the world stops.

Everywhere I look, there's a bad memory. She was in my house, in my bathroom, with my husband. I have to stop my thoughts from spiraling.

But I can't commit.

I can't decide if I can forgive him. It's been weeks, and I'm struggling.

I'm struggling.

"I'll think about it," I tell him.

He pulls out his phone when it dings with a text, and as he does, as he looks at it, my heart races. He used to text her. Maybe even when I was sitting right there. He glances at my face and freezes.

"God, Corinne, I'm sorry. It's just the office."

He holds his phone faceup so I can see it.

I relax when I see the familiar number.

It's still hard to swallow, though.

Jude eyes me. "Just looking at my phone is hard for you, isn't it?"

I nod. "I know it sounds silly. But you talked to her on it. She sent you pictures, and you arranged dates and…" My voice trails off, and I stare at the offensive object, at the orange-and-gray case that I've seen a million times before. It looks different to me now. Menacing, almost.

"Okay." Jude stands up and walks out of the room immediately. Curiously, I follow him outdoors.

He drops his phone on the driveway and stomps on it. It doesn't break.

He picks it up and throws it against the ground. It still doesn't break.

"Glad I invested in the titanium case," he says wryly, with a scowl.

"It's okay," I assure him. "I'll get over it. It's just a phone."

"It causes you pain," he points out stubbornly. "Hang on. I know what."

He tosses it on the driveway again, gets into his Land Rover and runs it over.

The glass finally crushes, and it feels amazingly good. He picks it up and hands it to me, and it's shattered.

"Thank you," I say limply. "I'll get you a new one tomorrow."

"Don't worry about it. I'll do it."

I drop it in the garbage, and we return to our dinner.

"When I get a new phone, I'll leave it on the counter when I'm home," he tells me casually after taking a bite of rice. "That way, if a text comes in, you'll see who it's from. I want you to feel comfortable."

I choke up and my eyes water.

"Corinne, it's okay," Jude promises. "If I can do anything to help you, tell me. I'll do it. No questions asked."

I nod because I can't speak, because words won't form. Jude gets up and leads me to the couch, his hands gentle. He sits with me, and we watch the fire burning.

"Don't leave me," he says finally. "Please. I love you."

My eyes are on his hands, his long fingers, and I picture him touching *her* with them.

"Did you hold her hand?" I ask him, and I know that's a stupid question. Who cares if he held her hand? But I do. It signifies love and tenderness.

He shakes his head. "God, no. It wasn't like that, Corinne. It wasn't sweet love and butterflies. It was sexual innuendo and kinky talk. That's it."

My hand curls around my belly, the belly that was almost empty because of her. No matter what, everything will be different now. I'll have to mourn the loss of my marriage the way I knew it.

If we stay together, it will all be different now.

I'm not the naive girl I once was.

She's gone forever.

I'll have to grieve her, too.

66

Jude

All my life, when I was upset, I talked to my brother.

We discussed everything.

Not being able to talk to him about this is killing me.

So I pretend. I go into my study and pretend that he's sitting in the chair across from me, like he has so many times before.

"I've never felt so helpless in my life," I tell him. I gulp at my water, and I imagine that Michel examines me with his watchful eyes, the way he has a hundred times before.

"You've done a terrible thing," he points out to me. "There are consequences. You've got to wait and see what happens. I wish I had better advice."

"Jesus." I gulp at my water again. "Don't sugarcoat it."

"Jude, whatever was wrong in your marriage, you should've addressed it. Sought counseling. You can't turn to someone else. If you've learned nothing else, I hope you've learned that."

"Yeah. I've learned that."

"How's Corinne?"

"She's as you would expect. Confused, devastated, sad. She's got an influx of memories about that Halloween, and all of the emotion from this, and the horror from Zoe's accident... and...*you*... Shit, she's having a hard time."

"What are you doing to help?" Michel's gaze is firm and unwavering. I feel like squirming beneath it.

"I'm there for her. That's all I feel like I can do. She doesn't want to talk about it. But I'm there for her when she does."

"Think about this from her perspective," Michel tells me. "It was horrific. She's been through a lot. You were unfaithful. Your lover tried to kill Corinne, and she did kill me. You've got to show Corinne that life is worth living, and that you're worth sharing it with. Earning back her trust will take time, but you can start by showing her the good stuff."

"The good stuff?"

I don't even feel dumb pretending to talk to a dead man. It's bringing me comfort, so fuck it.

Michel points at the newspaper on my desk, tapping on an ad from the local animal shelter.

Puppies need a forever home.

"You think a new dog is going to fix everything?" I ask dubiously.

"Hell, no. But a puppy will give her something to smile about. That's what you need to focus on. Giving her reasons to smile, every day, until one of these days, she smiles all on her own."

"You're right," I admit. "You actually make sense."

"Well, I'm fairly bright." Michel shrugs. "Particularly now. I'm omniscient."

That's exactly something my brother would say. I roll my eyes and get up, taking the newspaper with me.

I call the number from the car, and I drive to adopt a second dog.

It happens just that fast.

On the way home, the wriggly fat puppy in the passenger seat looks up at me with big brown eyes, and I pat his head.

"You're medicine, boy. I hope you're up to the task."

He wags his tail, and I turn into the drive.

I carry him inside, and we find Corinne and Artie in the sunroom. She is curled up on a lounge.

When she sees the puppy, her eyes widen, then soften. She glances up at me.

"What's this?"

"His name is Rx," I tell her, sitting him on her lap. "He's here to make you feel better."

She starts to scowl at me, but Rx puts a big puffy paw on her chest and leans his face against hers.

Her eyes soften further, and she hugs him, clasping him to her chest.

"I love that puppy smell," she admits without looking at me.

"I'll take care of him," I promise. "You won't have to do a thing."

"This doesn't fix things," she tells me seriously. "A puppy won't fix us."

"No," I agree. "But he made you smile."

She stares up at me with teary eyes, and for the first time this week, her gaze isn't guarded.

"Yeah, I guess he did."

"That's progress," I tell her.

"Yeah, I guess it is."

I leave her snuggled with the puppy. They're both asleep when I check on them an hour later, his face lying right next to hers with Artie nearby. I cover her lap with a blanket and tiptoe away.

67

Days and nights have been running together.

Sometimes I sleep, sometimes I don't.

I'm plagued by nightmares, of the past and of the present.

Of my rapist, of the murders, of my husband and Zoe, of Michel dying.

It's all *so much*.

But to my husband's credit, he's been doing everything in his power to make things right. He does little things for me every day, like running my bath towels through the dryer before I use them so they'll be warm, or putting a note on my bathroom mirror to tell me he loves me.

Or bringing me home something to love me.

Rx stares up at me now, his eyes so big and brown. He yawns, and he's got puppy breath.

"You need to go out," I tell him. "Before you have an accident."

I listen for Jude because I know he's still home. He's been home every morning since it happened. He hasn't gone running on the trails. He's tried to change everything about his life that might remind me of *her.*

He runs on the treadmill now, until I start to feel more comfortable. He didn't have to do that, but he insisted.

I lie still and listen to the whirring of the treadmill belt, and the pounding of his feet.

When it stops, I wait for him to come shower, but he doesn't. Minutes pass, and finally, I get up to check on him, carrying Rx with me. The doctor has cleared me to walk around the house a bit, and for that, I'm thankful.

Jude is in his den, on his computer.

When I walk in, he minimizes his screen quickly, and my heart pounds.

"What are you hiding?" I ask, because that's what I'm scared of now. *What he's hiding.* Is he chatting with someone again? Is he going to go back down that path?

He shakes his head and turns his computer around. "Don't be scared," he tells me softly. "I'm not doing anything wrong. Look."

There's a real estate website pulled up. He's looking at houses in other towns…in Denver, Kansas City, Miami, Seattle.

"I didn't want you to freak out," he tells me. "I didn't want you to feel pressured."

Relief floods me from my head to my toes because he's not doing anything bad. He's not texting someone, he's not chatting with a strange woman.

Maybe…

Just maybe…

Maybe he means what he says. Maybe I can lower my guard…just a little.

The fresh new houses stare at me from the screen, and the idea of starting somewhere new is suddenly appealing.

"Portland might be nice," I suggest, and my words are soft.

Jude startles, then smiles. "Really?"

"Yeah."

Without another word, I leave and let the dogs out and then make coffee for Jude.

He joins me and we curl up on the sofa and we start talking, and we don't stop for hours. We talk about where we went wrong, how we grew apart. We talk about how he should have reacted and how he didn't, and how we both felt when Zoe died. We talk about Michel and how devastated we are. We talk about all of it.

"How are we going to get through this?" I ask, and I realize that I'm afraid to hear the answer.

Jude is silent, and his head is bowed, and I have to strain to hear him.

"We've already been doing it, Co. We've been getting through every day, hour by hour. We swallow the pain like a pill and move forward. We've already been doing it."

"Tell me how it all started with her," I tell him. "Please. I need to know."

So he does. He tells me all of it. How he was flattered, how it felt validating. How he felt useless to me and important to her. And how she manipulated all of it.

"I'll never understand how I got to such a place," Jude finally says at the end of his explanation. "It was like I wasn't even myself. Looking back, it doesn't even seem like me. It seems like a bad caricature."

"It does," I agree.

"It's going to be a long road," Jude tells me, cupping my face with his hand. "For you to recover, I mean. It's been traumatic, and it kills me that I did this to you. But if you can just live one day at a time, and focus on the *now*, I promise you, I'll make it worth it."

I swallow, and there's a lump in my throat, and I want to believe him.

I desperately want to believe him. That has to be a start.

"I can't make love to you yet," I warn him as he kisses my forehead. "I just can't. I keep picturing you touching her and..." I shudder.

He lifts my chin with his finger.

"I want to tell you something. I never made love to her. Not ever. It was all so stupid and ridiculous, but she meant nothing to me. Less than nothing. *You* are everything, Corinne. Everything. Without you, I'm lost."

My chest rumbles, and I'm going to cry again, so I swallow it down. I do believe him. I believe that she meant nothing. He showed me the texts—all of them. From the very beginning, and even though it hurt, even though it shredded me, it painted a picture of a girl pursuing a married man. And while that's true, he still succumbed. So he's not faultless. That's what I can't get past.

"If that ever happens again, you have to shut it down," I tell him. "From the very beginning. You can't allow yourself to be flattered. You have to be firm."

"Don't worry," he says wryly. "I'll run in the other direction. I promise."

He leaves to get us milk shakes and then dinner, and then days turn into nights, which turn into days, which turn into a strange sort of healing.

Every day, Jude tries to prove that he's strong and true.

He texts me from wherever he goes, and tells me he loves me and holds me at night. Every night, I have nightmares... about Zoe dying, about Jude sleeping with her...about all of it. Sometimes I wake up screaming. When I do, Jude holds me and soothes me.

We decide to sell our house and move to Portland to start

over. I've always loved the mountains and the sea, and Portland is a metropolis near both, just waiting for us to start anew in.

On the night we sell our home, I stand in the doorway of our guest room, staring at the empty walls. It's how Jude finds me when he comes home from work.

Coming up behind me, he wraps his arms around my waist.

"Are you okay?"

I nod. "It's just… This house was supposed to grow our family. We were supposed to flourish here."

"Our new house is beautiful," Jude reminds me. "We're going to have our baby there, Co. She'll have a beautiful nursery, and then we'll have more babies. And our life is going to be grand."

"Make love to me, Jude," I say softly. He glances down at me sharply, and I nod.

"It's been a long three months, Jude. I think I need this… to heal. I need to make you mine again."

"I've always been yours," he growls against my lips before he kisses me. "I'll always be yours."

He carries me into our bedroom and lays me gently on the floor.

"Has your doctor approved this?" he asks, and he's so so concerned and gentle.

I nod. "Yeah. I can resume all normal activity. Our baby is fine."

We make love on the floor, surrounded by blank walls. It doesn't matter. My husband makes me his again, and his hands are everywhere and he's mine.

He's mine.

He doesn't fuck me, he makes love to me. My chest swells with emotion, and he's so gentle, so loving. He touches me with reverence and stares at me with such a soft look in his eyes. The gold in them turns liquid, and I kiss him softly, my lips melting into his. He pulls me close closer closer. He rocks with me, and we come together, and it's a meeting of souls, not just a joining of bodies. We're one again.

We're Corinne and Jude, and we both feel it.

"Don't hurt me again," I tell him afterward as my head rests on his chest. "Just don't."

"I won't." His words are quiet, his grip is strong. He holds me like the world is ending, and in a way, it did.

Our world ended. And then it started again. It started over, and it started better.

We're stronger now than ever before, and we won't be vulnerable to something like this again. I feel that in my bones.

I close my eyes tight and let my husband hold me, and I know that everything is going to be all right. Maybe not today, but someday.

I *am* strong, and our wounds will heal, and our scars will fade.

That's what scars do.

It has to be enough.

"Will you stay with me?" Jude asks, long after the flush in our cheeks has faded and we're still clinging together.

I nod, and my cheek scrapes against his chest.

I remember lying like this with him in Hawaii, on our honeymoon. We were on the cusp of a life together, and we were so naive and new.

We're battered now, but we're stronger.

We're older, but we're wiser.

We're better now. So much better than before.

"Yes," I tell him. "I'm staying. You're my home."

He *is* my home, no matter where we move or where we end up.

"You're mine and I'm yours," he promises me. "And that's how it will always be."

"I'll hold you to that," I tell him, my fingers lacing through his.

And I will.

EPILOGUE

Two years later
Jude

I stare at the paper in my hands.

Calvin Jacob Friess will be appearing in front of the parole board in fourteen days. I know Corinne will fly out there for the hearing. She's done everything in her power, along with our attorneys, to get her father granted parole. With her testimony about the rape he walked in on and how she herself killed Joe Gibson in self-defense, it does give him more credibility that he's not a monster.

He was protecting his daughter, something any man would do.

He's not a menace to society.

He's not even mentally unstable.

It was a lie he told to protect his daughter.

I put the letter in my study. I'll give it to Corinne tomorrow. For now, we've got another obstacle to hurdle tonight.

Venturing down the hall, I find my wife and daughter in our bright kitchen.

"We don't have to do this," I mention to Corinne as she tugs the Halloween costume onto AnnaBelle's writhing body.

"Hold still," Corinne tells her, laughing. AnnaBelle stares at her indignantly, her golden curls bouncing as she shakes her head.

"No," she pouts.

"Why did she have to learn that word so well?" Corinne sighs, straightening the princess crown on our daughter's head.

"Because she's petulant like you," I suggest. Corinne swats at me.

"But seriously," I add. "We don't have to take her trick-or-treating. She's not even two. She won't know the difference."

"But I will," Corinne says. "It's okay, Ju. I'm okay. It's only taken a year of intense therapy, but I can do it."

Corinne always handles things in that way, with sarcasm, and wry humor, and a little bit of self-diminishment.

"You're the bravest person I know," I tell her honestly. "You really are."

She rolls her eyes now and turns AnnaBelle loose. Our daughter runs away, with Rx right on her heels, chasing her princess skirt. The little-girl giggles echo through the halls of our Oregon home.

"It's going to rain," I tell her. "Will that be a trigger for you?"

Corinne chuckles. "It's Portland. It always rains. I've learned to deal with it."

She walks into the living room to empty candy into a bowl, and I follow.

"Want me to take AnnaBelle trick-or-treating, or should I stay here to hand out candy?"

"What? And miss her first trick-or-treating? I think not. We'll go for a while, take a bunch of pictures and then come back to pass out candy." Corinne kisses my cheek and turns.

She pauses, then turns back.

"Jude, want to hear something great?"

"Always," I tell her immediately. We've made a habit out of trying to make each other smile every day. It started out as a method of healing, but it's turned into something we truly enjoy.

"I'm pregnant," she says simply.

And my grin is as big as the ocean. I gather her into my arms in a bear hug, and my wife smiles into my neck.

"For sure?"

She nods. "Yeah. I just found out yesterday. I wanted to wait and tell you when the time was perfect...but I haven't made you smile yet today. So there you go. Your daily smile."

I shake my head. "You make me smile every day just by being here."

She could've left me. I know that. Yet she didn't. She chose to fight it out with me, and in doing so, our marriage has turned into something bigger and better than we could ever have dreamed.

Corinne squeezes me tighter, and for a second, a blissful amazing second, the world seems perfect.

"It's all working out," she finally says, with tears in her eyes and joy in her smile.

"Yes," I agree. "And it always will. We'll make it so."

We hold each other for a while, standing in the living room of the home we've made together, in this new life that we've built, while the rain starts lightly pelting the windows.

Corinne laughs. "I'll get the umbrella."

As she does, I finger the St. Michael's medallion that Corinne bought me last year.

"Michel is always going to watch out for you," she'd told me. "This will just be a tangible reminder of that." I'm not too proud to say that I cried. I wear it every minute of the day, and I do allow myself the luxury of thinking my brother is always with me.

One way or another, he is.

Corinne and I bundle up our daughter, take the umbrella and head down the driveway. Behind us, the jack-o'-lanterns on our porch twinkle as the candles inside of them burn.

I briefly wonder if my wife is okay, with all of the Halloween decorations around us, and she looks at me.

"Memories can't hurt us anymore," Corinne tells me softly, as though she can read my mind. "We're okay. We're safe."

And we really are.

Our daughter toddles to the neighbor's door, her candy bucket in her hand, a giggle on her lips, and Corinne and I share a smile, and her fingers flutter to cup her still-flat belly where my child grows.

We really are.

★ ★ ★ ★ ★

ACKNOWLEDGMENTS

To my beautiful best friend, Michelle Leighton. You kept my head above water when everything seemed dark and ugly. I don't know what I would've done without you then, and I don't know what I would do without you now. I hope I never have to find out.

To my husband. Sherrilyn Kenyon said: *The strongest steel is forged by the fires of hell.* We've certainly proved that to be true. We're stronger than ever, and we've worked for that. I love you. You're mine, I'm yours.

To my brother-in-law, E.L. I knew you would be helpful with this manuscript, providing insight with the whole "twin thing," but I underestimated exactly how helpful you would be. You're awesome at providing feedback, and you truly helped me make Michel shine. Thank you for that, big brother. You are my second favorite twin!

To my agent, Kevan. Thank you for believing in me so fiercely. You are a dream agent, a force to be reckoned with. I'm so glad to have you on my team. Thank you for always being in my corner.

To my editor, Kathy. Thank you for seeing this story and

deciding that it needed to be told. Thank you for believing in me and bringing me into the MIRA/HarperCollins fold. I look forward to seeing what else we can do together!

To Talon Smith and Jennie Wurtz. You were among the first to see this story and to tell me to *Keep Writing It*. I appreciate you both, so much. You always give me the honest truth, and that is so priceless. I love you both—forever and ever.

And...to my readers. You are my rock stars every day. It's because of you that I get to dream up fictional people and treat them as if they're real. On my darkest days, you guys are all beams of light. I thank you for that. Thank you for reading my stories and for making my dreams come true.